He'd just reached his limit.

Hilary heard the splash a few yards away.

The shock caused her to jackknife, and she went under, panic clutching at her as she caught sight of the dark shape coming at her through the water.

The second his body grazed against hers she knew him. She felt her own body explode in a myriad of stinging sensations when he dragged her against him.

They broke through the surface together, and then his mouth was on hers, hard and bruising, before they sank into the cool depths again.

This was not the gentle pressure of his first kiss, nor even the sweet, hard kiss he'd given her that morning. This was the demanding urgency of a need long denied, a frustration unappeased, a man claiming his woman in the final moments of conquest.

Dear Reader,

Merry Christmas! This is the season for good wishes and gift giving, and I hope that one of your gifts to yourself this holiday season will be the time to read this month's Silhouette Intimate Moments. As always, we've put together what we think is a pretty special package for you.

For starters, try Marilyn Pappano's *Room at the Inn*, a very special—and especially romantic—book set around a country inn, the holiday season and, of course, a man and a woman who are destined to be together forever. Snow is falling in tiny Angel's Peak, North Carolina, when Leah meets Bryce for the first time. How can she know that he's the man who will change her life and bring joy to her heart, becoming not only her husband but a father to the four children she loves so much? There's "room at the inn" for you, too, so why not join her for a very special Christmas?

Then, if you're tired of winter, escape into summer with ever popular author Heather Graham Pozzessere. *Lucia in Love* reignites Lucia Lorenzo's once torrid relationship with Ryan Dandridge. With her entire lovable, wacky family on hand, Lucia expects their reunion to be eventful, but never downright dangerous! And Ryan isn't the only threat; someone else is stalking her. Surrendering to Ryan might very well be the *best* thing she could do.

Complete this month's reading with new books from Mary Anne Wilson and Doreen Roberts, then look forward to next year and more compelling romances from your favorite authors, including Maura Seger, Linda Howard and Barbara Faith, to name only a few.

Happy Holidays!

Leslie J. Wainger
Senior Editor

Doreen Roberts
Forbidden Jade

Silhouette Intimate Moments

Published by Silhouette Books New York

America's Publisher of Contemporary Romance

SILHOUETTE BOOKS
300 East 42nd St., New York, N.Y. 10017

ISBN: 0-373-07266-X

First Silhouette Books printing December 1988

Printed in the U.S.A.

Books by Doreen Roberts

Silhouette Intimate Moments

Gambler's Gold #215
Willing Accomplice #239
Forbidden Jade #266

DOREEN ROBERTS

tries to apply Shakespeare's philosophy to her writing—make them laugh, make them cry, make them wait. She believes the element of suspense adds to a romance, and her first priority is her readers; she wants her stories to be as real to them as they are to her. She lives in Oregon with her husband of twenty-seven years, and their son is one of her strongest supporters.

Chapter 1

Through the thick blue haze of smoke, Simon King watched the girl in the tight orange dress approach, her hips swaying with exaggerated motion. His stomach muscles contracted with distaste as he raised his glass and downed the harsh whiskey.

She was pretty enough, he thought. She even looked clean. It was her age that got to him. She couldn't have been more than twelve or thirteen. He'd been in Bangkok two months and still couldn't stomach the sight of these children selling their bodies.

What made it worse was the knowledge that she'd probably been forced into the profession, sold to the brothel by a desperate parent who'd sacrificed the eldest child to save the rest.

He didn't know if it was the whiskey or the painted face of the child that made him shudder. She'd reached his chair and was standing with one hand resting provocatively on her bony hip. "You American?" she said softly.

When he nodded, her lips curved in a wide smile.

"You very handsome American," she announced. "You want good time?"

Simon reached into his shirt pocket and drew out a handful of the colorful Baht the Thai used for currency. "You can have this if you can answer my questions." He held out a couple of bills.

As he'd expected, her smile vanished and she backed away. "I know nothing."

Shrugging, he tucked the money back into his pocket.

Her gaze lingered there, disappointment visible on her face, then she turned and vanished back into the smoke, heading for the crowded bar.

Grimacing, Simon beckoned to the waitress. It had been the same story for the five days he'd been sitting in this dump. Ever since the unknown voice on the phone had tipped him off that Hal and Jerry frequented the Shanghai Saloon.

The girls had approached him constantly and had backed off once they'd realized he was looking for someone. He couldn't blame them; he'd heard enough to know that if they were discovered talking it would mean a vicious beating and probably imprisonment for a week in a rat-infested hovel.

The waitress loomed up at his elbow, an expanse of thigh displayed prominently in the waist-high slit in her dress. Simon gave her a cursory glance and lifted his empty glass in a gesture of demand.

Tight-lipped, she nodded and turned away.

Simon watched her weave her way through the men at the bar. She ignored their loud remarks and raucous laughter with an ease born of experience.

She'd probably been working this hole since she was a kid, Simon thought in disgust. He'd already tried questioning her and received the usual negative response. She'd been wary of him ever since.

She was on her way back to him when two men entered through the door on her right. Simon glanced at them, then away, then looked sharply back, a familiar tingle already moving up the back of his neck.

The taller of the two wore a thick mustache, which drooped on either side of his lower lip. The last time Simon had seen him, he'd had a beard, as had the thickset man standing next to him. Although the second was now clean shaven, there was no mistaking the beady eyes and pale, greasy hair he fruitlessly used to cover the bald patches of his head.

Jerry Carver. And his buddy Hal Vickers. Simon could feel the adrenaline pulsing through him as he shifted sideways to screen himself. Though he'd worn a beard himself in those days, he knew they would recognize him as easily as he'd spotted them.

Simon realized that with his unruly blond hair and mustache, not to mention his height, he stood out in this crowd anyway. And it wasn't likely the two had forgotten him. His eyes narrowed as he watched them push their way to the bar.

He was going to enjoy smashing this operation. He'd almost done it before, back in Oregon two years ago. He'd missed his chance then, but he was going to make damn sure he didn't mess up this time.

His flesh crawled as he watched Jerry slide his hand around a young girl's waist. There was only one person Simon wanted more than the bulky man at the bar, and that was Jerry's boss, Frank Chambers. This time he would get them both—whatever it took.

All he had to do now was wait. Sooner or later they would leave, and he would be on their tail. And there he would stay, like a burr in a dog's coat. Eventually they would lead him to Chambers, and the hunt would be over.

He gave the surprised waitress a wide grin and dumped an extra bill on her tray. "Keep it, honey," he murmured, "as a goodbye gift." Lifting his glass, he settled back in his chair for the long wait.

Hilary Barlow put down the phone in her hotel room with a frustrated sigh. Why hadn't it occurred to her that the

Department of Fine Arts would be closed before she could get there? She'd been tempted to explain everything over the phone to the woman who'd answered, but the woman's accent had been thick and heavy, so Hilary had decided to wait.

She hoped the officials spoke better English, since she couldn't speak a word of Thai.

Hilary frowned as she walked over to the window and pulled back the heavy drapes. She should have taken a crash course in the language before she'd come to Thailand, but she'd never been any good at learning foreign languages. She couldn't even master shorthand.

She pushed up the window and leaned out. Anyway, she would have hated being stuck in an office all day, she told herself. The heat came up to hit her, a suffocating contrast to the air-conditioned room. The tuk-tuk sound of a three-wheeled taxi punctuated the roar of traffic as it passed, three floors below.

Hilary sighed. Ever since she'd arrived in Bangkok, two days earlier, she'd been fascinated by the exotic city with its domed temples and colorful street vendors. Having lived in Los Angeles for most of her twenty-nine years, she was used to heat and noise, though she had to admit both were more pronounced in this land of ancient culture.

She would have been in her glory exploring the many intriguing glimpses into the past that Bangkok offered, if it hadn't been for the disturbing situation she found herself in. Even now she found it hard to believe.

She tugged the window down, shutting out the chaos of pedestrians and vehicles battling for space on the crowded street. As she fingered the tiny jade insect that hung from the gold chain around her neck, her eyes misted over. Her father would have loved to be here. She still found it impossible to believe he was gone. It had all happened so impossibly fast—the call from the hospital, her wild dash to get to Arizona, and the last, so few final moments of her father's life.

He should have been here instead of her. It had been his idea to exchange the priceless Buddha bequeathed to the Walter Somerset Museum in Los Angeles for the equally priceless jade scorpion that until today had belonged to a museum here in Bangkok.

The scorpion had always meant so much to him, and as a collector he had long had a dream to see it placed in the States, where he could visit it anytime.

Hilary wandered over to the armchair and sat down. Now he would never realize his dream. He had known, that last day, that he was dying. He'd told her he'd already authorized her to go in his place. Now, three months later, she was in Thailand and would have to live his dream for him.

She slipped off her shoes and wriggled her toes. Her first glimpse of the jade scorpion had taken her breath away. The carving that dangled from a chain around her neck—the carving that her father had carried with him for forty years—had been copied faithfully, from the tapering body and tail to the outstretched claws.

She recalled how she'd watched the official from the Department of Fine Arts remove the scorpion from the case and offer it to her with a deep bow. She'd held it in her hands, hardly able to believe she was actually looking at the original, which had been cut and ground into its exquisite shape for a Qing emperor more than two centuries before. Not until she'd brought it back to the hotel and taken another long look at it had she realized it was a fake.

Hilary pushed herself up from the chair and once more reached for the inlaid lacquered box that held the jade. She opened the lid and stared down at the carving, a small hope that she was mistaken after all still simmering at the back of her mind.

The scorpion, ten inches long, nestled on a cushion of silk, its brilliant green body glowing against the white fabric. It was a beautiful piece of work, she acknowledged as she lifted it out and turned it in her hands. Every detail had been so meticulously reproduced that it seemed almost alive.

Only someone who had studied photographs of the real thing would have detected the difference. Someone who knew it so well she could see that the green shading, which contrasted with the white in an emerald swirl across the ridged back, was not the same as the original.

At first she'd been unable to accept her suspicions. She'd spent most of the day hunting down bookstores and libraries to locate a picture of the carving and had finally found one in a tourist guide of the National Museum.

One look at the picture had convinced her that the scorpion sitting in her hands right now was not the original.

With unsteady hands, Hilary replaced the jade in the box, reached for the guide and studied the picture of the scorpion. The difference was subtle, but it was there nevertheless. That was what had made the curator's absolute refusal to believe her so incredible.

She'd shown him the evidence, and when he'd refused to even discuss the matter, she'd told him that she intended to go back to her hotel and call the Department of Fine Arts. She would insist that they send an expert out to check it.

Hilary shuddered. She'd been disturbed by the expression on the elderly man's face as he'd told her in his curiously flat voice that he was an expert himself and could assure her that she was mistaken.

Hilary closed the guide and stared moodily at the cover. The Department of Fine Arts was closed now, and she would have to wait until tomorrow.

How would her father have handled it? she wondered. Probably the same way. At the moment there didn't seem much else she could do.

Determined not to think about her father, she took another look at the guide. A short paragraph on the back page stated that the artifacts had been photographed especially for the new guide, which had been printed to coincide with the Songkran Festival. The date of that festival was listed as mid-April of that year.

Hilary felt a stab of excitement. If the pictures had been taken shortly before the guide was printed, then seven months ago the real scorpion had been safely in the museum.

Had it been stolen and replaced with a copy? Or had the Department of Fine Arts deliberately switched the carvings in an attempt to defraud the Somerset museum? Hilary shook her head. That was a little hard to believe. It was more likely to have been stolen. And, if that was the case, it had been stolen recently. In the past seven months. There might still be a chance to recover it.

She sat on the bed and stared at her bare feet in resignation. Maybe she should go to the police. But she didn't speak the language, and what would the police know, anyway? They'd take one look at the picture, just as the curator had, and tell her she was mistaken.

Any insistence on her part could be embarrassing under the circumstances. No. She had to get proof. At least she had an appointment at the arts department in the morning, and they would be able to give her the proof she needed. Until then, the scorpion, or its imposter, would have to wait. She stood and picked up her shoes.

In the meantime, she thought with a sigh of resignation, she might as well try some more of that ginger chicken they served in the restaurant downstairs, and follow it with a new discovery, a delicious Thai gelatin with coconut cream. Her mouth watering at the thought, she made for the shower.

Simon frowned in concentration as he tried to keep the little white car in sight in the honking, tire-squealing traffic. Having to brake constantly to avoid pedestrians and the slow three-wheeled *samlor*s, he almost lost his quarry several times. By the time the white car had finally jerked to a halt on Sukhumvit Road, his nerves were stretched to the limit.

His forehead still creased in a frown, he watched Jerry
and Hal disappear into a modern-looking hotel. They had
taken him by surprise. He'd expected them to spend at least
a couple of hours in the bar, but soon after they'd arrived,
Jerry had been called to the phone.

He and Hal had left immediately, and it had taken Simon some guesswork and luck to pick up their trail again.
Luckily they'd been held up by a traffic jam, and Simon had
crept in behind them, a couple of cars back.

The hotel must be popular, Simon thought as he walked
cautiously through the main doors. Several tourists stood at
the reception desk, all talking at once. The lone clerk behind the counter nodded and smiled but didn't seem to be
achieving too much.

Simon spotted Hal's dark head above the crowd and
edged closer, shielding himself behind the impressive bulk
of an American who appeared to have cornered the market
on cameras.

Over the babble Simon heard Jerry, in his harsh voice,
asking for someone. Straining his ears, Simon caught the
last name: Barlow. The clerk muttered something, then ignored Jerry, his attention on a new tourist.

Simon heard Jerry snarl, and, peering around the American's pudgy arm, he saw Jerry reach over and grab the
clerk's sparkling white shirt.

The little man's eyes widened in fright, and he stam-
mered something in Thai that Simon didn't catch. With his
shirt still grasped in Jerry's fist, the clerk leafed through a
stack of cards in front of him.

Simon narrowed his eyes and concentrated. Although he
couldn't hear the clerk, he was close enough to see him
mouth ''320.''

Satisfied, Simon dropped back and stationed himself behind one of the wide pillars that supported the flamboy-
antly carved ceiling. He watched his quarry enter the
elevator and remained in place until the two men reap-

peared, twenty minutes later. He didn't move until they'd crossed the foyer and left the hotel.

He was halfway to the doors when they opened and a stream of tourists poured into the lobby. Cursing quietly as he stumbled over suitcases, Simon reached the doors, only to be stopped by another human tide surging through the narrow space.

By the time he finally burst out into the street, the little white car had disappeared into the night. Seething with frustration, Simon turned and scowled at the hotel. It looked as though he would have to pay this Barlow a visit. Room 320, the clerk had said.

As he strode back into the hotel, he hoped passionately that Barlow wasn't one of Chambers's gang of thugs. If the man didn't know who Simon was, he might be able to gain his confidence and learn what he needed to know.

The first thing he had to do was get a look at Barlow. He didn't recognize the name, but he was sure that if the guy had been part of that Oregon mess two years ago, he'd know him.

Simon sauntered over to the public telephone, dialed room 320 and waited, cursing inwardly when a female voice answered.

"Mr. Barlow, please," he said briskly, disguising his voice with a heavy accent.

"There is no Mr. Barlow," the low female voice answered. "Who are you?"

Simon raised his eyebrows. Barlow, a woman? An upset woman, by the sound of it. Jerry and Hal's visit must not have been a friendly one.

He frowned. Jerry could be extremely unpleasant when he wanted to be. Especially with a woman. What was her connection with them?

"So sorry," he said smoothly. "The letter here say Barlow, room 320. I thought you were man."

"Letter?"

"Yes." Simon relaxed. The woman sounded a little calmer. "Someone left letter for you. You come to desk and get it?"

"I'll do that. Thank you."

He replaced the receiver, his brow creased in thought. A woman. Whatever she had, it was important enough for Jerry and Hal to hotfoot it across town to get it.

She had to be a go-between of some kind. Simon knew Chambers, and he would never trust anything important to a woman. She was probably just a messenger. Still, she had to be connected in some way and could therefore lead him to Chambers.

If not, it would mean another stint at the Shanghai Saloon. And that was getting dangerous. Someone there was bound to tip Hal and Jerry off that he was looking for them. He was surprised somebody hadn't done it already. It was only a matter of time.

He couldn't afford to let those thugs know he was in town. Not until he got a firm lock on Chambers's hideout. The man was as slippery as a wet fish. One word of warning and he'd vanish as thoroughly as he had from the Oregon mountains.

Simon waited impatiently, his gaze on the elevator door. He would have to somehow engineer a meeting with the Barlow woman and hope she could tell him something he could use.

He hunched his shoulders as he jammed his hands into his pockets. He hated it when a woman was involved. He hoped with all his heart that it wouldn't come to a showdown with her.

Half an hour earlier Hilary had finished an enjoyable dinner, in spite of her worry over the scorpion. She was actually beginning to have second thoughts about the whole thing when the knock came on her door.

The shorter of the two men in the doorway gave her a smile that reminded her of a comic-strip cat.

"Good evening," he said smoothly. "Miss Barlow?"

She nodded, eyeing them both warily.

"My name is Brent, and this is Sam Connors," the man said, waving a hand at his tall companion. "We're from the Department of Fine Arts, and we'd like a minute of your time, if it's convenient?"

Hilary hesitated. Something about him bothered her. His safari suit, with its creased pants, looked far too casual for business, and he talked as though he were a child reciting the lines of a play.

"I won't keep you a minute," he said with another forced smile.

Maybe it was customary for Thai businessmen to dress this way in the evenings, Hilary decided, and stepped back, inviting them in with a gracious gesture.

Mr. Brent explained that he wanted to examine the carving, and Hilary watched him, becoming increasingly uneasy as he studied it, then held it to the light.

It occurred to her that it was rather late in the evening for officials to be paying a visit. And did Americans work for the arts department in Thailand? It didn't seem likely, especially men like these.

When he handed the scorpion back to her with a solemn smile and informed her that it was indeed the genuine article, she thanked them and ushered them out the door, telling them she was late for an appointment.

She was still puzzling over the whole incident when the phone rang and she was once again plunged into confusion.

Now she replaced the receiver and stared at it, her mind racing. Who would have sent her a letter at this hotel? No one knew she was here. She hadn't even told her mother, who Hilary knew would have kept digging until she'd found out the reason for her visit.

She could just imagine her mother's reaction if she knew why Hilary had come all this way. The subject of Hilary's father had been forbidden ever since the divorce.

Well, she wasn't going to find out anything sitting there, Hilary decided. She would go down and get the letter and then make up her mind what to do. She picked up her lacy wrap and drew it around her shoulders.

The curator must have told the arts department where she was staying, she thought as she let herself out of the door and locked it. She hadn't mentioned it when she'd called them, but she had told the curator the name of her hotel.

She stepped into the elevator and pushed the button for the ground floor. But why would the curator have even spoken to the arts department? He'd been so insistent that she was wrong. And if those men weren't from the arts department, then who were they? She was still worrying with that question when the door slid open at the foyer.

Simon jerked to attention as the elevator opened. An elderly couple walked out first, followed by a slim, dark-haired woman in a pale blue dress.

The woman walked with a brisk, light step to the desk, which had been cleared of everybody except for three businessmen carrying briefcases.

It came as a shock to Simon when he heard her say, "I'm Hilary Barlow. I believe you have a letter for me."

Simon thought his jaw must have dropped six inches. He didn't know what he'd been expecting, but it sure wasn't this refined-looking woman.

He studied her. Not too tall, around five foot four, as far as he could judge from there. Her dark brown hair was straight and smooth and swung just below her jawline.

The dress had a flared skirt, but he got the impression she had slim hips and long legs for her height. He was intrigued by her face, which was in profile. She had well-defined cheekbones and a proud nose. Her tan suggested that she came from a state in the Sunbelt. Probably California, he guessed, judging by her voice on the phone.

Her mouth was what caught his attention, though. It was a generous mouth, full lipped and provocative, an interesting contrast to her otherwise finely chiseled face.

Aware that he was staring, he hastily removed his gaze and was surprised to find his pulse quickening. It wasn't often that he was interested at first glance. In fact, now that he came to think about it, it had been a hell of a long time since he'd been interested in anyone.

He looked back at her. Now that he'd seen her, he was even less happy with the prospect of his next move. But it had to be done. He squared his shoulders and moved forward, hoping his guidebook Thai stood up to the occasion.

Hilary stared at the clerk in confusion. His accent was strong, but he'd made himself quite clear. There was no letter waiting for her at the desk.

"Are you sure?" she insisted, looking around as if expecting to see it lying on the counter. "Weren't you the one who called me just now?"

The clerk shook his head, lifting his hands in a helpless gesture. "I not call you."

"Who did, then?" Hilary could feel a pulse at her throat beginning to throb. All this was becoming too much for her. Something was going on—something she didn't understand.

"Look," she said desperately. "Someone called my room and said that there was a letter with my name on it waiting for me here at the desk. Who else was working here? It was only a few minutes ago—" She broke off when a deep, husky voice spoke behind her.

"Can I be of help here?"

Hilary swung around, her breath catching as she stared up into cool blue eyes.

"Thank you," she said, captivated by his sensuous mouth and thick blond mustache. His hair, bleached even lighter by the sun, looked as if it hadn't seen a comb in several hours but somehow managed to make him look rugged more than untidy.

"It's all right, though," she added, finding her voice. "I guess there's just been some kind of mistake."

She watched, fascinated, as he spoke in short sentences to

the desk clerk. The man behind the counter broke out into
a smile and answered rapidly, waving his hands around as
he poured forth a stream of words.

Hilary's quick glance assured her that the blond man's
body was every bit as impressive as his face. His lightweight shirt and pants outlined his lean figure, and she could
guess at the solid muscle in the firm thighs and sunburned
arms.

He probably had an ego to match, she told herself as she
pulled her gaze away. Even so, she couldn't help the little
jump of her heart when he smiled down at her.

"There was some sort of mix-up," he told her. "The other
clerk must have called you, but someone else picked up the
letter, a Mr. Barton. I guess the clerk didn't read the hand-
writing too well."

"Oh." Hilary gave a little breathless laugh. "Well, that
at least explains something. With everything that's happened to me today, I've had enough of mysteries."

"Mysteries? That sounds interesting. How about joining
me for a drink and telling me about it?"

Every instinct told her to politely refuse. She knew nothing about this man except that he was American and extremely attractive. And kind. He *had* come to her aid, after
all.

But what if he'd done it just to pick her up? She almost
laughed out loud at the absurd thought.

"Thank you," she said regretfully, "but I'm rather tired.
It's been a long day. Thank you for sorting this out for me—
I don't speak the language. I'm afraid that makes things a
little awkward at times."

"You're here alone?"

He seemed determined to talk, and Hilary had to admit
she felt flattered. Something about the way he looked at her
made her feel attractive.

"Yes." She smiled up at him, liking the way his eyes
crinkled at the edges when he returned the smile. They were
nice eyes, very light blue, almost gray. Dangerous eyes.

She dropped her gaze quickly. Now, what had made her think that? Something warned her not to tell him the real reason for her visit. She might be tempted to go into the details of her discovery, and she wasn't ready to do that with a stranger.

"It's a wonderful city," she blurted out to cover her discomfort. "I'm looking forward to exploring it all. There's so much to see, what with the temples and museums and all those wonderful shops. I don't know where to start first." She told herself wildly to stop babbling. What did he care what she was doing?

But he did seem to care; he appeared fascinated, even. He was leaning against the counter, his elbow supporting him as he studied her face. Hilary shifted her weight, uncomfortable under that intense gaze.

"My name is Simon," he said, holding out his hand. "It's nice to meet another American. You sure you won't change your mind about that drink?"

"Hilary." She felt her mouth widening in a self-conscious smile at his easy assumption of a first-name basis. She took his hand, then wished she hadn't when his strong fingers closed around hers to send electric signals up her arm.

"Hilary," he repeated. "A pretty name—I like it."

The way his voice had caressed her name made it sound exotic. She could feel herself weakening and, with an effort, withdrew her hand from his grasp. "Thank you. I've enjoyed talking to you, Simon, but I really must go now."

"You're going to make me drink alone, huh?"

Some little demon deep inside her head made her say, "You don't have a wife to drink with?" Horrified, she clamped her mouth shut as warmth flooded her cheeks.

He gave her a slow grin that sent tingles down her back. "So that's what you're worrying about. I'm not married, Hilary. I swear."

"I don't—I didn't mean—" She took a wobbly breath and sidestepped around him. "Thanks again, Simon," she muttered. "Good night."

Her embarrassment was complete when the unfamiliar high heel of her sandal turned under her and almost sent her sprawling into the elevator doors. Knowing he must be staring after her, she waited until the door had closed behind her and then collapsed against the wall with a low groan.

Simon stared at the elevator. Something didn't add up. He had the feeling she was hiding something, and yet ... what was someone like that doing working for a hood like Chambers? Either she was extremely clever with her cover, or Chambers's taste had improved considerably. Neither of which was likely.

He pushed away from the counter with an irritable sigh. He must be slipping. It wasn't often that he got turned down. He was just out of practice, he told himself.

Disgruntled, he beckoned to the clerk. It would have to wait until the morning now. And this time Hilary Barlow wouldn't get away so easily. Simon booked a room for the night, then walked to the elevator.

It wasn't until he opened the door of his room that he realized just how much he was hoping he was wrong about the woman. Something about her, a certain kind of warmth in her expressive dark eyes, appealed to him.

He knew it wouldn't be easy to play the heavy with a woman like that. He had the distinct feeling that Hilary Barlow was vulnerable, and he hadn't had much practice in dealing with vulnerable women. Most of the women he met were just as tough as he was.

Simon fell into an uneasy sleep, unsure of whether he was dreading or looking forward to the morning.

Hilary, on the floor above him, wasn't managing quite so well. She'd lost the light blanket twice and had to retrieve it from the floor. Plumping the pillow furiously for the third time, she sighed out loud.

Her mind would not shut off. Every time she closed her eyes she saw a rugged face with a sensuous smile and a gaze that turned her muscles to cookie dough.

She tried to concentrate on the jade scorpion and only succeeded in tightening the tension behind her eyes. Who were the two men who had come to her door that evening? Why couldn't she just accept that they were from the arts department and that the scorpion she had been given was the original?

Because she knew it wasn't. Ever since her father had told her about it, the carving had been almost an obsession with her. She knew it like the back of her hand. The picture in the museum guide proved it was a copy. Why wouldn't the curator listen to her?

The answer to that hit her with such force that she sat bolt upright. What if the curator was in on the theft? He could have sent the two men to her hotel to convince her not to go to the arts department.

She lay back down, her heart thumping. It was easy enough to find out—since the curator was the only person she'd told the name of her hotel, all she'd have to do was ask the officials tomorrow if they'd sent the men.

She'd show the officials the carving and let them do the tests that would prove it a fake. Then that nasty little man, the curator, could be taken into custody. She could only hope he'd tell them where the real carving was. There was no way she was going home without it.

Closing her eyes, she deliberately blocked the day's events out of her mind and concentrated on going to sleep.

The sun woke her up the next morning before she was ready. She lay there for a while, letting the day seep into her consciousness. Lazily she reached for her watch and peered at the tiny hands that pointed to ten past eight. Her appointment was at ten-thirty, so she had plenty of time to shower and eat breakfast.

Pushing her hair out of her eyes, she slipped out of bed, her breath catching as the memory of Simon's face returned. Impatient with herself, she kept her mind on her coming appointment, but despite her good intentions, her pulse fluttered as she walked into the hotel dining room.

A quick glance around assured her he wasn't there, and she fought back the treacherous disappointment as she allowed the maître d' to show her to a table.

She was acting silly, she told herself as she studied the menu. So he'd asked her for a drink last night. The minute she was out of sight he'd probably picked up the next available woman who'd passed by.

She could just imagine the type of woman he'd go for— no doubt something in the cool, sophisticated blonde department, preferably dripping with diamonds and stinking of Chanel.

Annoyed at herself, she stared at the list of items on the menu. How could she be so catty? She didn't even know the man, and it wasn't fair to prejudge him just because he happened to be one of the most attractive men she'd ever been that close to.

"Aha. Took a quick course in Thai, did we?"

The voice had been just as pleasantly husky as last night, and as she looked up with a start, Hilary wondered why she detected a hard edge to it. Her stomach took a wild leap when she met the cool blue gaze.

He was standing behind her, looking pointedly at the menu.

Confused, she looked down, and felt the familiar warmth creep into her face when she realized she'd been staring at unintelligible rows of squiggles.

Quickly she turned to the English translations and gave an embarrassed laugh. "I guess I'm not awake yet. My mind was on other things."

She thought she saw a flicker of skepticism cross his features, then it was gone as a smile took over.

"Must be important," he said lightly. "Mind if I join you?"

It would have been churlish of her to refuse, she thought. Especially if, as Hilary suspected, he'd already told the maître d' he was sitting there. Positive she wouldn't be able to eat a thing, she gestured at the empty chair and said,

"Not at all. I'd enjoy the company." She hadn't the faintest idea why he was being so attentive, but she decided she might as well try to enjoy it, since it wasn't likely to last long.

She ordered an omelette and fresh fruit from the waiter, and smiled when Simon did the same. He returned the smile, but she had the odd feeling that it was an automatic gesture.

She sensed a certain tension about him, as if he wasn't nearly as relaxed as he was pretending to be. She almost forgot her uneasiness when he launched into a discussion on the importance of a sensible diet, a discussion that lasted throughout the entire meal.

"So, what are your plans for today?" Simon asked casually when they'd both cleared their plates and were left with coffee.

Hilary started guiltily. She didn't want to discuss her problem with a total stranger, even if he was a good-looking, charming stranger.

When she viewed her dilemma in the cold light of day—or rather the warm wash of sunshine—she found it hard to believe she hadn't overreacted about the whole thing. After all, it was possible that she'd been mistaken about the scorpion. The curator had suggested that photographs could be misleading. Light changes, angles, could make a difference.

Possible, she thought, but not likely. She was as certain as she could be without positive proof that the scorpion was a fake. And the two men who had visited her last night were just as phony.

The arts department should be able to settle it, one way or the other. Then she would have to decide what to do next.

Covering her apprehension, she gave Simon a bright smile, then realized he was still waiting for an answer to his question about her plans. "Oh!" Why did he make her feel like a tongue-tied adolescent? "I haven't really decided yet," she said with a rush. "I thought I might look at a temple or two."

"*Wat.*"

Hilary blinked. "I said I thought I might look—"

Simon grinned. "No, the Thai call a temple a *wat.*"

"Oh." He was obviously the type who liked to air his knowledge, she thought. "Whatever," she said coolly. "Anyway, I suppose if I'm going to spend the day sight-seeing, I'd better get a move on."

She reached for the bill, but he beat her to it.

"I'll take care of this. My thanks for letting me share your table."

She hated to be obligated like that, but there wasn't much she could do, short of arguing about it. Nodding her thanks, she gathered up her purse and stood.

"Would you consider a companion for the day?" Simon asked, smiling up at her. "I'm supposed to be taking pictures for a travel magazine, so I'll be touring the city, too. I'd really enjoy the company, and I could show you where all the best sights are."

"You're a photographer?" Hilary said in surprise. Somehow she hadn't imagined him being anything quite so ordinary. An airline pilot, perhaps. He had an aura of confidence about him, a hint of controlled power that intrigued her.

"One of the best." His eyes challenged her. "How about it?"

If she hadn't had that appointment, Hilary reflected, she might have been tempted. Very tempted. Maybe it was just as well. Men like Simon were not in her league.

She softened her response with a smile. "Maybe another time." She couldn't mistake the spark of frustration in his gaze. It made her uncomfortable, and she quickly left the dining room.

For some reason he was being remarkably persistent—and she wasn't foolish enough to think he was taken with her.

It was her sister, Andrea, who had all the looks in the family and the confidence to go with them.

Hilary gave herself a mental shake. It had been a long time since she had given her sister a second thought, and she found it humiliating to be doing so now, just because an attractive man had paid attention to her.

Uneasy at her train of thought, Hilary bent her concentration on her appointment, which she was anxious to get over with. Outside the hotel, she climbed into a taxi and gave her destination.

She had calmed down a little by the time she arrived at the arts department building and was ushered into a quiet office on the ground floor. To her dismay, it wasn't the friendly official she'd met the day before but a solemn-faced man who rose from behind a desk to greet her.

She didn't catch his name, but the nameplate on the desk said Phong. Relieved to hear him speaking in English, Hilary introduced herself and asked the question that had been burning in her mind since the night before.

"Did you send two officials to my hotel last night?"

An odd expression flickered across the man's face. "I did not," he said carefully.

Hilary's heart was hammering. "I have something rather disturbing to tell you, Mr. Phong," she said, trying to keep her voice steady. "The scorpion I was given in exchange for the Buddha is a fake."

She drew the box out of her bag and laid it on his desk. "If you take a look at the photograph in this guide, you'll see I'm right." She placed the book next to the box. "The shading on the back and tail is different from that in the original."

Phong lifted the scorpion from its box and examined it. Hilary waited, her pulse throbbing, as he compared the photograph with the carving.

"You see?" Hilary said eagerly, leaning forward to point at the jade. "The shading here, and here—it's narrower and doesn't reach to the end of the tail like the one in the photograph. It's close, but—"

Phong interrupted her. "Miss Barlow, I apologize for contradicting you, but I see no discrepancy here. The carving is most certainly the same as the one in the picture. Surely you are not suggesting that we are capable of cheating an American museum."

Hilary colored, remembering her doubts of the night before. "Of course not," she said quickly. "But I am saying that the real scorpion could have been stolen and replaced with a copy."

"Is that so?" Phong reached for an intercom on his desk and pressed a button. Something about the way he settled back in his chair, linked his hands and stared at her made Hilary nervous.

"I can assure you, Miss Barlow," he said, "that it would be impossible for anyone to steal an antique from the museum. Our security system there is one of the best in the world. The combination is known only to the company that installed it. It is impossible that such a theft could have taken place without our being aware of it."

"But the curator must be in on it," Hilary said desperately. "He had to be the one who sent those two men last night—" She broke off as a sharp rap sounded on the door.

Phong said something in Thai, and a uniformed man entered and stood just inside the room.

Hilary gave him a quick glance, then turned back to Phong. "I'm sure that if you run the tests on the scorpion you'll see I'm right." She leaned forward to give emphasis to her words. "I just *know* the curator is behind all this."

Phong unlinked his hands and also sat forward. "Miss Barlow," he said in a cold voice that raised the hairs on the back of Hilary's neck, "I don't have to remind you that this is an important cultural exchange between our countries. I'm quite sure you would wish to avoid the embarrassment of making such unjustified accusations."

She watched him replace the scorpion in the box, her mind racing. "Maybe," she suggested quietly, "I should talk to the police about this, or the American Embassy. I think perhaps they'll listen to me."

"And I think not." Phong nodded at the man by the door. "Miss Barlow, you will achieve nothing but an awkward situation for yourself and for the gentlemen responsible for your trip to our country. I can assure you the scorpion is genuine, and I shall attest to that to whoever wishes to question it."

Hilary stared at him in seething frustration. The man was dense and incredibly stupid, but he was right. As long as he was convinced she was mistaken, nothing she could do would change the situation. She would have to find the proof herself and shove it under this man's nose.

Before she could answer, she felt fingers clasp her arm firmly. She glanced up at the guard's relentless expression. At the same time, Phong's next words chilled her.

"I would suggest, Miss Barlow, that you forget this unfortunate conversation and return immediately to the United States. You would be wise to deliver the scorpion to the museum in Los Angeles before something else...unfortunate happens."

Unfortunate? To the scorpion or to her? Hilary wondered, feeling the cold seeping through her body.

Chapter 2

Simon stood in the shade of a small bushy tree, squinting against the sunlight as he trained his eyes on the impressive building into which Hilary Barlow had disappeared.

He couldn't imagine what she was doing in there, but sooner or later he was going to find out. The more he was around that mysterious lady, the more curious he became.

He hadn't expected her to accept his invitation that morning. First of all, he'd caught her reading Thai after she'd told him she didn't understand it. Then her hesitation about her plans had made it pretty obvious that she was evading his questions. She had to fit into this deal somewhere.

What bothered him was the way she'd declined. That aloof little smile as she'd walked away from the table had ruffled his feelings more than he cared to admit.

She could have at least looked as if she regretted her refusal. Once or twice he'd caught a spark of interest in her wide-set eyes when they'd talked, yet she'd dismissed him as though he were an errant schoolboy when he'd suggested they spend the day together.

Impatient with himself for letting it matter, he leaned against the frail tree trunk. He didn't like to think his ego could bruise so easily. He was even mildly surprised he'd given it a second thought. The days were long gone since he'd really cared what anyone thought of him.

Not that he cared now, he assured himself. It was just that he couldn't seem to connect the soft-spoken, seemingly guileless woman to a monster like Chambers.

But if she wasn't involved with him, why had his goons visited her late at night? He hunched his shoulders and shoved his hands in his pockets. Again he hoped he was wrong.

If he was, it meant he'd lost the trail again, but somehow the thought of Hilary Barlow working for Frank Chambers made his stomach turn.

Inside the building, Hilary stared at the man behind the desk. Was he actually ordering her out of the country? She was still trying to think of a suitable answer when he spoke again.

"I'm sorry, Miss Barlow, but I am a busy man. The guard will show you out. Have a good trip back to America." His voice was a pleasant monotone, but she had no doubt about the significance of his words.

Hilary gritted her teeth. "I'm not leaving this country," she said fiercely, "until I've proved to you that I'm right. There is no way I'm taking a fake back to the States."

The guard's fingers tightened on her arm, and she glared up at him. "Get your hands off me," she demanded. "I'm not a criminal."

Phong said something quickly in Thai, and the guard dropped his hand. "He doesn't speak English," Phong explained to Hilary. "If you go with him quietly, it won't be necessary for him to hold you."

There was nothing more she could do there, Hilary realized. She had to get back to her hotel room and give herself time to think.

In a daze she allowed the officer to lead her out of the office and across the marble floor to the building entrance. A splash of sunshine shone through the dusty windows and sparkled in a pool of light at her feet. It dazzled her, and she was still blinking as she went through the door. She didn't see the two men until they were standing on either side of her.

Her mind froze in panic as she stared into cruel gray eyes. These were the men who had come to her last night, pretending they were from the arts department. She tried to dodge them, but they each grabbed one of her arms.

"Too bad you didn't listen to us, lady," said the shorter man. "You should've kept your mouth shut. Now we're gonna have to shut it for you."

Hilary's fear evaporated under a rush of anger. "I know you're involved in this somewhere," she said recklessly, "and I know that curator at the museum is in on it, too. I'm going to make sure you all end up in jail, so you'd better get out of here before I scream my head off and bring the guards out here."

He stretched his lips over uneven teeth in an unpleasant grin. "Open your mouth and I'll shut it with my fist. We're gonna take you somewhere where nobody's gonna find you."

The fear returned, clawing at her stomach with icy fingers. She didn't have the breath to scream if she'd wanted to, she thought wildly as the two men marched her onto the sidewalk.

She had been propelled forward several paces when a noisy group of teenagers drew up in front of them, laughing and playfully shoving one another.

One of them collided with the tall man who held her, loosening his grip. Hilary saw her chance. Tugging her arm free, she stomped on the instep of the small man and jerked her arm out of his grasp.

Leaping aside to avoid two tourists, she reached the curb and gave a hunted look around. The street was jammed with buses and cars, and she focused on a gap in front of a motorcycle.

Since the traffic was moving slowly, she just might make it, she decided. Thankful for the foresight that had prompted her to wear flat sandals, she plunged into the street. Dodging left and right, she felt her stomach flip when she heard shouts behind her and the pounding of feet.

Her mouth dry with fear, she spotted the bus bearing down on her and made a frantic lunge for the sidewalk, crying out when she felt her arm caught in an iron grip.

"Come on—this way!" a deep voice demanded.

She barely had time to register the grim mouth beneath the blond mustache and a knife-sharp gaze before she was whisked almost off her feet in a headlong dash for the corner.

She had no idea where Simon had come from, but she'd never been so glad to see anyone in her life. Sobbing for breath, she raced to keep up with him.

He took the corner like a greyhound, dragging her with him, his fingers biting painfully into her bare arm. Her elbow caught a slight woman in the shoulder, spinning the dazed woman around.

"Sorry," Hilary gasped while Simon pulled ahead, towing her behind him as he threaded his way through the crowd of astonished pedestrians.

Hilary and Simon had gone almost the length of the block when he skidded to a halt and pushed her through the open doorway of a tiny shop. Unable to see in the dim light, she stopped short, gasping when Simon crashed into her.

He swore and glanced behind him. "Keep going," he ordered, "out the back."

What back? Hilary thought desperately as she lunged past the startled shopkeeper and his racks of silk dresses. She pulled up short at a beaded curtain at the back of the shop, only to be shoved through the doorway by Simon's none-too-gentle hand.

The beads rattled as she flung them aside, and she winced when a strand of them swung back and rapped her smartly on the cheek. Beyond the curtain was a small storeroom that was stacked from floor to ceiling with crates.

An unfamiliar pungent aroma made her wrinkle her nose, but she had no time to think about it as Simon pushed past her and rattled the handle of the narrow door in the corner.

It opened abruptly, letting in smoky sunshine and the smell of exhaust fumes. Hilary dragged air into her lungs as Simon grabbed her arm and tugged her outside, shutting the door behind them.

Breathing hard, Hilary looked at him. Sweat beaded on his forehead, dampening the blond strands of hair. His eyes glittered with an expression that made her feel almost as nervous as she'd been in the official's office. She opened her mouth to speak, but he gave her a sharp shake of his head.

"Not now. We're not out of this yet."

Hilary found the "we" faintly comforting. Even so, her heart pounded furiously as she followed him down the narrow alleyway.

He led her quickly down two more blocks, past modern buildings with gaudy business signs, quaint shops and tiny restaurants shaded beneath brilliant red-and-gold awnings, then through yet another alley and across a street crammed with vehicles, before he finally came to a halt.

He and Hilary were alongside a small expanse of grass and spindly trees. Simon pointed to a blue compact parked at the curb. "There's my car. Get in fast, and keep your head down."

She did so, curling up into a tight ball, her chin on her knees, as he bounced into the seat next to her. She felt the car jerk forward, stop, then swerve out into the traffic.

After a few moments she turned her head sideways and swallowed at the close proximity of a very well-developed thigh. "Thank you," she said faintly. "I can't tell you how glad I am you were there."

As soon as the words were out of her mouth it occurred to her to wonder why he *had* been there. He seemed to be popping up every time she turned around. Had he been following her?

Her heart plummeted as the possibility formed in her mind. If so, he was probably mixed up in all this, too. Had she escaped one dilemma only to find herself in a worse one? Her fears were intensified when Simon answered in a brusque voice, "Don't get too excited about it. By the time I'm through with you, you'll probably wish you'd taken your chances with Hal and Jerry."

"What's that supposed to mean?" She sat up, alarmed by this new threat.

"It means," said Simon grimly, "that we're through playing games." He stamped on the brake to avoid a bus that roared into his path in a cloud of black smoke and fumes.

"I've got to hand it to you," he went on, turning the wheel with sure fingers. "You put on a hell of an act. Wherever did Chambers find you?"

"Chambers?" Hilary's voice was a squeak, and she cleared her throat. "Who's Chambers?"

Simon's gaze was lethal when he glanced at her. "Come off it. I must admit, you had me going for a while there. I almost believed that innocent tourist act—till Chambers set his bloodhounds on you. What did you do, try to double-cross him? He won't like that, you know. He doesn't like being crossed."

Hilary couldn't remember having been more confused, or more scared, in her life. She was in the middle of a terrible nightmare, with no hope of waking up. There seemed no end to this stream of calamities, each one getting progressively worse.

Out of all the people who'd threatened her since the moment she'd set eyes on the scorpion, this man seemed the most dangerous. She clenched her shoulder bag as she fought to control her rising panic.

"I have no idea what you're talking about," she said stiffly. "I don't know who this Chambers person is. I've never heard of him. As for those two men, I don't know who they are, either, except that they're some kind of crooks." She could feel his eyes on her but refused to turn her head.

"Save it till we get to my apartment," he said gruffly. "You can do all the talking you want then."

She felt a jolt all the way to her toes. "Your apartment?"

"My apartment. I don't want any interruptions while you're telling me what I want to know."

"I thought you were staying at the hotel," Hilary said, eyeing the door handle. Could she possibly jump out of the car? They weren't traveling all that fast.

"I was, last night. That was for your benefit."

"Oh." For a minute she forgot about escape as she stared at his grim profile. So she was right. He'd engineered that whole thing last night. And this morning.

Why had he helped her get away from those two thugs if he was involved with them? And who was Chambers?

She had to get out of there. She was moving her hand carefully toward the handle when the car jerked to a stop.

They were on a side street, she discovered, outside some rickety buildings that looked as if they wouldn't survive the next strong wind.

As if Simon had anticipated her intentions, he was out of the car and around the hood before she had time to think about escaping.

He tugged the door open, reached inside and grasped her arm. "Let's go. And don't try anything stupid. The only thing you'll run into in this neighborhood is trouble."

Hilary could believe that. A couple of youths in filthy T-shirts and jeans lounged against a wall that was covered in graffiti. The boys' expressions made her feel as if spiders were crawling over her skin.

Farther down the street, an old man with a beard that reached almost to his knees shuffled toward them, mumbling to himself while he nodded continuously. He was followed by a giant of a man who walked as if he were treading on hot coals, his huge hands swinging loosely at his sides.

Hilary found it almost a relief to feel Simon's strong fingers on her arm as he guided her through the cracked front door and up a narrow staircase.

She wasn't sure what she was expecting, but after seeing the chipped paint on the walls and the broken railings of the staircase, the comparative cleanliness of the tiny living room came as a pleasant surprise.

She sat on the shabby couch while Simon walked over to a bookcase and switched on the fan on top of it. When he flicked on a ceiling fan, Hilary began to feel a little better. It was still very hot in the small apartment, but at least the air moving past her cooled her a little. Even so, she longed for the air-conditioned comfort of her hotel room—or, preferably, her own apartment in California.

She looked at Simon, gripping her bag when he threw himself down beside her on the couch. She would have felt a great deal more comfortable if he'd taken the armchair on the other side of the room.

He leaned back and brushed at his forehead with the back of his hand. "Okay," he muttered. "Let's start at the beginning."

"The beginning of what?"

He dropped his hand and gave her a look that fairly made her cringe. "I don't have a lot of patience," he said a little too quietly, "so, for both our sakes, drop the innocent act."

"It isn't an act." She was beginning to feel more angry than scared. She'd been threatened, manhandled and ordered out of the country. All that had been bad enough, but this man, who managed to look attractive in spite of the scowl on his face and the fact that he was very likely a criminal, was one minute saving her neck and the next coming on like Attila the Hun.

He wanted an explanation, he could have it. And then she was going to demand an explanation herself. "I came here," she said in a low voice full of fury, "to make an international cultural exchange—an antique jade Buddha from a museum in L.A. for a jade scorpion from a museum here. After I was given the scorpion, I realized that it was a fake. I reported it to the curator, who told me, in so many words, that I was crazy.

"Then last night those two men turned up at my door and said they were from the Department of Fine Arts and that the carving was genuine. I knew they were lying, so I went to the arts department this morning to report my suspicions. The official there refused to listen to me and accused me of trying to create an international embarrassment. He actually threatened me and suggested—strongly—that I return to the States immediately."

She stopped for breath, her skin prickling as Simon's intense gaze rested on her face.

"Why would he do that?" Simon said, folding his arms.

Hilary tried not to notice the way his biceps bunched below the rolled-up sleeves of his shirt. "Because," she said, "the man's an idiot. I told him about the two men and that I thought the curator of the museum was involved, but he refused to even consider the possibility."

A tiny frown appeared between Simon's blue eyes. "Why do you think the curator is involved with anything?"

"You know the answer to that one," she said shortly. "Those two men are no more arts department representatives than they are Santa's helpers. Since the curator was the only person who knew where I was staying, he had to have sent them last night . . . as well as you."

Simon pushed himself to his feet and ran his hands through his hair. It would explain a lot if she was telling the truth. His gut feeling had been telling him all along that she didn't cut it as part of Chambers's charming little setup.

But this business about a carving had him mystified. Had she stumbled onto something else that Chambers was into? A sideline? Not that it would surprise him. Offer that creep a ticking time bomb and he'd grab it with both hands if there was a profit in it.

Hilary watched him, a small hope beginning to take form. He didn't seem like one of them. She remembered him smiling at her across the breakfast table that morning and hoped desperately that she'd misjudged him.

He paced up and down in front of her, his brows drawn together, his hands shoved deep in his pockets.

She couldn't help noticing the way the thin fabric of his pants stretched across the tight muscles of his behind, any more than she could help the little jump her pulse gave when she stared at it. She looked up quickly when he came and stood in front of her.

"All right," he said, "Vickers and Carver paid you a visit last night and said they were from the arts department. What did you tell them?"

Hilary's brow wrinkled. "They said their names were Brent and Connors."

"They lied. Actually, most people know them as Jerry and Hal. Jerry—the short one—is the meaner of the two."

"I didn't tell them anything," Hilary said, suppressing a shudder. "I knew something was wrong, but I pretended to believe them. I thanked them and they left."

Simon dropped onto the couch again. "And this morning?"

"They were waiting for me when I came out of the arts building." She looked down at her hands, unnerved by his shoulder being so close to her own. "The short one told me that I should have kept my mouth shut. That they were going to take me somewhere where no one else would find me."

"They must have figured last night that you hadn't swallowed their story," he muttered. "I'm surprised they didn't stop you from going in."

"Maybe their friend at the museum found out the time of
my appointment and they waited till then. I was about
twenty minutes early, so I must have arrived before they got
there." She looked at him anxiously. "I guess it didn't help
when I lost my temper. I told them I was going to see them
both in jail, as well as their curator friend."

"Not a smart move," Simon said, though he felt like
smiling in spite of himself.

"No," Hilary said unhappily. "I guess not."

Simon looked at her. Now that he knew she wasn't part
of this setup, he was noticing all kinds of things about her.
The way soft strands of her hair drifted across her forehead. The faint dimple at the corner of her mouth, which
came and went as she talked. The sprinkling of freckles
across her nose. The sudden flare of warmth in her eyes—
He dragged his thoughts to a stop. What was he doing? He
had a job to do, and he had to get her out of the way if he
was going to do it. And now he'd probably lost track of
Chambers again.

"The best thing you can do is fly back home, today," he
said, deciding he would worry about Chambers later. "I'll
take you back to your hotel and pick up your things and
then take you to the airport—"

"Wait a minute," Hilary said, interrupting him. "I'm not
going anywhere until you tell me what all this is about." Her
rush of relief at her discovery that Simon was not a threat
after all had made her feel as if she'd just drunk a glass of
champagne.

"Believe me," Simon said heavily. "The less you know
the better."

"Maybe, but I still want to know." She stared defiantly
into his eyes, refusing to look away even though she could
feel little shivers of awareness chasing down her spine.

"I don't know much myself," Simon said finally. "I do
know that whatever you've stepped into could be very dangerous, as you've already discovered. We're dealing with a

violent and unpredictable man here, and the best thing you can do is go home while you still can."

"Chambers, the man you were talking about earlier?"

Simon sighed, and nodded reluctantly. It would have been better if she hadn't known that. If word got out that she could name the head of the organization, her life wouldn't be worth peanuts.

"What does he have to do with the scorpion?" Hilary demanded. "And where do you come into it?"

Simon shrugged. "I don't know what the deal is on the scorpion. I want him for something very different."

"Are you a policeman or something?"

She leaned toward him, and he felt his pulse rate accelerate. He had no business telling her anything, he reminded himself. But something told him she wouldn't give up until she knew it all. And the more she knew, the more danger she'd be in.

Racked with indecision, he wrestled with his thoughts. Maybe if he told her enough to frighten her, he finally decided, she'd get a move on. After all, she'd be on her way home tonight, so it couldn't do that much harm to tell her.

He had no idea what time the flight left for L.A., but he knew she had better be on it.

"I'm working for the U.S. government," he said slowly. "Drug Enforcement Administration. Chambers is running a high-stakes operation, and I'm here to put a stop to it. Not that I'm having much luck at the moment. That's why I tagged onto you. I was hoping you could give me a lead on him."

Hearing the frustration in his voice, Hilary eyed him with sympathy. "Are you working here alone? What about the Thai government? Can't they help you? Surely they'd be just as anxious to find him as you are."

Simon gave a short laugh. "They've got their hands full. The Golden Triangle is teeming with warlords and opium kings. One more, especially if it isn't one of theirs, won't make that much difference."

"The Golden Triangle?" asked Hilary, fascinated with the exotic name.

"It's an area in northern Thailand that borders Burma and Laos—so called because of the huge fortunes made in opium."

He shook his head in disgust. "The poppies are grown in the hills there, and the opium is refined into heroin then smuggled back to the States, where thousands of kids get hooked on it and spend what's left of their lives in hell. Chambers was involved in the same little game back in the States till we caught up with him." He added vehemently, "This time I'll see he gets what he deserves."

Hilary could feel chills sliding down her back. Something about the way he'd said the words made her feel almost sorry for this Chambers.

"The tough part is finding him," Simon went on, his voice reflecting his impatience. "I've come close enough a couple of times, even tracked down one of his refineries, but by the time I got there, it had been abandoned. This is a land of smugglers, from jade and drugs to refugees. Tracking down one criminal is like looking for a four-leafed clover.

He gave her a wry smile. "And then if I find him, I have to have proof that he's involved. We know what he's doing, but proving it could be something else. I don't have any legal authority in Thailand, but if I have the proof I need, I can take it to the government and they'll do the rest."

She nodded. "But why did you think I knew anything about him?"

Simon's eyes narrowed as he looked at her. "I followed our two Prince Charmings to your hotel last night. When they went up to talk to you, I figured you were a contact. They are Chambers's head honchos, and they're every bit as poisonous as he is."

"Oh." Hilary swallowed. "Then Chambers must be involved with the theft of the carving."

"It looks that way. So now that you know, let's get going." He started to get up. "I'll call the airport and check on the flight."

"You won't need to do that."

He stood and looked down at her. He didn't like the way she'd said that—or the way she looked at him with that grim determination in her eyes.

"I'm not going," she said firmly.

His heart sank. He'd suspected as much; she was going to give him an argument. "Yes, you are," he said just as firmly.

"No." Hilary stood, her arms folded defiantly under her breasts. "I told Mr. Phong at the arts department, and I'm telling you. I'm not going back until I have the real scorpion in my hands."

"And just how," Simon said carefully, "do you propose to do that?"

Hilary gave him a level look. "Not me. Us. You're looking for Chambers. Since it appears that he's the one who stole the carving in the first place, then I'm looking for him, too. We'll find him together."

"Forget it. You're going home."

"Everyone keeps telling me to go home. I'm sick of people ordering me around. Are you going to help me, or do I have to do it alone?"

Reason with her, Simon thought desperately. It scared him to know he was tempted to give in. "You don't know that Chambers has the carving. Or even that he's involved at all."

"You said yourself that he had to be," Hilary insisted. "Why else would his men be knocking at my door? The curator must have called him, and he sent Jerry and Hal to my hotel."

"All right." Simon thought quickly. "I'll find the carving for you when I catch up with Chambers. I'll get it all straightened out, and you can come back for it later."

"No way. First of all, you wouldn't be able to identify the original. For all we know, he could have other copies of it." She paused. How could she make him understand? "Apart from the fact that I've been entrusted to bring the scorpion back, I have a personal interest in the carving," she said, choosing her words with care. "It's very important to me that I see it safely delivered to the museum."

"Want to tell me about it?"

His eyes questioned her, but there was no threat in them, only a desire to understand.

She lifted the chain around her neck and showed him the carving. "This is a copy of the scorpion," she said, hesitating over the words. "It belonged to my father. It was his wish that the original be placed in the L.A. museum." She couldn't explain now, she realized. Her father's death was too fresh in her mind. It was still too painful to even think about.

"I just need to see it where it rightfully belongs," she muttered finally, deciding that it would have to be enough.

Simon reached out for the jade and took it in his fingers. "It could be very dangerous," he said quietly. "I wouldn't be doing you any favors by letting you stay. I know how Chambers operates. You could be a threat to him. He won't be satisfied until he knows you're out of his hair. He'll go on looking for you."

His fingers brushed her bare skin above the neckline of her dress, sending a heated response down to her thighs. Rejecting the sensation as a momentary weakness brought on by her emotional state, she chose to ignore it.

"Then you need me," she said, determined not to give up.

Simon raised his eyebrows. "How do you make that out?"

"You want Chambers, don't you?" She met his gaze squarely. "You don't know where he is, and you don't know where his men are. If they come looking for me, you won't have to go looking for them."

He stared down at her, fighting his conscience. In spite of his severe misgivings, he had to admit it made sense.

It was a long shot, but long shots were all he had left. It beat sitting around the Shanghai Saloon for another few days. There were no guarantees they'd go back there anyway.

Chambers's headquarters were somewhere near Chiang Mai, in the north. Once Hal and Jerry's business here was done, they'd be going back there and he'd lose them again. If Chambers was involved in some deal with the museum, that would at least explain why they were in Bangkok.

He could go and have a chat with the curator, he argued silently, but that would tip off Chambers that he was on his trail. No, his best bet was to lie in wait and hope that Hal and Jerry showed up. He'd make *sure* Hilary was safe, he assured himself.

After all, she was the one insisting that she help him. It wasn't as if she were doing anything she didn't want to do.

With the distinct feeling that he was burning bridges, he gave her a reluctant smile. "I guess you have something there," he said, spreading his hands out in defeat. "I just hope you realize what you could be getting into."

"You're a United States government agent. I have complete faith in your ability to protect me."

Her smile caught him off guard, and he found himself responding with a warmth that was as unsettling as it was unfamiliar.

His ego was feeling a hundred percent better, he decided as he returned her smile. "I guess we have a deal, Miss Barlow." Holding out his hand, he experienced a sensation he'd almost forgotten as her soft palm pressed against his hardened skin.

This time Hilary couldn't ignore the impact of his touch. She was really being very stupid, she told herself, but she couldn't escape the little thrill of excitement at the thought of working with a man like Simon.

"I don't know your last name," she exclaimed as the realization hit her. "And how did you know mine?"

His eyes mocked her when he started speaking in a heavily accented voice. "So sorry. The letter say Barlow, room 320. I thought you were man."

"That was you!"

Simon nodded. "I heard Jerry ask for you at the counter. I had to figure out a way to meet you."

His reminder that their meeting had been arranged brought her back to earth with a thump. She pulled her hand from his, her excitement evaporating. She was indulging in a fantasy that was not only juvenile but dangerous. People could get hurt that way, and she wasn't about to let that happen.

He was making it pretty obvious that his interest in her was purely business. As soon as they'd obtained what they were both after, they would go their separate ways. Considering what he did for a living, she thought it was the best thing that could happen.

She'd been right earlier. She wasn't in his league. Nor did she want to be. She knew what she wanted out of life, and she wasn't going to settle for less.

"You still haven't told me your name," she said brightly.

"Simon King. At your service." He inclined his head in a stiff little bow.

"I'm glad to know you, Simon King." She resisted an impulse to hold out her hand again. Keep it light, she instructed herself, fervently hoping that it was possible.

"Well, I guess the next thing is to take you back to the hotel." Simon looked at his watch. "We've missed lunch. We can get something on the way back, if you're hungry."

She was very hungry, she discovered. "Do you think Hal and Jerry will be waiting for me when I get back to the hotel?" she said nervously, the thought taking the edge off her appetite.

"Don't worry. I'll check it all out before I let you go in." Simon switched off the fans, then opened the door and stood aside to let her pass. "I still have a room booked at the hotel. You can stay there for now."

She brushed past him, her face tense, and for a moment he had an insane urge to take her in his arms and reassure her. Impatient with himself, he locked the door and followed her down the stairs.

The roadside stall he chose obviously met with Hilary's approval. She was so enchanted he couldn't help watching her. She seemed absorbed as the man deftly turned the sticks of barbecued meat on the grill, then speared a square of pineapple onto one of them to finish it off.

Simon watched as she touched the meat with the end of her tongue, experimenting with the taste of it. He felt a tug of regret. If things had been different, he might have enjoyed showing her the sights of Bangkok.

She had none of the pretenses displayed by most of the women he'd met. She didn't hide her pleasure behind a veneer of bored sophistication; she expressed it with smiles and gestures and with an honest delight that he found enchanting.

When she tugged on his arm so he'd come and see the display of colorful parasols on the stall a few feet away, he couldn't resist. He fished in his pocket for his wallet, handed the grinning woman a bill and chose a buttercup-yellow one edged in white lace.

"To match your dress," he said as he handed it to her. He watched, intrigued, as color flooded her cheeks. He hadn't realized that there were still women who blushed.

At a complete loss for words, Hilary spun the parasol gently around in her hands. It had been a spontaneous gift and she knew better than to put any significance to it, yet she felt a warm glow spreading through her body that had nothing to do with the hot sun.

"It's beautiful," she whispered at last. When she dared to look up, she could almost swear she saw an answering spark in the cool depths of his eyes. She dropped her gaze quickly, before she let her imagination run away with her again. "Thank you."

"You're very welcome." Simon cleared his throat. "I guess we should be getting back to the hotel."

She nodded, holding back a sigh of reluctance. For a little while she'd almost forgotten why she and Simon were together. She closed the parasol and climbed back into the car.

"Give me your room key," Simon said as he slid in beside her. "When we get there I'll go in first and check everything out, then come back and get you."

Hilary kept her gaze straight ahead as they followed a ramshackle pickup truck down the street. She hadn't really thought until now about what she was doing.

She had to admit she wasn't too comfortable with the situation. There had been something so evil about those men, especially Jerry. She hoped passionately that Simon would be able to handle them if they came looking for her.

She sent him a sideways glance and relaxed. He looked so capable, so confident, that somehow she knew he would take care of her. That instinctive trust was what had convinced her to stay and fight this out.

When she left Thailand it would be because she wanted to and not because she'd been ordered to go. And the devil himself couldn't make her leave without taking the real scorpion with her.

She'd made the right decision in staying, she told herself. The only one she could live with. And she would be safe with Simon.

By the time he pulled into the hotel parking lot, Simon was seething with impatience. Now that the decisions were made, he wanted to get on with it and get it over. He hoped that Chambers's boys showed up before nightfall.

Hilary would be safe in the room he still had booked. Not that he expected them to turn up in the middle of the night. If they didn't get there before she went to bed, they were more likely to be waiting for her when she got up in the morning. Only he'd be there first.

Once he was on their tail again, he'd leave word for Hilary to stay put in the hotel until he got back. She wouldn't like it, but she'd be out of danger until he got this thing wrapped up.

"Stay here until I come back for you," he told Hilary, climbing out of the car. "I'll leave the keys in it so you can keep the air conditioning running." Dazzled by the grateful smile she gave him, he hurried into the hotel. Once he was on the third floor it was only a matter of minutes before he'd assured himself that Hilary's room had been untouched.

He would help her pack everything, he decided, check her out and move her to his room. Jerry and Hal would probably ask for her at the counter first, but if they decided to take a look at the room to make sure Hilary had left, they'd find it empty.

They'd figure that she'd gone home, he hoped, and go back to their own business. And he'd be right behind them. As long as Hilary stayed put, she'd be safe.

He would have felt a lot better if she'd caught that flight out. But he'd known she wasn't about to give up that easily, and he couldn't take the chance that she'd do something stupid and not only endanger herself but foul up the whole game in the process.

He hit the button for the elevator, trying to decide where in the foyer he would lie in wait for Hal and Jerry. He was still thinking about it as he crossed the parking lot to the car.

Then everything was obliterated from his mind except for one cold, sickening fact. The car, along with Hilary, had vanished.

Chapter 3

Hilary was idly watching a stray cat foraging for food among the garbage cans when two familiar figures crossed the parking lot a few yards in front of the car.

She shrank back against the seat, feeling the solid thump of her heartbeat as she recognized the heavy man in the floral shirt. Jerry and Hal were already coming to look for her.

It took her a minute or two to realize that they were walking away from the hotel. Had they been up to her room? Had they seen Simon? Hurt him? She panicked for a moment, then realized there hadn't been enough time for that.

It was obvious Simon hadn't seen them, or he would have been right behind them. She leaned forward slightly so that she could watch the two men climb into a small white car.

Now Simon was going to lose them again, she realized with a rush of dismay. What if they didn't come back? *Where was Simon?*

She looked back at the hotel, willing him to come out. What was she going to do? Hal and Jerry had already started the engine. Any second now they would be pulling out of the parking lot and the trail would be lost again.

Even as she turned her head, the white car rolled forward and paused, ready to weave into the traffic. There was only one thing she could do, she decided.

She slid into the driver's seat, let off the parking brake and shifted the gear lever. It should be easy enough to follow them, she assured herself. The traffic was moving slowly; all she had to do was find out where they were staying and get back to the hotel, she hoped before Simon realized she was missing and started worrying about her.

She drove several blocks, then saw with a surge of panic that the white car was approaching a busy highway. She allowed three cars to pull in front of her before she followed her quarry into the fast-moving traffic.

She realized frantically that she had no idea where she was or how she was going to get back. A sign loomed up ahead, and she squinted in the bright sunlight to read the words. She could just make out the fact that she was traveling north before she passed beyond it.

She saw the white car change lanes and speed up. Battling with indecision, she increased pressure on the accelerator.

She kept two cars between her and the men she was following and gritted her teeth. She'd come this far; she might as well stick with it, she told herself. After all, this was nothing compared to the Santa Monica Freeway at rush hour.

Praying that Hal and Jerry left the highway before they got too much farther, she relaxed her hands on the wheel. It was up to them now.

In the parking lot, Simon whirled in a full circle, his hands clenched. His worst fears had been confirmed: neither his car nor Hilary was anywhere in the area.

Swearing, he strode back to the hotel entrance, sorting out all the possibilities. There weren't that many. And the most likely one was the one he was deathly afraid of.

If Hilary had been kidnapped by Hal and Jerry, she would probably be taken to Chambers's hideout. Once there, she would be almost impossible to find.

Simon knew that better than anyone. Although the back-street stool pigeons were willing to talk if he made it worth their while, every lead he'd managed to dig up had finished in a dead end.

Frank Chambers was clever, and he was loaded. In Thailand, probably more than anywhere else in the world, money could buy a man enough security to keep him safe from everything short of a nuclear bomb.

Simon reached the hotel counter at a run. "Hilary Barlow," he snapped to the surprised desk clerk. "Have you seen her?"

The man shook his head.

"American, dark hair, about so high." He held his hand at shoulder level. Not that he had much hope, but it was worth a try. "There was a mix-up about a letter last night," he said urgently. "I talked with you." For a moment his pulse leaped as the little man's face cleared.

"Ah. Letter for Miss Barlow. I have it."

"You have a letter for her?" Simon stretched out his hand. "Let me see it."

The clerk looked at him doubtfully. "Letter for *Miss Barlow*."

Simon relaxed his face into a smile. "Miss Barlow and I are very good friends. You remember, last night? She asked me to pick up her letter for her." He waited in an agony of impatience while the clerk hesitated. Maybe the letter had nothing to do with her disappearance. And maybe it had.

Finally the clerk reached into the racks behind him and withdrew an envelope. "You give Miss Barlow," he said sternly.

Simon had to stop himself from snatching it from his hand. "I promise," he said, and withdrew into a corner to open it. His hand shook as he tore the end off the envelope and extracted the slip of paper inside.

Written in block letters were the words, *KEEP YOUR MOUTH SHUT IF YOU WANT TO STAY ALIVE.*

He didn't need a signature to know who the message was from. He crumpled the paper into a tight ball, his face creased in thought. It had been hand delivered. Had Hal and Jerry brought it here themselves?

He went back to the counter, tapping his foot irritably while the clerk had a long, pleasant conversation with a young couple who had obviously just arrived.

"Who delivered the letter?" he said when the clerk turned to him at last.

The clerk shook his head as if he didn't understand.

"The man who brought this here." Simon held up the envelope. "Did you see him?"

The clerk nodded. "Two men." He held up his fingers. "One big, one small. American. They call first."

"Called? Miss Barlow?"

Again the clerk nodded. "She not here. So they bring letter."

"When?" said Simon urgently. "When were they here?"

The clerk spread his hands out. "Just now. Ten minute, maybe?"

Simon's heart dropped. Ten minutes. They must have seen Hilary when they left. He'd just missed them. They'd probably come and gone while he'd been upstairs, checking her room.

He paced back and forth, furiously thinking. Hal and Jerry had decided to ensure Hilary's silence. They'd called her, and, when they'd found out she wasn't there, decided to leave her a letter, no doubt hoping she'd be scared enough to get on the next plane.

Then, on the way out, they'd seen her in the car and forced her to go with them. But why take the car? Why hadn't they just taken her in theirs?

Something didn't add up, and he didn't like what he was thinking. It occurred to him that she could be part of this setup, after all. Suppose she'd seen him follow her this morning and *staged* that little scene with Hal and Jerry outside the arts department?

She could have called them from there; he'd seen them arrive shortly before she'd come out. Then she could have had them deliver the letter, and, knowing he would think she'd been kidnapped, taken off in his car once he was inside the hotel.

It was the last thing in the world he wanted to think, but he'd been in enough tight spots to know he had to explore all angles of every situation.

There was one way to find out. He returned to the desk and asked the clerk to get him the phone number of the Department of Fine Arts.

Back in his room, he dialed the number, cursing loudly as the ringing on the other end went unanswered. He would have to wait until tomorrow.

Even before he'd replaced the receiver, he knew she couldn't be in on it with them. She couldn't possibly have made all that up about the scorpion—not with that innocent look in those beautiful brown eyes—and if it was true, why would she have told him all that if she was involved?

He remembered how her mouth curved into a smile and how her slender body moved when she walked. He thought about the parasol, her blush when he'd given it to her and the sparkle in her eyes when she'd thanked him.

No way. He had been around too long to be taken in by an act like that. She was genuine. He'd stake his life on it.

Which meant she was in Hal and Jerry's hands—or, worse, had been taken to Chambers. Groaning, he flung open the door. He couldn't let himself think about that. And he couldn't lie around here without doing something.

Somehow he had to pick up the trail again, and he knew just where to start. This time he'd use muscle instead of money to make someone at the Shanghai Saloon talk, and first thing in the morning he was going to pay a little visit to the museum and the arts department. If they knew anything—anything at all—he was going to know it, too.

The clerk looked surprised when Simon checked out at the counter. "You leaving?" he said. "Miss Barlow leave, too?"

"No," Simon said shortly. "Just me."

Outside the hotel, he hailed a cab. Now he would have to rent another car, he thought irritably. And it was going to be a little hard to explain what had happened to the other one.

He gave the driver the address of his apartment and leaned back, closing his eyes. What had he been thinking of? He should have insisted that she get on the next plane back to the States. He had acted irresponsibly. He never let his personal feelings cloud his judgment, and yet he'd given in to the plea in a pair of warm brown eyes.

It was just as well this was his last job, he thought ruefully. He was softening up—something an agent couldn't afford to do.

He wouldn't let it happen again. If he got her back safely, he was going to put her on the next flight out, no matter what she said. He just prayed that he found her in time to do that, before Chambers got his hands on her.

Hilary blinked rapidly in an effort to stay awake as she peered at the blur of lights winking in the darkness ahead. She'd been driving for eight hours with only one break. She'd had a short stop in a one-street town, where, after a fruitless search for a phone, she'd managed to grab a mug of sweet-tasting tea at a roadside stall while she waited for Hal and Jerry to emerge from a bar.

Now her back ached, and her right foot had been numb for the best part of an hour. She was passing through another town, she realized wearily. She'd been driving on a country road for so long it was wonderful to see buildings again.

The white car stopped at a light ahead of her, and she braked sharply to avoid coming up right behind them. They must have noticed her by now, she thought uneasily. They had passed through several small towns; it became less feasible with each one that only by coincidence would she still be on the same road they were on.

She hoped, with every strained nerve in her body, that this town was their destination. Apart from the fact that her gas tank was just about empty, the longer she was on their tail, the more suspicious Hal and Jerry could become about the blue compact that had been behind them since they left Bangkok.

There was also the inescapable fact that she was reaching the point of exhaustion. The two men ahead of her had probably changed places after their stop. She'd been at the wheel the entire trip and had already had to jerk herself upright a couple of times when she'd begun to doze off.

She could have wept with relief when the white car turned onto a side street. Slowing at the corner, she edged the car forward just in time to see the taillights disappear around the next corner.

She cut off her own lights and let the car roll at a snail's pace, the muscles in her back complaining painfully as she leaned over the wheel to peer into the darkness.

She was in a quiet suburban neighborhood, she realized. The unpaved road cut through a stand of tall palm trees and leafy oaks. Small houses were scattered drunkenly along the street, the yellow glow from their windows spilling onto coarse grass.

Hilary's eyelids dropped with fatigue as she strained to see the white car through the trees. It took all her concentration to maneuver in the dim light, and when the brake lights glowed red ahead of her, she was unprepared.

Cursing under her breath, she slammed on the brakes and cut the engine. Praying they hadn't noticed her, she waited while the silence enveloped her like a heavy cloak.

She heard a car door slam, but it was impossible for her to see anything in the darkness of the trees up ahead. When she'd sat there for a full three minutes without detecting any sign of human life, she drew a shaky breath.

She eased the door open and carefully slid out, her legs threatening to buckle under when she stood. After closing the car door just enough to extinguish the overhead light, she moved forward on tiptoe, keeping close to the trees.

The white car was parked a few feet down the street. Nothing stirred in the shadows around it. She paused, listening for any sound that would alert her of someone's presence, but the silence remained undisturbed except for the insistent chirping of cicadas and the low, throbbing croak of frogs.

Moving a step at a time, every nerve tensed for flight, she edged forward, searching the car and the area surrounding it. She made out a lopsided sign hanging from a thick tree trunk but found it difficult to read in the soft light from the crescent moon.

When she drew nearer she gave a small sigh of frustration. She couldn't read it anyway; it was written in squiggly Thai. She scanned the two houses that stood between her and the one where the white car was parked.

The car was empty. They had to be in the house. And the house was in darkness. Breathing easier, she felt it safe to assume they were here for the night.

This could even be the hideout that Simon had been searching for, she thought with a surge of excitement. She couldn't wait to get to a phone and call him. Not that she could tell him much; she'd have to rely on memory if she was going to bring him back here.

Thinking of the rugged blond agent sent a quiver through her. He was probably hunting all over town for his car. He might even think she'd stolen it, she realized guiltily. If only she'd had time to call him when she'd stopped. But she'd been afraid to move out of sight of the tavern, in case she missed Hal and Jerry coming out.

She spun around, impatient now to call Simon. She prayed that he would still be at the hotel, the only place she knew where to contact him.

She reached the car and felt immense relief as she closed the door. The worst part was over. She would find a hotel, call Simon and sleep.

Committing to memory the street patterns, she drove toward where the lights seemed brightest and found herself crossing a bridge that spanned a narrow river.

In contrast to the area she'd just left, here people were strolling across the street. On her left were a cluster of bright lights reflected in the dark water, and she was elated to discover that it was a small inn, or "guest house," as the proprietor informed her in fractured English.

Hardly bigger than a large house, it was nevertheless clean looking and, in her state of weariness, incredibly inviting.

The phone was a public one situated in the downstairs hallway. It took her several minutes of exchanging gestures and smiles with a charming and helpful young woman, and sorting out the intricacies of the Thai coins, before she finally heard the solid sound of the phone ringing in the Bangkok hotel.

She'd been so excited at the prospect of speaking to Simon that she was speechless when a polite voice informed her that he had checked out of the hotel that afternoon.

Why had she expected him to be there? she thought dismally. Of course he would be back at his apartment, and she hadn't a clue of the address.

Answering her question, the voice assured her that when Simon had checked in he had given his address only as America.

Hanging up, Hilary dialed for the operator but after several frustrating minutes was told there was no listing for Simon King.

She stared at the flowered wallpaper, fighting the temptation to burst into tears. She was so tired, she couldn't think. Maybe after a night's sleep she could decide what to do.

On an impulse she called the hotel again. "If Mr. King should call or come in," she said wearily, "please tell him to leave his number. I'll call you again in the morning."

She was tempted to give the number of the guest house but decided against it. If it got into the wrong hands, she could be in a lot of trouble.

She barely had the strength to slip out of her dress and sandals and crawl into the comfortable, narrow bed. Tomorrow, if all went well, she could contact Simon. Feeling better, she sank almost immediately into a deep sleep.

Simon let himself into his apartment and threw his keys on the table, scowling as they skidded off again and landed on the floor.

He'd spent the entire evening talking, offering bribes and threatening—all to no avail. He knew no more now than he had when he'd started.

He'd left the Shanghai when it had become obvious he was getting nowhere, and then had scoured the streets, looking for likely prospects who would spill anything for a couple thousand baht. That was less than a hundred dollars, but to the hundreds of vagabonds who roamed the streets it was food for a starving family or relief from the ever-constant craving for drugs.

Chambers's boys had covered their tracks well, Simon thought angrily as he slumped onto the couch. Through either hard cash or threats. Simon knew both of those would have exceeded his own efforts.

He leaned his elbows on his knees and ran his hands through his hair. It had been a tough night, and thoughts of Hilary were tormenting him.

He could still smell her flowery fragrance, and he kept hearing her low, musical laugh as he'd heard it at the roadside stall when he'd teased her about the sauce on her chin.

When he closed his eyes he saw the determined set of her mouth as she'd told him she wasn't leaving Thailand. Her warm, kissable mouth.

His thoughts came to a halt as he realized he was wondering what it would be like to kiss that mouth. That kind of thinking, he warned himself, was dangerous.

He stared down at his hands, his heart filling with a cold dread. She was in trouble, and so far he'd been helpless to find her. How would he live with himself if anything happened to her?

Maybe he should call the hotel in case she'd turned up, he thought, then shook his head. It was almost two in the morning. He had to get sleep, renew his tired body and mind, and then he would go on looking. He'd bring in reinforcements if he had to, but somehow he would find her.

Half an hour later he knew he wasn't going to get any sleep until he'd at least tried the hotel. He reached for the phone, willing himself not to hope for too much. It rang for so long he was at the point of hanging up when the tired voice answered.

"This is Simon King," he said, and heard the dejection in his own voice. "I don't suppose Hilary Barlow has come back yet."

He almost dropped the phone when after a moment's silence the voice said, "She call. She want your number. Say she call again in morning."

His relief sent the blood rushing through his body, revitalizing him. "Is she all right? Did she say where she was?"

"No. She say she call in morning."

Simon recited his phone number rapidly into the phone, questions chasing through his mind. Had Hilary escaped? If so, where was she? At least she'd been able to call; he had to be satisfied with that for now.

He would have to wait till the morning to find out what had happened. The night seemed to stretch ahead of him, intolerable and endless. The million questions he had for her burned in his brain, but behind them one little fact burned hotter than the rest.

He couldn't wait to see Hilary again. The knowledge nagged at him, making him restless, and he'd barely fallen asleep when the strident ringing of the phone woke him.

Her voice was music to his ears. "Where are you?" he demanded as soon as she'd said his name.

"Chiang Mai. I think that's how you pronounce it. It's a nine-hour drive from there."

"I know where it is," Simon said grimly. "How the hell did you end up there?"

"I followed your friends Hal and Jerry. I saw them coming across the parking lot and you weren't anywhere around. I didn't want to lose them, so I followed them."

Simon digested that in stunned silence. Of all the things he'd imagined, it hadn't been that. "That was a damn stupid thing to do," he said once he'd found his voice.

"Thanks," Hilary said dryly. "I'll remember that next time."

He made a mental note to explain a few things to her when he caught up with her again. "So what happened?"

"Nothing much. I followed them to this house on the outskirts of the town, then I found an inn and called the hotel. They said you'd checked out."

"Nothing much," Simon repeated, swallowing his anger. "You follow two dangerous criminals for over four hundred miles in a strange country—I'd say that was quite a bit."

On the other end of the line, Hilary frowned. "You sound cross," she said warily. "I was trying to help. You were nowhere around, and I knew if we lost them we might not get another chance." In an effort to reassure him, she added, "Besides, I'm used to driving. I do it for a living."

When he didn't answer, she became nervous. "Simon?"

"I was just wondering why Hal and Jerry took off in such a hurry. It had to be important for them to take their attention off you. Or *almost* off you."

"What does that mean?" Hilary said, gripping the phone more tightly. She listened while Simon read out the note they'd left. When he'd finished, she suggested, "Maybe they figured I'd been frightened enough and would do what they say."

"They don't usually give up so easily. Where are they now? Still at the house?"

"I hope so." Hilary glanced at her watch. "That's why I called you early, before I go back and check on them. I didn't want them to leave without my seeing them."

She winced as Simon's deep voice roared over the line. "Now, you listen to me! You are going to stay put. You are not going anywhere without me."

"They might leave. I didn't come all this way—"

He interrupted her with a word that made her eyes sparkle with resentment. "Where are you?" he demanded. "What's the name of the inn?"

Hilary spelled it out for him. "It looks out onto the river, next to the bridge as you come into town."

"I'll find it," he said quickly. "I'm going to grab a plane, and I'll be there later this morning. You wait for me there. You understand? You give me your solemn promise that you will wait until I get there."

Reluctantly, Hilary promised. She replaced the receiver with a mixture of emotions. He'd sounded furious. She hoped he'd recovered from his bad mood by the time he arrived, for she had a strong feeling that Simon King in a temper would be a formidable sight.

In spite of her apprehension, she couldn't suppress the leap of her pulse when she thought about seeing him again. She knew it might not be very sensible of her, but he was an attractive man and she couldn't help it if she enjoyed looking at him.

As long as she didn't expect anything more than that, she told herself sternly as she went in search of breakfast. She'd have to be her sister, Andrea, before that man would give her a second look.

She was sitting on a bench at the river's edge later that morning when she saw him walking toward her with a loose, easy stride. Her good intentions disappeared like dust in the wind as a sweet longing suffused her body.

The sun painted golden streaks in his wind-ruffled hair, and as he drew closer, she noticed that his eyes were the same smoky blue as the sky above him.

It wasn't only his looks, she thought, feeling her pulse dance with wild rhythm. He was a strong man, a tough, dependable man, yet she was aware of an underlying sensitivity in him that was at war with the facade he presented. She'd sensed it in his apartment, when he'd fingered her jade, and again when he'd handed her the parasol with a wariness that suggested he was unsure of her reaction.

He looked sure enough of himself now, she reflected uneasily. One glance at his mouth confirmed her suspicions. The full lip beneath his mustache was set in a hard line. He was still angry.

He sat down on the bench next to her without saying a word, his eyes focused on the sparkling water.

"That didn't take long," she said brightly. "It's a lot quicker than driving."

He looked at her then, a long, hard look that only made her pulse race faster.

"That was not only stupid but incredibly dangerous," he said harshly. "Those men would have had no mercy if they'd caught you. They have too much to lose."

"I was very careful. I'm a good driver, and I didn't do anything reckless." She hated the resentment that crept into her voice. "I thought you'd be pleased."

"Pleased?" He made an explosive sound of exasperation. "Do you have any idea what I went through last night? I combed every back-street alley, looking for someone who could give me information. I thought Jerry had grabbed you in the parking lot. I was going crazy imagining the horrors they were dishing out to you. And believe me—none of it would have been an exaggeration.''

Something in his voice chilled her blood, and she laid her hand on his arm. "I'm sorry. There wasn't time to think. I knew how important it was to keep on their tail, and it was the only thing I could think of.''

He stared at her in silence for another minute or so, then groaned and pushed himself to his feet. "I know," he said more quietly, "and I do appreciate what you did. Now, I want you to tell me where you last saw Jerry and Hal, then you have—" he glanced at his watch "—just over an hour to catch your plane. I'll take you to the airport myself.''

"Plane?" Hilary stared at him, hoping he didn't mean what she thought he meant.

"I've booked you a flight to Bangkok," Simon said firmly. "Your connecting flight to L.A. is also booked. I've packed everything you left in the hotel. Your suitcases are sitting in the lobby of the inn.''

Simon watched her face change, and he felt as if he'd just kicked a puppy. Steeling himself, he hung on to his resolutions. She had to leave, and the sooner the better. Not only was she a danger to herself; she was a danger to him.

He hadn't mistaken his reaction when he'd first caught sight of her sitting so peacefully by the river. He'd expected to feel relief, even pleasure, at seeing her again.

He hadn't expected the rush of excitement that made him want to grab her up in his arms and kiss the mouth that had teased his mind all night.

He'd tried to tell himself that it was a natural reaction, just as his anger had been. After the kind of worrying he'd done, relief could produce all kinds of emotions.

It was when he'd sat down beside her—and had had to force himself not to touch her—that he'd realized his feelings were a little deeper than that. It wasn't what he wanted or needed. And he had better put a stop to it before it got out of hand.

It was a measure, he thought ruefully, of how tired he was of this life-style and its casual relationships.

Looking down at Hilary's stricken face, he felt a surge of regret. Maybe it was because instinctively he knew that she wasn't the kind of woman who could accept his limitations. She would play for keeps, and that was something he wasn't prepared to give.

Hilary stared into Simon's relentless gaze in stunned disbelief. How dare he dismiss her as though she were some errant child who'd stumbled in his way! This was as much her mission as his. Getting slowly to her feet, she faced him.

"I appreciate your bringing my things," she said as steadily as her fury would allow, "but I have no intention of going home. I told you that yesterday. I was under the impression that you'd agreed with me."

"I agreed with you long enough to get you back to the hotel." His voice held a note of warning. "I intended to leave you safely in my room while I took care of the situation."

"I see." Feeling herself trembling on the edge of hot temper, Hilary clenched her fingers. "Then you lied to me." She was satisfied to see a spot of color appear high in his cheek.

"For your own good." He folded his arms. "You wouldn't listen to reason."

"And you weren't listening to *me*." She gave up the struggle to control her rage and stepped closer to him. "Just like everybody else, you think you know better than I do what is good for me. Well, let me tell you, Mr. King, I am an adult and am perfectly capable of making my own decisions. And not you or that blockhead at the arts department or your precious Chambers and his gang are going to dictate to me when I go home."

She'd been flinging her arms around while she delivered her speech, and her words ended on a gasp as Simon grabbed her wrists and pinned her arms against his chest.

The odd gleam in his eye diffused her temper faster than it had materialized, and she went limp in his grasp.

"One of the things you have to learn about Asian culture," he said quietly, "is that it's considered very bad manners to display emotions in public. Especially anger."

Anger was far from the emotion she was experiencing. With her arms pressed tightly against the solid mass of his chest, she could feel the warmth of his skin through his thick cotton shirt.

In the tense silence between them, she could hear the gentle slapping of the river against the banks and the laughter of children flying kites several yards away, but most of all she was conscious of her heart slamming against her ribs as she felt the heat of his body so close to her own.

Gathering her senses, she tried to pull away from him, but he held her, his eyes compelling her to look at him.

"I suggest we finish this conversation in the privacy of your room," he went on, still in the same, quiet tone.

"All right." She let out her breath as he released her. "But I'm not going to change my mind."

He didn't answer, and, much to her relief, when she stumbled in the long grass he made no move to touch her. She was still trying to slow down her heartbeat.

She hadn't realized that her room in the inn was so small. His broad shoulders seemed to take up most of the space as he sat on the edge of the bed.

Refusing his gesture to join him, she stood with her back to the wall, putting as much distance between them as was possible.

Simon looked at her rebellious expression, and felt a moment of indecision. For once in his life he was out of his depth. He could hardly carry her bodily onto the plane. Even if he did, there was no guarantee she wouldn't turn around and come right back.

What he would like to do was literally shake some sense into her, but he was reluctant to get that close to her again. He seemed to have an uncontrollable urge to kiss her every time he got near her.

He knew full well that if it hadn't been for the fact that they'd been in public just now, he would have given in to the temptation.

Even now he could feel his body sending off urgent signals—which he was doing his best to ignore. "Look. I'm sorry if I upset you," he said, shifting to a more comfortable position on the bed, "but you have to understand that we are up against major-league players here. I can't afford to take risks with your safety."

"You're not taking the risks. I am. I'm here of my own free will. You've explained the situation, and I accept it. Now, why can't you accept it, too?"

"Maybe because I know better than you what the risks are," Simon said evenly.

Hilary sighed. "I think it all depends on why you're taking the risks and if the end results are worth it. I happen to think they are."

"It's that important to you?" He folded his arms, his gaze intent on her face.

"I don't like being ordered around, and I like even less being called a liar."

"You didn't leave your Mr. Phong much choice," Simon said reasonably. "The Asians are very hot on saving face. Even if he'd agreed with you, he could hardly admit it, not until he'd found out what was going on. He's probably looking into it right now, and you'll find it all resolved sooner or later."

"That's not going to get the scorpion back, is it?" Hilary said irritably. "Besides, there's a little more to it than that."

She knew by his expression that he was waiting for her to go on. This time, she decided reluctantly, she would have to explain.

He waited in silence as she sat gingerly on the edge of the bed.

"My father arranged the exchange," she began, her voice low. "He'd been fascinated by the scorpion ever since he'd been given the copy of it by a Burmese native forty years ago."

Her fingers strayed to the jade on the chain around her neck. "He read in the paper several months ago that an American had been presented with a jade Buddha in the nineteenth century by a member of Siamese royalty. When the late owner died, he left it to the Walter Somerset museum, in Los Angeles. Since the Buddha had once belonged to royalty, the Thai government was eager to get it back, but the museum didn't want to give it up."

She smiled, though she knew her eyes were damp. "That's when my father got the idea. He'd studied the scorpion. It had a long and interesting history and, in his opinion, was much more fascinating than the Buddha. It took him months of hard talking, both here and in the States, before he got both sides to agree to an exchange."

She swallowed, took an unsteady breath and went on. "He was so excited about it all. He called to tell me he'd actually been entrusted to make the exchange, and went on for an hour about how much he was looking forward to it and what a great contribution it would make to the museum."

She fought back the tears she felt gathering behind her eyelashes. "Then, three months ago, he had a heart attack. When I got to the hospital he told me that he'd authorized me to go in his place in case he didn't make it. He died the next day."

She looked up, and Simon felt his heart contract when he saw the tears clinging to her eyelashes.

"He was so proud of what he'd achieved," she went on, "and that he'd been entrusted to make the exchange. Now I've been entrusted with it, and I will not let him down, or the people at the museum who allowed me to come in his place. I will not go home until I've done everything in my power to get the scorpion back."

Simon couldn't bear to see that look on her face a minute longer. How could he argue with her? He knew what it was to lose; his loss still hurt, and hers was so recent.

He knew that no matter what he said or did, she would go on looking in spite of him. And if she insisted on staying, she was safer with him than on her own.

He reached out and gently brushed the tears away with his thumb. "We'll find it," he said softly, "and we'll bring it back. We'll hunt Chambers down, and if he doesn't have it, we'll make him tell us where it is. One way or another we'll see that the scorpion gets to the States."

Her eyes brimmed with new tears as she gave him a bone-shattering smile that stirred more than his blood. She was just feeling gratitude, he told himself. That's all it was. And it would be grossly unfair of him to take advantage of that.

"Thank you," she said simply.

The warm expression in her eyes was almost his undoing. With considerable effort he pushed himself up from the bed. "Oh, my motives aren't purely unselfish ones," he said lightly, "After all, if I catch Chambers with the carving, I'll have a heck of an excuse to bring him in for questioning."

He kept his back to her, afraid of what he might see on her face. He was already regretting his rashness. He'd have his hands full from now on, in more ways than one. He wasn't sure whether he was more worried about Hilary's safety or about his potent reaction to her whenever she was near him.

Either way, he told himself, his last assignment promised to be an interesting one. He only hoped it didn't turn out to be more than he could handle.

Chapter 4

I don't know the name of the street, but I can show you where it is," Hilary said. The temperature, much to her relief, seemed cooler here than in Bangkok, and she'd been able to change into light blue cotton pants and a striped camp shirt, thanks to Simon's delivery of her luggage.

Simon, meanwhile, impatiently paced up and down in the lobby of the inn. When Hilary joined him, he had to admit the wait had been worth it. She looked cool and casual and seemed to be bursting with an enthusiasm that he found hard to share at the moment.

The more he'd thought about them joining forces, the less he liked it, but he couldn't deny that he was impressed by Hilary's spunk.

"In that case, you'd better show me the street," he said as they walked out to the car. He stopped Hilary in the act of opening the door on the driver's side. "You may be an expert," he said, holding out his hand for the keys, "but I prefer to do my own driving. You can concentrate on the navigating."

"So, what do you drive in the States?" he asked as they crossed over the bridge. "Race cars?"

"Limousines," Hilary said absently. She was trying to remember on which street they had to make the turn. "I work for a company that hires out chauffeur-driven limousines."

Everything looked so different to her in daylight, she mused. Natives and tourists alike balanced on bicycles, taking what seemed to her to be incredible risks. They had to navigate among not only buses and slow-moving ox-drawn carts but also the three-wheeled taxis that were propelled by the furiously pumping feet of the drivers. It was quite a departure from the noisy engines of the *samlor*s in Bangkok.

"You drive limousines in L.A.?" Simon sounded impressed. "You must meet some pretty interesting people."

"Some." Hilary leaned forward, frowning. "But I just drive them around. I don't socialize with them." She added dryly, "I leave that sort of thing to my sister."

Simon shot her a quick glance. "You don't get along with her?"

She looked at him, startled. Her comment had just popped out without her thinking about it. Her tone of voice must have given her away. "Let's just say we're very different."

"In what way?"

Hilary sighed. He could be very persistent. "Andrea is a professional model and is like my mother—tall, beautiful and very sure of herself. Andrea has worked very hard for her career and fully deserves her success, but it didn't leave much time for us to become close. She goes her way, and I go mine."

"And your mother?"

"My mother works for Andrea—she's her agent. She was the one who encouraged Andrea to try for a modeling career."

"I see," Simon said thoughtfully.

Hilary had the strong impression that he did see, more than she wanted him to. She wasn't sure she liked him knowing how isolated she felt from her family.

"You must miss your father very much," he added. His sympathetic tone threatened to bring tears to her eyes again.

"In a way, I lost my father a long time ago." She blinked, hard. "My parents were divorced when I was nine. I kept in touch with my father over the years, but it was never quite the same."

She was relieved when she saw the turn and gestured abruptly with an upraised hand. "Wait. I think this is it."

Simon obediently turned left and then, at Hilary's signal, yet another left.

"Park here," Hilary said in a sharp whisper as they bounced along the unpaved road. She could feel her lungs tightening with tension, shortening her breath. "It's just through those trees. There's a sign hanging from one of them. I couldn't understand the writing on it."

Simon nodded. "Right. Which house?"

"I'll show you."

She had the car door open when he laid a hand on her arm. "Why don't you just tell me? I'll take a look and come back for you."

"Are we in this together or not?" she said in a low, fierce voice.

He sighed. "I guess we are."

"Then come on." She slipped out of the car and waited until he closed the door on his side. In the quiet neighborhood it sounded like a bomb going off. Giving him a quick frown, she walked slowly past the watchful houses. The sign still hung, creaking as it swayed in the warm breeze.

"Down there," Hilary said through lips that felt like old leather. "Third one down on the right."

She interpreted his look of protest and glared at him. "I'm coming," she said firmly.

He raised his hands in defeat and trod the several yards necessary to bring him level with the wide steps that led up to the veranda.

Hilary, creeping close on his heels, felt exceedingly grateful for his powerful body between her and the house. Then she gasped in dismay. "Their car! The white car—it's gone."

"Yeah, I noticed," Simon said easily. "It looks as though our friends have left."

"When did you notice?" Hilary glared up at him.

"Back by the sign." He grinned down at her. "I would have mentioned it, but you were having such a good time."

Her discovery that she was clutching a handful of his shirt heated her face. "That was a dirty trick," she muttered.

"Just getting you in practice for when things get tough." His smile faded as he looked at her. "And believe me—they will get tough. Lesson number one—never underestimate the enemy. They could have parked the car out of sight and been waiting for us behind one of those windows."

Hilary shot a nervous glance at the windows, which were covered by heavy bamboo blinds. "So what are you going to do?"

"Knock on the door and invite myself in."

He reached inside his shirt and revealed something that had been hidden up to now by the heavy cotton fabric. Even with her arms pinned to his chest, Hilary hadn't realized that he was wearing a shoulder holster.

The sight of the small black revolver in his hand did more to undermine her courage than anything had so far. For the first time, she was beginning to appreciate the danger. Now she understood Simon's reaction to her drive from Bangkok.

She suddenly knew she couldn't possibly have handled this all by herself, and she felt a surge of gratitude that someone as dependable as Simon was at her side. Even if his motives were more for his benefit than hers.

"I'm sorry, Hilary, but I'm going to have to insist you wait for me back at the car."

She knew he would take no argument from her this time, and she had to admit to a sense of relief as she walked back quickly through the trees. He'd done it on purpose, she thought. He'd let her come far enough with him to get a real sense of the danger.

Till now she'd had a vague sense of unreality about everything, but for the first time she was beginning to understand that Hal and Jerry had meant it when they'd said they would take her where no one else would find her.

They'd been actually threatening to kill her, she realized with a shock. Not that it would change her mind, she decided, but she'd certainly think twice before she went charging off on her own again.

She stood behind a thick tree trunk. From there she could watch Simon as he walked carefully up the steps, and she knew by the set of his shoulders just how tense he was.

It was so quiet she could hear the distant tinkle of temple bells mingling with the faint hum of traffic from the main road. She watched Simon pull open the screen door and rap loudly on the sturdy door behind it.

She drew back when the door opened a crack. She couldn't hear what Simon said, but her stomach flipped over when she saw the door begin to close, only to be blocked by Simon's foot.

He gave the door one heave with a brawny shoulder and it crashed open, swallowing him up in abrupt and deathly silence. Hilary winced as she felt the rough bark bite into her palms, and she released her hold on the tree.

Staring at the still-open door, she tried to organize her scattered thoughts. There had been no shot, no sound at all, once Simon had slammed through the doorway.

There was no movement, either. She waited an eternity for some sign of life from the silent house.

The steady buzz of insects in the grass drummed in her ears as all her senses heightened. She could feel the sun burning her shoulders, and her nostrils filled with the sultry perfume of some bright red blossoms growing nearby.

When a bare arm appeared in the doorway and beckoned to her, she let out her breath in a rush of relief. Hurrying forward, she had reached the steps when it occurred to her that it could have been anyone's arm.

Simon's sleeves were rolled up above his elbows; anyone could have done the same. She peered up at the screen door, but it had swung closed and restricted her view. Carefully she placed her foot on the bottom step and put her weight on it, wincing at the resulting creak. Wisps of hair clung to her damp forehead, and she brushed at them with the back of her hand.

Another step, and then another, and she was within reach of the door. The insects seemed to buzz even more loudly as she leaned forward and peered through the screen.

From that angle she could see only the corner of the room, and it was obscured by the shadows the blinds created. Aware that she was holding her breath, she released it, jutting out her bottom lip to direct it up her face in an effort to cool herself.

The screen door opened easily at her touch, and she held it ajar with her foot and leaned into the doorway. The silence, dark and threatening, waited for her.

She could see more of the room now. The floorboards were covered with some kind of matting. A low, round table stood next to a curly-backed cane chair in the corner.

She raised her hand and saw it trembling visibly as she rested it on the doorjamb. Then the air in her lungs jolted out of her mouth in a shrill scream as a tall, lean figure stepped from behind the door.

Simon! She cut the scream off with her hand and glared at him. "God, you scared me. I thought you were one of Chambers's thugs." She looked past his shoulder. "I take it the birds have flown the nest."

"The vultures have gone, but they left us a sparrow."

Hilary wrinkled her brow, and in answer he stood back and waved her inside.

She stepped into the cool, shaded room and at once noticed the tiny figure cowering on another cane-backed chair. At first glance she thought it was a child, then, as her eyes adjusted to the light, she realized it was an elderly woman.

Hilary felt a wrench of pity as she took in the frightened dark eyes staring from a wrinkled face. The woman's silver-gray hair was pulled back in a severe bun, and her flowered print dress looked as if it would fit someone three times her size.

Hilary took an anxious step forward. "Is she hurt?"

"No. Just scared. She wasn't expecting me to come crashing through the door." When Hilary glared at him, Simon lifted his hands in a gesture of apology. "I didn't know she was there. She didn't speak when she opened the door. I thought it might be one of our boys."

"Poor thing. She must have been terrified." Hilary hurried over to the petite figure and squatted on her heels. "It's all right," she said in a soft voice. "He won't hurt you. He's a nice man."

"Thanks," said Simon dryly, "but you're wasting your breath. I can't get a word out of her. I doubt she speaks English anyway, and she probably doesn't understand my version of Thai."

Hilary took the woman's thin hands in hers, disturbed by the lack of flesh that covered the bones. "She might not understand the words, but she'll get the meaning."

After a long moment she heard Simon cross the room behind her. "I'm going to take a closer look around," he said, his voice unusually gruff, "see if I can get some clue of where our boys might have gone."

She barely nodded. The bony hands lying in hers had ceased to tremble, and the dark eyes were watching her curiously.

Hilary smiled. "Are you feeling better?" She patted the hands and let them go, then moved over to the other chair. She dragged it across the room and sat next to the old woman, giving her another warm smile.

"Hilary," she said, pointing to herself. "Simon." She jabbed a finger at the doorway through which Simon had vanished.

The woman's eyes followed the movements with interest.

"You?" Hilary pointed at the woman.

She'd almost given up when a soft whisper escaped the woman's lips.

"May Song."

Hilary almost laughed in delight. "May Song."

The woman nodded.

"Simon—" Hilary pointed at the doorway "—he didn't mean to frighten you. He's looking for someone." Her words died on her lips as she realized that Hal and Jerry had probably spent the night in this house. May Song must know them.

The old woman suddenly shrank back in the chair.

"No," Hilary said quickly, realizing May Song must have seen the change in her expression. "It's all right." She reached for the wrinkled hands again. "We won't hurt you." Somehow she knew that this fragile little woman couldn't possibly be one of them. They must have forced her to give them a room in her house.

Struggling to communicate her understanding of the situation, Hilary leaned forward. "Hal and Jerry are bad men." Frowning, she shook her head.

"Simon is a good man." She nodded, smiling broadly. "Simon will find the bad men." She brought the flat of her hand down hard on her knee. "He'll take care of them." She waited, staring anxiously into May Song's face, willing her to understand.

The dry lips moved slowly, the words slipping out so softly Hilary wasn't sure she understood. "Husband— Chen."

"You speak English," Hilary said with a rush of excitement.

May Song moved her head in a slight nod. "Little."

"Where is your husband?" Hilary waited again while May Song studied her face.

"You not hurt Chen?" she said haltingly at last.

"Of course not." Hilary gave an emphatic shake of her head.

"He?" May Song's hand lifted in the direction of the doorway.

"No." Again Hilary shook her head, praying that Chen wasn't one of Chambers's cronies. "I told you, Simon is a very nice man."

The woman's face softened. "Pretty man."

"Very pretty man," Hilary agreed gravely. She jerked her head up when, from beyond the doorway, Simon cleared his throat.

"They left it as clean as a bathed baby," he said as he came into the room.

Hilary studied his face, but except for a slight gleam in his eyes that could have meant anything, his expression was one of pure innocence.

If he'd heard her, she thought, he at least had the decency not to mention it. "This lady's name is May Song, and she does speak English. A little, anyway. She seems to be worried about her husband, Chen."

Simon came and hunkered down by the old lady. "Tell me about Chen," he said gently. "Where is he? Did he go with the Americans?"

May Song nodded, her eyes darting back and forth between Hilary and Simon. "*Make* him go," she said in a thin, high voice.

Simon patted her arm. "Don't worry. We'll find him. Do you know where they went?"

Hilary could see the struggle going on behind May Song's anxious eyes. "Tell us," she encouraged the woman. "We'll help him."

The silence stretched for several seconds before May Song answered. "They take him, carve jade." May Song emphasized her words with a fluid movement of her hands.

"He's a carver?" Simon frowned. "He works for Chambers?"

May Song nodded. "Chambers make him. Many times. Chen not want to go. Chambers say Chen not work, his men hurt me—my children—the children of my children."

Her voice had risen in her agitation, and Hilary put her arm around the trembling shoulders. She looked beseechingly at Simon, who answered her with a nod.

"I get the picture," he said quietly. He stood up, leaning over May Song, his face grim. "You tell me how to find Chambers," he said in that soft voice that gave Hilary chills, "and I promise you Chen will never have to work for him again."

The old woman stared at him for a long moment. "If I tell you—Chen get hurt."

"May Song. If I can't find Chambers, I can't help Chen. He could get hurt if I don't help him."

After another long silence, May Song's voice shook as she struggled with her words. "Men bring jade from Burma. Americans meet them at border. At dawn—three days." She held up three fingers.

Simon nodded. "Where at the border?"

Again May Song hesitated. "Chen—if rangers take him, he die in prison. Chen old man. Not live in prison."

"Rangers?" Hilary asked quickly.

"Thai Army Rangers. They patrol the border." Simon bent his knees, and Hilary felt a wave of tenderness as she saw May Song's frail hand swallowed up in his big, square one. "I promise you, May Song," he said, his voice gentle, "I will do my best to protect Chen. If he's being *forced* to work, it's unlikely that he'll be put in prison. I will do everything in my power to see that your husband returns safely home. You have my word of honor as an agent of the United States government."

May Song's eyes widened, and Hilary leaned forward in concern.

"You government man?" May Song gasped.

Simon gave her an encouraging smile. "Don't worry. Chen will be safe with me. Now, tell me where the meeting is to take place."

Hilary watched, holding her breath as dark brown eyes stared into light blue ones. Then, as if satisfied by what she saw there, May Song said, "East of Mae Sai. Twelve kilometers." She sank back in the chair as if exhausted by her revelation.

Simon straightened up with a satisfied sigh. "All right," he said softly, laying a hand on May Song's shoulder. "If Americans come back, you tell them nothing."

The old woman nodded. "Nothing," she repeated in a tired voice.

"Let's go." Simon moved to the door and waited as Hilary got slowly to her feet.

"Don't worry," she said, smiling at May Song with what she hoped was a confident expression. "Simon will keep Chen safe. I know he will."

May Song nodded again. "Nice man."

"Very nice man." She gripped the thin hands one more time. "Goodbye, May Song, and try not to worry."

May Song's smile made her eyes almost disappear. "I wish luck for you and pretty man," she whispered.

Walking back to the car, Hilary felt a stirring of anger toward Chambers. May Song had seemed so helpless and so worried about her Chen.

"Will she be all right?" she asked Simon as she waited for him to unlock the door.

"For the moment." Simon held the door while she slid onto the furnace-hot seat. "As long as they don't find out we were there."

"She won't tell them," Hilary said quickly.

"No, I don't think she will." He joined her, then switched on the ignition.

After a few seconds cool air bathed her face, and she leaned forward to get the full benefit from the vents. "So we're going to the border?" She had managed to sound casual in spite of the quivering excitement in the pit of her stomach.

Simon reversed the car, spun the wheel and put the gear lever into Forward. "I guess that's our next move."

Hilary sent him a narrowed look. He'd sounded off-hand. She'd been expecting a violent argument, with him giving all the excellent reasons why she should be left behind.

"I am coming with you," she said, her voice accusing.

"I know."

He kept his gaze on the road, and she wished she could see his eyes. Not that they gave much away, she thought ruefully.

"May Song said three days," Simon said when they were back on the main highway. "That makes it dawn Sunday. So we'll leave tomorrow. There's an Akha village not too far from Mae Sai. I've met the *buseh* there. We'll stay there tomorrow night while I check out the area. There's less chance of Hal and Jerry spotting us. That'll give me all of Saturday to scout the area."

"What's a *buseh*?" Hilary was trying to deal with the sensations his casual statement about staying the night had aroused in her. It had sounded so intimate. And she'd discovered that she couldn't think intimate with this man, casual or not.

Not that he meant anything by it. When he'd said they would stay the night, he hadn't meant together, of course. She moved her thoughts off that subject before they became too potent. Just the mere idea of sleeping with Simon King was enough to bring hot color flooding her face. She caught up with his words in midsentence.

" . . . so he's more or less the leader of the village. You'll see when you get there."

"I'm looking forward to it." Hilary hoped she sounded as if she'd heard every word. "Is it far from here?"

"About a three-hour drive. We'll leave here in the afternoon and arrive at the village in time for dinner. The villagers always enjoy guests."

He gave her a quick glance. "Pack a sweater. It's cooler in the hills."

"What about you? Did you bring clothes with you?" She didn't remember seeing any other luggage but hers at the inn.

"I booked a room at a rooming house before coming on to the inn. Hotels are not the best place to stay if you want to keep a low profile."

"I guess not." Hilary frowned. "Is it far from the inn?"

"Downtown Chiang Mai. It's not too far. I've stayed there before."

She looked at him in surprise. "So that's how you knew where the inn was. You must have spent some time here—you seem to know your way around."

He shrugged. "I heard that Chambers's headquarters is somewhere around here, in the hills. I was trying to hunt down some more information when I got a call from a contact in Bangkok. He'd seen Hal and Jerry hanging out in a bar. So I flew back there in the hopes of picking up their trail. I wondered at the time what they were doing in Bangkok, when the headquarters are up here near Chiang Mai."

He brought the car to a halt behind the inn. "It's all beginning to piece together now. That deal with the jade in Bangkok, and now this meeting with the smugglers at the border—it looks as though Chambers is into a good deal more than drugs."

"You think he did steal the scorpion, then?" Hilary said breathlessly.

"The scorpion, and probably a lot more." Simon leaned on the wheel. "I think he's got quite a deal going. It looks as if Chen could be making copies of jade antiques. Since they have to be carved from Burmese jade—which is the only jade that has the imperial green shading—and the only way to bring jade out of Burma is to smuggle it, that would explain why they're meeting with the smugglers.''

"How come you know so much about jade?" Hilary said, impressed.

He shrugged. "I know a lot about the illegal activities in this country. It helps to know what you're up against. At a guess, I'd say that Hal and Jerry are systematically stealing the antiques from the museum and replacing them with Chen's copies.''

Hilary gasped. "But those carvings are priceless! And, most of them, well-known. They wouldn't be able to sell them.''

Simon gave a short laugh. "You'd be surprised what a collector would be willing to pay just for the satisfaction of owning a valuable antique, even if he was the only one who would be seeing it. It happens all the time. Paintings, jewelry, old books—anything rare enough to tempt a collector.''

"That's disgusting," Hilary said, outraged. "That's putting commercial value on something that should belong to everyone to enjoy. That's like . . . trying to buy the Statue of Liberty.''

"Or the Grand Canyon.''

His smile made her forget her anger. She watched his mouth, fascinated by the way his mustache lifted higher on one side than the other.

"I guess we think alike on that score, at least," he said softly.

She lifted her gaze and forgot her answer when she saw the warmth in his light blue eyes. "At least." It was all she could find to say.

"We think alike on something else, too." His voice had dropped to a husky whisper.

"We do?" *I seem to be reduced to two-word sentences,* Hilary thought helplessly.

"I think *you're* very nice, too.''

"Oh. Thank you." She smiled, finding it impossible to look away.

His smile widened to a grin. "Do you really think I'm pretty?"

She heard the laughter in his voice and felt a flush spread all the way down her neck. "I was just agreeing with everything May Song said."

She turned and fumbled for the door handle, then froze when she felt his fingers on her arm.

"I'm sorry," he said, sounding as if he meant it. "I couldn't resist seeing that blush again."

Not knowing how to answer that, she kept silent, her nerves tingling as he gently took hold of her chin and turned her face toward him.

No longer teasing, his eyes held a softness that liquefied her entire body. "I think you're pretty, too," he said quietly. "I didn't mean to make fun of you. Forgive me?"

His fingers tightened on her face, and she just had time to wonder what it would be like to kiss a man with a mustache when he leaned forward and touched her mouth with his.

Simon had intended it to be no more than a light kiss just to make amends for his teasing, but the second his lips met hers, he knew it would have to be more than that.

He felt her slight resistance as she recovered from her surprise, then excitement skittered along his nerves as she returned the pressure, her soft mouth moving against his.

He lifted his head a fraction while his mind battled with the heated response flowing through his body. He knew he should draw back, but her mouth was so close to his—warm, inviting and impossible to resist.

Hilary closed her eyes when he moved his hand to the back of her neck and lightly brushed her lips with his mouth. A mustache could be incredibly sensual, she discovered as it feathered against her skin and sent little rivers of heat coursing through her veins.

He teased her mouth, barely touching her as he moved his lips back and forth. Impatient now, she tried to deepen the kiss, and felt keen disappointment when he pulled away.

She opened her eyes and met the full force of his gaze. The heat there quickened her pulse, and she parted her lips in an unsteady sigh.

It was all Simon could do not to accept the invitation in that soft sound. He was more shaken than he wanted to admit by the sensations rushing through his body. He was afraid to take the kiss any further, knowing that once the fire in his body was ignited, he might not be able to prevent it from exploding into a roaring furnace.

It had been a long time since he'd felt this way. He had the feeling he was racing out of control, like a runaway train. He was heading for a tunnel where, though the journey was unseen, the destination beckoned with a blinding light.

But it was a dangerous journey, and one he wasn't ready to embark on. Even so, he felt the sting of regret as he leaned across Hilary and opened her door.

"I've got a couple of things to take care of," he said casually, "then I'll come and pick you up. You might as well see something of the city while you're here."

"I'd like that." She managed a quick smile and swung her legs out of the car. "How long?"

Simon glanced at his watch. "Three-thirty? We'll do some sight-seeing and then I'll take you to dinner."

"Wonderful. I'll enjoy that." She managed to hold the smile until he'd waved goodbye and pulled away from the curb. Then, wistfully, she walked into the inn.

She must have mistaken the warmth in his gaze, she thought. It had been a light kiss, a friendly kiss, nothing else. That it hadn't blossomed into something meaningful bothered her more than was sensible.

Annoyed with herself, she walked into her room and dropped onto the bed with a sigh. If she was going to spend the next couple of days with Simon King, she had better get one thing straight in her mind. He wasn't interested. She just wasn't Simon King material. For the first time in her life she wished she looked more like her sister.

Angrily she grabbed the pillow that Simon had flattened with his weight, and plumped it back into shape. That kind of thinking, she decided, would not do her any good at all.

If Simon King preferred sophisticated, glamorous women, it was nothing to do with her. She wouldn't be one of them for all the tea in Thailand. Not even for Simon King.

She was Hilary Barlow, unique in her own way, and she was darn proud of who she was. It had taken her a good many years to reach that conviction, and she wasn't going to let a sexy-looking blond agent make her lose it.

Feeling better, she lugged her suitcase onto the bed and sorted through it for something to wear that would be suitable for both sightseeing and dinner.

Simon drove carefully through the motley traffic, his mind on the woman who had just reduced him to a whirlpool of mixed emotions.

He was like a child playing with matches. Sooner or later the whole thing was going to go up in smoke, and he would be helpless to stop it.

Why was he torturing himself like this, then? Why didn't he just take off for the hills, leaving Hilary a polite explanation, before he did something they would both very likely regret?

Because he couldn't do that, he told himself. He swore under his breath. He couldn't just run off and leave her to sweat it out, wondering what was going on.

Besides, knowing her as well as he did now, he was sure she would probably just take off after him. She had the location; there was nothing to stop her from hiring a car and taking a shot at it herself.

She wouldn't get very far, of course. He frowned, thinking of her stranded in the hills, alone, vulnerable and very probably terrified.

No, he couldn't take that chance. He would have to take her as far as the village. At least then she would be safe while he attended the meeting at the border.

He would just keep a lid on his sexual responses and hope this assignment was wrapped up before he succumbed to her tempting mouth and seductive eyes.

He'd have to make sure that such an opportunity didn't arise, and he'd have to be extra careful when he was alone with her. Because, judging by his reactions just now, he had some doubts that he'd be able to resist temptation.

He clamped down on the interesting visions that thought conjured up. "Simmer down, King," he muttered aloud, "before your libido leads you into more trouble than you can handle."

Feeling restless and uneasy, he let himself into his cheap but comfortable room on the fourth floor of the rooming house.

His reservations still hadn't faded when he left an hour later to pick up Hilary. When he arrived at the inn, she was waiting for him, looking cool and fresh in a mint-green sleeveless blouse and a white pleated skirt.

Her white strap sandals had low heels, he noted with approval. With the amount of walking he planned to do, she didn't need to be tottering around on those spiky things some women thought were so essential to an outfit.

He was tempted to take her arm but thought better of it. He didn't need the touch of her smooth, bare skin under his fingers to remind him of his weakness where she was concerned.

Disconcerted at the direction his mind was taking, he avoided commenting on her appearance, then felt like a heel when the pleasure in her eyes dimmed a little.

"You look very nice," he said finally, when they were once more in the chaotic traffic. "Green looks good on you." It complemented those lovely eyes and put auburn highlights in that rich brown hair, his thoughts added treacherously.

"Thank you." Hilary felt the rush of pleasure at his comment and cautioned herself, He's just being polite. Don't put meanings into his words that just aren't there. "You look nice, too."

What he looked was extremely handsome, she amended silently. His blue-and-gray shirt and light gray slacks looked cool and comfortable.

She couldn't help noticing that the hair on his forearms was darker than the thick blond thatch on his head. As was the little she could see of his chest hair at the opened neck of his shirt.

She tried to visualize him without a shirt and knew just how big a mistake that was when she felt the irritating warmth of yet another blush. Cursing the miserable habit, she stared out the window, praying that Simon wouldn't look at her until the redness had faded.

She couldn't contain her gasp of pleasure when the car turned a corner and she caught sight of an imposing tiered dome topped by a golden spire that gleamed in the sun.

"There are more than three hundred *wat*s in Chiang Mai," Simon said, following her gaze. "Look there."

He gestured with his hand, and she saw a cluster of smaller temples, one with a similar domed roof and others with squared roofs, all of them intricately carved in fairy-tale coils and spirals.

Beyond them, the lush slopes of the mountains, shrouded in gray mist, rested against the hazy blue sky. "It's such a beautiful city," she said in a hushed voice. "There's so much color and variety. All these gorgeous exotic flowers and the temples and buildings—all so brilliant and yet none of it seems to clash."

"It's also known for it's beautiful women," Simon said, slowing down for yet more bicyclists.

Hilary gave him a quick glance, but his expression was quite serious.

"You'll find Chiang Mai quite different from Bangkok," he went on. "It's smaller, of course, and its people have different customs, dialects, architecture, dances. Even their food is different. It was isolated from Bangkok until the late 1920s. Before that it could be reached only by river or on the back of an elephant, through the jungle."

"Really?" Hilary looked at the dozens of tourists crowding the street and tried to imagine them all attempting such an arduous trip. "I bet there weren't many tourists here then."

Simon laughed. "Only those crazy enough to try it. We're coming into the old part of the city now," he said as the car crossed over a narrow stretch of water. "The area is bordered by a moat, and this is where you'll see some interesting temples."

Interesting didn't describe it, Hilary decided as the afternoon slipped by much too fast. When Simon insisted on taking pictures of her, she laughingly protested at first, then managed to ignore his camera as she discovered new treasures at every turn.

The massive pagodas were a medley of styles, and their guardian lions and angels, their gilded umbrellas and gold filigree edges, their quiet chapels, or *bots*, enchanted her beyond measure.

Standing barefoot in front of a giant Buddha, Hilary felt a deep sense of awe. Six hundred years ago men and women had stood on the spot where she stood now. She could only guess at the thoughts they'd had, the sensations they'd felt.

It was an eerie feeling, almost as if she could shut her eyes and hear their whispers, captured forever in the inner sanctuary of the ancient temple.

Outside again, in the warm sunshine, she heard the bells that hung from the temple's eaves chiming softly in the perfumed breeze.

"They sound as if they're singing," she said, slipping her feet into her sandals again.

"Who?" Simon looked at her, his eyebrows raised in question.

"The temples. The bells make it sound as if they're singing."

"I guess they do." He gave her one of those half smiles that always managed to make her spine tingle. "You're quite a romantic, aren't you?"

Hilary shrugged. "I think it's a romantic place. It's hard not to get fanciful when you're surrounded by all this ancient culture."

The expression in his eyes put a little leap in her pulse. "I'm glad you're enjoying the tour," he said, widening his smile.

"I am." She grinned at him. "I'd almost forgotten why we're here."

"We're here to enjoy the sights," Simon said firmly, and, much to her consternation, took hold of her hand. "And there's a lot more to come. Dinner under the stars, with live music, and afterward a stroll through the night bazaar before I take you back to the inn. How does that sound?"

Aware of the warmth creeping up her arm from the firm grip of his fingers around hers, she put her heart into her smile. "It sounds incredible," she said softly.

His gaze caught hers and held, in a long, suspenseful moment when she felt sure she would melt from the fire that engulfed her.

She saw his jaw tense, and she felt as if she and Simon were being drawn together by some invisible force, a force they were both trying to resist.

She wondered briefly what would happen if she stopped resisting, but before her mind could answer that question, Simon dropped her hand.

"I'm glad it meets with your approval," he said in the casual tone that meant he was dismissing whatever thoughts he'd had at that moment.

Shrugging off her disappointment, she followed him to the car and settled back to enjoy the drive to the open-air restaurant he told her about on the way.

If she'd thought the temples were romantic, Hilary decided with an almost painful yearning, the restaurant was a hundred times more so.

The soft music carried on the warm night air, and the pungent aroma of sweet perfumed flowers, the ripples of lights on the water, all added up to an unbearable longing as she listened to Simon talking in his low, husky voice.

With candlelight flickering between them, she watched him while he told her about the history of Thailand and about the villages that were scattered throughout the hills.

He never talked about himself, she realized. In all the hours they'd spent together, he'd never once mentioned his family or his background or his life in the States.

She wondered if he'd ever been married. She found it hard to believe some woman hadn't fallen for the easy charm, the hidden sensitivity behind his lethal strength.

The band began to play a haunting tune with a slow, pulsing rhythm that seemed to tug at her heart. Her eyes strayed to the dance floor, where couples entwined in each other's arms swayed beneath a sky sprinkled with stars.

She felt a thrill course through her from her head to her toes when Simon asked softly, "Would you like to dance?"

She nodded, knowing she'd never wanted anything more in her life. He stood, holding out his hand. Afraid to breathe in case she woke up, she took his hand and followed him onto the floor.

When he turned to take her in his arms, she felt a moment's panic, conscious of the fact that no matter how sternly she talked to herself, she was inescapably attracted to this man, and in a way that could only hurt her badly in the end.

Raising her chin, she looked into his eyes and, abandoning all common sense, stepped into his arms.

Chapter 5

She fitted against him perfectly, just as he'd known she would. Her light fragrance pleased him more than the exotic perfume of the night-scented blossoms. It suited her personality, refreshingly natural and sincere.

He folded his arms around her, his stomach muscles contracting as her hair brushed his jaw. She felt so soft, so incredibly soft.

Her breasts cushioned his chest as he drew her closer with his palm in the middle of her back. One small hand rested in his; the other burned into his shoulder through his shirt.

She wasn't looking at him, but he didn't need to see her eyes to know that she was as aware of him as he was of her. He could feel it in the faint tremble of her hand and in the unsteady rhythm of her breathing.

He knew the chance he was taking, but he felt safe in the knowledge that on a crowded dance floor he would have no opportunity to go beyond the limits he'd set for himself.

He just wanted to be close to her. Ever since he'd tasted the sweetness of her lips, he'd wanted to know the touch of her body against his. What would it hurt, he told himself, to take one small step over that invisible line. Only one step, and he could still back out.

When...how...had she slipped past his guard enough to tempt him like this? Was it the way she blushed so easily, was it her impulsive courage, or was it the moment when she'd knelt in front of a frightened old lady, nothing but compassion in her mind?

Or was it simply the person she was—the person he hoped he'd captured with his camera? The warm, open, enthusiastic woman who'd laughed at the antics of a pet monkey they'd seen that afternoon, silently gazed at a Buddha in obvious reverence and talked about ancient ghosts and singing temples?

Whatever it was, he knew it could be very dangerous. No other woman had affected him so thoroughly and with such apparent ease. When she'd looked over at the dance floor with longing in her eyes, he'd known the reason he'd brought her there.

Even if he hadn't admitted it to himself at first, he'd known he wanted to hold her close like this and had planned it from the moment he'd picked her up at the inn.

It scared him, more than anything he could remember since that terrible day his mother died. It was as if his emotions had been buried in the aftermath of that day and had lain dormant until now.

He'd met a number of women through the years, but none of them had ever uncovered these feelings he was experiencing.

The throbbing beat of the music seemed to echo in the most sensitive parts of his body, tormenting him with an urgency he hadn't known he was capable of.

He pulled Hilary to a stop against him as another couple danced too close, and in his doing so, his hips collided with hers. He felt her shudder as his body embarrassingly betrayed his feelings.

She gave him a startled look, her lips parted, her eyes wide with an answering emotion that made his blood pound in his head.

He wanted her. And, in the same moment, he knew he couldn't allow himself the luxury of satisfying that need. In the past he'd chosen his women carefully. Sophisticated women, women who knew what they were getting into and were willing to take the consequences.

He'd never promised them anything beyond the moment, because he'd known he could offer nothing more. And as much as he wanted Hilary, he knew that she would never be able to understand that.

With a reluctance that was almost a physical pain, he lowered his arms and stood back. "We'd better be moving if you want to see the night bazaar," he said, his voice rough with emotion.

Hilary emphatically did not want to see the night bazaar. At least not right now. What she wanted was to stay in his arms, feel the music seep into her body as she moved with him.

She'd felt his heat beneath her hand, a liquid heat that flowed between them, welding them together. His hard, lean body had excited her, the touch of his thigh against hers, his firm chest pushing against her breasts and the wild, intoxicating evidence of his response.

Now, deprived of that heady warmth, she felt the coolness of the night creeping between them. "I'd like that," she said, summoning a smile. She had her pride. He'd reacted like any normal male under the circumstances and had rejected his feelings as soon as they'd become apparent. He couldn't have given her a plainer message.

He didn't speak to her while they drove to the market. Hilary sat stiff backed and depressed, her attention only half on the brightly colored lights of the city.

She knew she was being foolish. Hadn't she told herself right from the beginning that Simon King was not for her?

She knew what she wanted, and it wasn't a charming, unpredictable adventurer.

She had watched her childhood crumble after she'd been separated from the father she adored. She had seen her mother grow old before her eyes as a second marriage failed, and she had suffered the agony of watching her mother try desperately to recapture her youth with a younger man, only to have her third marriage end in disaster.

If it hadn't been for Andrea, Hilary thought in silent regret, her mother would not have survived. In turning her attention to pushing Andrea in her career, her mother had salvaged her own crushed pride and found a reason to go on.

Her mother's experience had almost put Hilary off marriage altogether, except for her longing to have a family. A real family, children who had both a mother and a father who would stay together for the rest of their lives.

And, Hilary promised herself, she was going to be very sure of the man she married. Safe, secure, dependable and willing to make a lifetime commitment. That's what she wanted, and unless she found him, she'd stay single.

She looked up with a start as the car halted. She hadn't even noticed that they'd arrived at the bazaar. By the time she and Simon had visited every stall, the atmosphere between them had returned to an easy companionship, much to Hilary's relief.

The noisy, bustling crowd, the fascinating array of handcrafts and clothes, all helped to dispel her depression. She found herself enjoying the excitement of watching Simon bargain for her selection of an exquisite inlaid mother-of-pearl jewelry box and shared in his laughter when he presented to her, with a flourish, his gift of an ivory elephant.

She agonized over her choice of a gift for Simon and finally decided on a small silver bell. "To remind you of the singing temples," she said when she handed it to him.

He took a long time to answer, turning the intricately embossed piece over in his hand, then letting it swing gently to hear it's chime. "Whenever I hear this," he said slowly,

"I'll remember the temples of Thailand." His eyes met hers. "And you."

She swallowed past the lump in her throat and turned her head, pretending to look for yet another stall. It was several minutes before she felt composed enough to speak, and by then they were walking back to the car.

"It was a wonderful day," she said, hugging her purchases to her chest. "I'll never forget it. I think Chiang Mai is the most beautiful city I've ever seen."

"You'll be seeing quite a different version of Thailand tomorrow." Simon opened the car door and took her packages from her. "Don't bring more than you can comfortably carry. We have to trek some of the way on foot."

"We do?" Hilary watched him place her parcels on the back seat. "Is it far?"

"No more than a mile or so. But it's uphill, and quite a climb."

She thought about the things he'd told her about the village. It sounded primitive and utterly fascinating. "I'm looking forward to it," she said truthfully as she watched him climb into the front seat next to her.

Once again it occurred to her how little he talked about himself, and this time her curiosity got the better of her. "Where do you live in the States?" she asked when he was guiding the car into the still-busy traffic.

"Oregon."

She waited several moments, then prompted him, "In Portland?"

"Yes." He shot her a quick glance. "Have you been there?"

"No. I have a friend who went to live there, though. He was transferred there and was upset at first, but when he wrote, he couldn't stop raving about it."

"It's a nice city." He was silent for a moment, then startled her by asking, "How come you're not married?"

With the question coming so close on her previous thoughts about the subject, she felt flustered and sought the right answer. "I guess it's the same old cliché. I just haven't met the right man," she said at last.

"What kind of man are you looking for?"

He sounded as if he really wanted to know, and she decided to tell him. "I want a man who will be a partner and a friend, as well as a lover," she said quietly. "Most of the men I meet either are immature and looking for a substitute mother or behave as if they own me and order me around."

"And which category do I fall into?"

His tone was light, but she interpreted an underlying tension that intrigued her. "I would suspect," she said, careful to keep her tone just as light, "that you fall into the latter."

Her answer seemed to please him, and it was several moments before it occurred to her that he had neatly turned the conversation away from himself.

Determined not to let him get away with it, she studied his face and said boldly, "How about you? Have you ever been married?"

He shook his head. "My job isn't exactly compatible with marriage."

"What about family?" Hilary persisted. "Do they live in Portland, too?"

She could see the tension in his jaw as he stared straight ahead. Since he was obviously reluctant to talk about it, she wondered why she was pursuing the subject, except that it seemed important that she know everything about him. Or as much as he was willing to tell her.

It didn't seem as if he was going to tell her anything else, and she had just about given up when he spoke.

"Like you, I have a sister," he said in a tight voice. "She's married, very happily, and helps her husband with their resort in the Oregon mountains, when she's not busy with her son. My mother is dead, and my father remarried and lives in Portland, too."

She'd heard the pain in his voice when he'd spoken of his mother. "I'm sorry." She touched his arm in silent sympathy, her own loss touching her in a brief agony of pain.

He gave her a quick look, then turned away.

"Well, we have something in common," Hilary said brightly, striving to ease the thickening atmosphere. "We've both lost a parent and we both have a sister." If only we both wanted the same things, she added silently as the car came to a gentle stop.

To her surprise, she saw that they were outside the inn. "Thank you for a very special day," she said as Simon hauled himself out of the car to help her gather up her purchases.

"You're welcome." He handed her the last one and stood looking down at her, his expression unreadable in the shadows. "Sleep well, Hilary. I'll call you in the morning."

She nodded, her heart jumping when he leaned forward and left a soft kiss on her lips that promised to stay there the entire night.

Without speaking, he left her, and she waited until the taillights had faded into a blur before she walked into the inn. Sleep well, he'd told her. She wondered if she'd be able to sleep at all.

What with the anticipation of the next day and the memories of this one, the night would be a long one. As for the empty ache deep inside her, she wasn't sure whether it had been caused by the memory of her father or by Simon's casual kiss.

To her surprise, she fell asleep almost as soon as her head touched the pillow, and when she opened her eyes to the new day, she felt refreshed. Though her apprehensions about the search for the scorpion had returned, she was longing to see Simon again.

It was several hours before he finally called her. He'd had phone calls to make, he explained, and they had taken some time to go through. He would be there within the hour.

Hilary had packed her small travel bag early that morning, mindful of Simon's warning to keep it light. After several minutes of indecision about whether or not to take the fake carving with her, she decided to pack it. She was reluctant to leave it behind, even if it wasn't the genuine article.

She put on her cotton pants again and topped them with a white cotton sweater, then agonized all morning over her choice of clothes.

Simon's glance of approval when he picked her up reassured her. He waited for her while she informed the owner of the inn that she would be gone for a few days.

Simon looked rugged and very capable in his chinos and safari shirt, she decided privately when she rejoined him. All he needed was a safari hat and a rifle, and he'd look like the Great White Hunter.

Thinking of the rifle made her remember his revolver, and as she followed him out into the warm afternoon, she wondered if he was wearing it. He'd left her in no doubt that he was experienced in handling a gun, a fact that made her feel more nervous than reassured. It reminded her of how little she really knew about him.

To her surprise he led her to a square-looking car perched on thick, high wheels. He must have caught her look of apprehension and grinned at her as he pulled open the door.

"We're going to need this baby where we're going. I hope you have a head for heights."

"Not really," Hilary murmured as she clambered aboard. Maybe this wasn't the time to tell him she got dizzy standing on a living room chair. "You said hills, not mountains."

"It's the same thing," Simon said cheerfully, throwing himself in beside her. "Don't worry. I've done it before. It's not as bad as it looks."

"Is that supposed to make me feel better?" She clutched the dashboard when the vehicle roared into the street and veered sharply when a motorbike scraped by in front of it.

"You'll be so impressed with the view, you won't even notice." He straightened the car and she tried to relax, hoping he was right.

"I don't want to put a damper on your mood," he added when they'd negotiated the stream of bicycles, pedicabs and buses and were on a highway, "but I want to make sure you fully understand the risks you're taking. Yesterday was a fun day, but now that could all change very fast."

A fun day, she thought wryly. That was all it had meant to him. For her it had been a day that would take a long time to forget.

"We're going close to the border," Simon was saying, "the area where I strongly suspect Chambers has his hideout. At the moment he has no idea we're on his trail, but if he gets one whiff of it, he'll send his goons out looking for you."

"Hal and Jerry," Hilary murmured, feeling a flutter of misgiving.

"Right. And that's not all. There are bandits in the hills who steal everything they can lay their hands on. Watches, jewelry, clothes—anything they can sell. They're a modern version of the holdup men of the Old West."

"If you're trying to scare me," Hilary said nervously, "you're succeeding."

"I'm only trying to warn you." He sent her a quick smile. "Just don't go anywhere alone, or you might really have something to be scared about."

"Tell me about Chambers," she said, not wanting to dwell on his last remark. "I gather you've had dealings with him before."

"Yeah. A couple of years ago. I'd been sent into the Oregon mountains to track down a drug lab he was operating up there."

Hilary's heart skipped a beat when she saw the hard line of his jaw. She was sorry she'd brought the subject up and was trying to think of something else to talk about when Simon continued, his voice low and bitter.

"I was holding the evidence in my hand—all of it, the entire operation—when Chambers walked in on me. It was a moment of carelessness on my part, and it almost cost me my life. Chambers told me in minute detail what his plans were for me, then had me tied hand and foot for five days, leaving me to sweat it out."

Hilary squirmed, her imagination providing what Simon had left out.

"It wasn't so much the danger," he went on. "It was the humiliation of being helpless, with three grinning apes on guard day and night. When you destroy a man's dignity, you scar his soul. Chambers will pay for that."

She had no doubt at all that he meant it. She only hoped she wasn't around to see it. "How did you get away?" she asked unsteadily.

"I had some help. My sister and the man who's now her husband managed to track me down and get me out of there. I went back for Chambers, but he'd already made his getaway."

"And now you're on his trail again."

"And this time I'm going to get him."

And do what? she wondered. What was a man like Simon capable of? She hoped, for her sake and his, that he stayed within the boundaries of the law.

She enjoyed the ride so much she was able to put her misgivings aside. The sight of what appeared to be a tiny doll's house, which was brightly painted and perched on a pole at a crossroads, caught her attention, and she was fascinated by Simon's explanation of the "ghost house."

"The Thai put them up to prevent accidents," he told her. "They believe that the spirits live in them. Almost every Thai family has a house for Chao Thi, the good spirit. If you come across one, you'd better pay your respects before you leave, so you don't offend the spirit, or the family."

"I'll remember that." She leaned back with a sigh. "This really is an exotic country. Even the air feels different, though it's cooler than I thought it would be."

"Just be glad you came in November. Around May the heat is unbearable, especially in Bangkok." The Jeep slowed as he touched the brake. "It's always cooler up here, in the hills, as you're about to find out."

Hilary swallowed. Maybe it wasn't going to be as bad as she'd imagined. After all, how steep could it be if the villages were built up here?

Very steep, she found out in the next few minutes. The track wound a precarious path up a ridge, then, to her horror, plunged along the spine of the hill. She took one agonized look at the sheer drop on either side of the narrow trail and squeezed her eyelids together.

"You all right?" she heard Simon say, but she could only manage a nod, as her lips were too frozen to move. She was glad when he didn't pursue the subject but concentrated on guiding the clumsy vehicle.

"You can open your eyes now," he said after a few minutes, and she saw they had reached the end of the ridge and were soaring through a forest of waving bamboo and tall teak trees.

When the Jeep emerged she saw that they were alongside a vast open field. On the other side of the road, the steep hillside appeared to have been devastated by a forest fire. Blackened stumps rose out of the bare ground, looking like stunted telephone poles.

"The villagers' way of clearing the fields," Simon told her when she remarked on it.

Hilary watched with interest as they approached a smaller field in which several women worked, bent almost double. "What are they wearing on their heads?" she asked, wondering if she was observing some kind of ceremony.

"It's their tribal dress." Simon slowed the Jeep. "They wear them all the time. Wait till you see them up close. They're quite impressive."

"Is this the village, then?" She twisted in her seat as he nudged the car up an even narrower trail.

"This is as far as we ride." He parked in a small clearing and jumped out. "We won't have to hike far." He pulled her bag from the back seat and handed it to her, then lifted out a bulky backpack.

The climb that followed exhausted her. The trail seemed in places to be at a ninety-degree angle. She was sure that without Simon's constant tugging on her hand, she would never have made it.

They climbed in silence, needing all of their breath, and the forest echoed all around them in stereophonic sound. Parrots, screeching raucously, streaked through the leafy branches, scolded by an occasional chattering monkey that was angered by the disturbance.

Hilary, on hearing a faint, low-pitched growl somewhere in the distance, almost lost her footing and had to be hauled upright by Simon's powerful grip.

She answered his raised eyebrows with a firm nod and continued climbing behind him, grateful again for his reassuring presence. She barely had enough breath left to answer him when they finally reached a narrow plateau and stopped to rest.

"I'm fine," she gasped in reply to his query, "but I'm not sure I'll be able to get down again. How on earth do people manage to live up here?"

Simon laughed. His breathing was considerably less labored than hers, she noticed. "They're used to it," he said. "They climb it every day to the fields and back, and carry water, as well."

"The women, too?" Hilary exclaimed, aghast at the thought.

"It's one of the women's chores to keep the household supplied with water, as well as firewood, rice and feed for the stock. They start when they're around eight years old and keep at it until they're too old."

"And what do the men do?" Hilary asked tartly. "The cooking and cleaning?"

Simon grinned. "Actually, they do a lot of the cooking. They prepare the meat and vegetables while the women take care of the rice."

He laughed outright at Hilary's expression. "Come on. You'll find it all works out equally in the end. That should please your feminist instincts."

They walked side by side up the trail, and when he laid an arm across her shoulders, her legs became even more unstable than they were already.

She and Simon had gone only a few more paces when they were confronted, from out of nowhere, by a group of near-naked, silent, wide-eyed children.

Simon halted, murmuring a greeting in Thai that brought no response from the curious faces. He dropped his arm from Hilary's shoulders and stepped forward, reaching into his pocket.

The children's dark eyes followed every movement as he held out his hand toward them. One by one, they shyly stepped forward and accepted the candy he offered.

Hilary felt a warm rush of delight as their solemn expressions turned to smiles and they began chattering excitedly to one another as they led the way up yet another steep slope, then scampered on ahead.

Arriving at the top, breathless and exhausted, Hilary was relieved to see the wide, thatched roofs of several bamboo houses that were sprawled in a large, cleared area between the trees.

The houses rested on stilts, with steps going up to the raised platforms. Hilary was surprised to see not only chickens but goats and pigs in the fenced areas around the buildings. As she and Simon neared the first one, two men came out to greet them, their hands clasped together as if for prayer.

Simon repeated the greeting he'd given the children and received a smiling response from the men. In halting English, the taller of the two men spoke.

"Welcome to our village. We happy to greet you, Simon King."

"Thank you." Simon took Hilary's arm and drew her forward. "This is Hilary," he said, and the men nodded and smiled.

Simon introduced them. At least Hilary supposed that's what he was doing, since she couldn't pronounce either name.

He then held a brief conversation in hesitant Thai and broken English with the two men, then turned to her.

"They're pleased that we're staying for a couple of nights," he told her, "and we've been invited to the *buseh*'s house for dinner. This man's wife will show us where we're staying."

As he spoke, a movement in the doorway of the house caught Hilary's attention. She held her breath as a woman emerged wearing a loose indigo-blue jacket over a bodice of the same color, and a matching skirt, which ended above her knees.

Multicolored tubing covered her calves, and her feet were bare, but it was her hat that held Hilary's gaze. It was adorned with rows of silver coins and balls, colored beads, and ornaments of red and yellow feathers that hung from it and twirled with every turn of her head.

Fascinated, Hilary followed the woman along a path that led away from the main group of houses to a much smaller house. Nestled in the trees, it was hidden from the main village.

She was so fascinated by the woman's outfit she barely noticed Simon's laugh at something the woman had said, and she was utterly charmed when the woman left them with a smiling bow and frequent nodding.

Hilary had entered the house and was taking her first good look around when she realized that Simon was still with her, and apparently making himself at home.

He had stacked his backpack against one wall and sat on one of the thick cushions on the floor, removing his boots.

She looked at him, wondering how she was going to phrase the question. He looked up and raised his eyebrows at her.

"Something wrong?"

Hilary cleared her throat. "I was just wondering, er, are we staying here—together?"

She was glad to see that his face remained impassive, though she wasn't sure she liked the gleam in his eyes. "It's all right," he said evenly. "There are separate bedrooms."

"Oh." Hilary looked around, but there were no rooms, only shoulder-high partitions dividing the whole house. "Where?" she said as casually as her voice would allow.

He jerked his head toward the partitions. His mouth, beneath his thick mustache, was perfectly serious, though amusement gleamed wickedly in his gray-blue eyes. "In there."

"I see," Hilary said faintly. She studied the bag she was still holding, unable to meet his knowing gaze. "And ... where are the bathroom facilities?"

"Out there."

Hilary looked up sharply. "Out where?"

"Out there," Simon repeated gently, "in the forest. I told you it was primitive."

"You didn't tell me it was this primitive," Hilary said crossly, dumping her bag on the floor and dropping onto a cushion. It was surprisingly solid and comfortable, she discovered, in spite of its rustic appearance. "You told me that there are guided tours to these villages and that tourists visit them all the time."

"They do." Simon stretched out his long legs and studied his feet. "And there are several villages that are equipped to deal with tourists in at least a reasonable amount of comfort. Unfortunately, this isn't one of them."

"And," Hilary said frostily, "I suppose you preferred one that was ... unequipped." Her voice dropped on the last word in disgust.

"I chose this one," Simon said quietly, "because I've been here before, I know the *buseh*, it's close to the border, and it's off the beaten track so there's less chance of being spotted by one of Chambers's gang. Or the bandits. They usually hang around the more profitable villages, which have rich tourist guests."

Hilary knew she was being unreasonable, but she was hot and tired and hungry. The knowledge that she was unlikely to see a shower for several days did nothing to improve her disposition.

And she dared not let herself think about food. Heaven knew what they ate in this neck of the woods—probably raw meat and roots.

"Cheer up, Hilary," Simon said in a hearty voice that made her want to choke him. "It's not that bad. We have food and shelter, and even privacy. What more could you ask?"

"At least an indoor bathroom," she retorted. "What about snakes?"

"There are a few you have to be careful of," Simon admitted, "but as long as you keep to the trails and stay away from the long grass, you shouldn't have a problem."

He grinned when she scowled at him. "You don't know how honored we are," he said cheerfully. "They gave us the bridal house."

She stared at him, heat flooding her face. "The what?"

"Bridal house." He was obviously fighting the urge to laugh, which only added to her discomfort. "It's where the betrothed couple stays for seven days before they're married, to see if they're compatible."

"You're joking," Hilary said desperately, knowing he wasn't.

He placed a hand on his chest. "On my word of honor. You don't have to worry, though. I won't take advantage of the situation."

Hilary's outraged expression was too much for him, and the force of his explosive laughter rocked him backward.

With a guttural sound of exasperation, Hilary scrambled to her feet and went outside to cool off her flaming face. It was several long minutes before she felt ready to go back.

There were no windows in the house, though suffused light filtered through the bamboo walls, giving the interior a shadowy half light that was both cool and intimate.

The only furnishings in the living area were the cushions, a very low table and, in the center of the room, a small fire pit covered by a grill.

No couple, Hilary thought grimly, would be in doubt as to their compatibility by the end of seven days here.

Simon's voice greeted her from the end of the house, and she jumped guiltily. She could just see his head above the partition as he moved around.

"Your room is the one in the middle," he said, his gaze on whatever he was doing. "You'll find it comfortable enough, though I'm afraid there isn't a dressing table or closet or attached bathroom with a shower—"

"All right." Determined to make the best of it, she gave him a good-humored smile. "I get the picture. It just took a bit of getting used to." She picked up her bag and moved around the partition into the center room. A short-legged cot stood in one corner, with a wooden chest placed next to it.

"If you want a shower," Simon said from the other side of the partition, "there's a very nice waterfall a short distance from here."

Of course! Hilary thought helplessly. What else?

"It's kind of a communal thing, I'm afraid—" his head disappeared from view briefly, then popped up again "—but if you time it right, you'll get some privacy. The villagers usually use it early in the morning, so it's safe enough now." He grinned at her over the partition and then moved into the opening that served as a doorway.

The first thing Hilary registered was that there were no doors between the partitions and the only thing dividing Simon's room from hers was little more than a screen.

The second thing that registered was that Simon was wearing a pair of very brief, ragged cutoffs and nothing else.

Simon saw her bemused expression and cursed inwardly. He should have put a shirt on, he told himself. He'd acted without thinking. Or had he? Hadn't a small part of him wanted to see what her reaction would be if he walked in on her when he was half-naked?

Even as his mind formed the doubt, he dismissed it. He knew better than to tempt fate that way. As it was, he felt rooted to the spot as Hilary's gaze burned over his body.

He couldn't believe that he was at a loss for what to say next. He, Simon King, who always knew the right words for any occasion, was actually floundering for a remark to defuse a tension that hummed with electricity.

They were like two bare wires—one touch and the sparks would set off a charge that would consume them both. He held his breath, knowing he should back off and not sure how to do it.

Hilary, caught in the same heated current, stared in helpless fascination. More than once she'd pictured him bare chested, but, faced with the reality, she was stunned by her own reactions.

He stood with his feet braced apart, one hand holding a towel. His legs were long and tanned, with muscular thighs and calves. Dark blond hair covered his chest to a point a few inches above his navel, then crept down behind his waistband.

She closed her eyes briefly to escape her imagination filling in the rest. Hot, pulsing need throbbed through her, shocking her with its intensity. She'd heard about women being turned on by a man's body but until that moment she'd never fully appreciated the impact of that statement.

If just the sight of him could have this effect on her, she thought wildly, what would his touch do to her? Desperately she blocked out the erotic visions that were crowding her mind.

She didn't know if she was relieved or disappointed when Simon said a little huskily, "I'm going to take a dip now, if you want me to show you where the waterfall is."

She focused on his face and made an effort to recover her poise. "I didn't bring a swimsuit," she said, and the moment the words were out of her head, she knew what his answer would be. This whole thing was beginning to seem like a bad Tarzan movie, she thought desperately.

He didn't disappoint her. "I didn't, either," he said deliberately. "It isn't necessary around here. If you want to wait till I get back, I can show you the way then."

She knew her face must be the color of a ripe strawberry. "Thank you. I'd appreciate that."

He nodded, paused as if he wanted to say something else, then apparently changed his mind, spun around and went back through his room to the door at the other end of the house.

Hilary sat on her bed, grateful to take the weight off her trembling legs. She couldn't do this, she thought, close to hysteria. She could not spend the night in these isolated, intimate surroundings and be separated from that man by nothing more than a bamboo screen.

She was going to end up making an utter fool of herself. How could she let herself get so batty over a man like Simon King, especially since his sole purpose in life seemed to be to embarrass her?

How could he do that to her? Standing up, she kicked at her bag with her sandaled foot and winced as her bare toe stung with the contact.

He could do that to her because it hadn't occurred to him that there was a problem, she thought miserably. As far as he was concerned, there *was* no problem. He hadn't even flinched when she'd told him she had no swimsuit. He couldn't have cared less if she'd gone swimming in the nude with him—that was how little effect she had on him.

For a moment there, when she'd first seen him standing in the doorway, she'd imagined she'd detected a hint of excitement in those cool blue eyes. And he *had* kissed her twice, and there *had* been that moment last night, when they'd bumped against each other on the dance floor.

She sighed. It must have been the music or something. And his kisses had been the casual ones of a friend, nothing more. If he'd been the slightest bit interested in her, he would not have ignored that moment just now. She was practically panting after him; he had to have known it.

Though what she would have done if he had made a move, she didn't want to think about. Simon King was not the man for her. He didn't fit into her plans. He wasn't the marrying kind; he'd told her so.

So why, she asked herself wretchedly, did she have the unsettling conviction that if he asked her to give up her plans and share his dangerous, unpredictable life, she would do so, without reservation or question?

That, she told herself, was probably the most stupid, ridiculous and thoroughly immature thought she'd ever had. It didn't help to know that without a doubt, despite all that, it happened to be the truth.

Chapter 6

The dinner that evening turned out to be far better than Hilary's nervous expectations. The exotic flavors of the meat and vegetables delighted her, and she enjoyed the smoky-flavored rice liquor that was passed liberally around.

She sat cross-legged on a mat at a low table that was similar to the one in the bridal house but much larger. Uncomfortable at first because she was the only woman in the company of five men, she felt flattered when Simon explained it was a great honor for a woman to eat with the men.

Though it offended her sense of feminism, she was willing to see it as a way of life both expected and accepted by the women of the villages. She just felt very glad that she didn't have to live that way.

Simon was obviously well liked by the other men, who all went to great pains to understand his limited Thai. When she could do so without being noticed, Hilary watched him, learning more about him as the evening hours drifted by.

She observed that he enjoyed the company of men, laughing at their comments with a deep-throated chuckle that skimmed along her skin like a tangible caress. He was intelligent, grasping at once, from gestures and the few odd-sounding English words, what each man was trying to say, while Hilary was still working on the first word. He was sensitive to her feelings, making sure she understood what the conversation was about and including her whenever possible.

She watched the way his eyes crinkled when he laughed and that endearing one-sided uplift of his mustache when he was merely amused. At one point he surprised her in her scrutiny, and she felt a deep, intimate tug as his ice-blue gaze collided with hers and held for several seconds, until he was interrupted by the man sitting next to him.

Put all that and his good looks on a well-developed physique, and he was the kind of man women fantasized about. Sensitive yet tough, determined yet considerate, intelligent and endowed with a sense of humor—what more could a woman ask for?

Commitment, she answered herself sadly. Simon was a beautiful man to look at, and fun to be with, but it was all on the surface. It didn't go any deeper than that. Not for her, anyway. And maybe, knowing Simon, not for any woman. He was married to his job, to the excitement and the danger, to the freedom and the pride of achievement.

She sighed. What a waste. What a criminal waste.

She forgot her somber thoughts when Simon informed her after the meal that they had been asked to join the younger village members at their dancing ground.

She and Simon were escorted to the area by a giggling group of teenagers, which reminded Hilary that some things were universal. The dance floor was a large clearing of bare earth and surrounded by three long wooden benches placed at right angles to form an open-sided square.

The music was provided by the girls singing their low, chanting melodies in unison while they danced in circles, then in circles within circles. Shoulder to shoulder, using simple steps to basic rhythms, they moved slowly around the square, their silver hats gleaming in the moonlight.

The boys sat on the benches, watching them, sometimes joining in the chanting music with their deep voices. One boy sat with a cylindrical drum made of animal skin stretched over a hollow log. His pulsing accompaniment to the chanting added a primeval beat that Hilary found almost unbearably erotic.

She was painfully conscious of Simon's powerful body next to her on the bench and was almost tempted to accept the girls' invitation to join in the dance, just to remove herself from the exquisite torture.

She was delighted when the two young girls, accepting her polite refusal, turned to Simon and tugged on his hands. Good-naturedly he jumped up, and she was reduced to an even worse misery as she watched his hips swaying seductively while he joined the giggling girls in a passable imitation of their rhythmic dance.

Sitting there, listening to the ancient chanting under a starry sky, she found it difficult to remember the reasons she and Simon had come there and what could be ahead of them.

He returned to her amid a burst of applause, his wide grin bringing a heady response that she couldn't suppress.

"You have hidden talents, Mr. King," she said lightly, to hide her rush of emotion. "I had no idea you were such a proficient dancer."

His eyes challenged her as he looked down at her. "You'd be surprised what I'm proficient at."

His smile destroyed what little composure she had left. She pulled her gaze away from his and pretended a great interest in the next dance, trying to ignore his soft chuckle as he sat down next to her.

She spent the next hour trying to avoid the brush of his bare arm against hers, and it was with a mixture of relief and regret that she watched the dancers signal an end to the evening.

The walk back to the house was pure agony for Hilary. She tried desperately to act as if the thought of spending the night in that cozy atmosphere wasn't affecting her one bit, but she knew she'd failed miserably when Simon remarked that if she kept shaking the oil lamp she'd been given, there'd be no fuel left by the time she reached the house.

He was holding his as steady as a rock, she noticed with more irritation than was necessary. Just once, she thought passionately, she'd like to see him disconcerted. If she thought it would do her any good, she'd teach him a lesson—though she hadn't the faintest idea how she would achieve that.

Back in her room, conscious of the fact that he only had to look over the top of the partition to see her, she kept one eye on it as she undressed quickly, slipped her brief cotton gown over her head and scurried into bed.

She reached for the lamp to turn it off, but her hand froze in motion as Simon's voice came softly from the next room.

"Good night, Hilary. Sleep well."

"Good night," she whispered back, then chided herself for wishing he'd been tempted—just once—to peek.

On the other side of the bamboo partition, Simon lay in an agony of frustration. He'd been a fool to think he could carry this off without it bothering him.

Bothering him. He gave a silent, mirthless laugh. That was the understatement of the century. His whole body was on fire. He was going to go out of his mind—the woman was driving him crazy.

Every look tonight, every touch, had been loaded with sexual awareness. He'd have to be a saint to ignore it, and he was no saint. He couldn't believe he hadn't taken her up on the promise that had been burning in her gaze when she looked at him.

Not that he didn't want to. It was all he could do not to go around this stupid little piece of bamboo that was separating them and do what his body and his mind were urging him to do.

It had been almost more than he could bear that afternoon, when he'd kept guard on her at the waterfall—unknown to her, of course. He'd been so tempted to look at her, and had thought of nothing else the whole time he'd waited for her.

He'd spent the entire evening letting his imagination draw for him what he'd been too afraid to see earlier. Afraid that if he'd given in to that temptation, he'd have given in to the rest.

Since when did he play Sir Galahad, anyway? he asked himself dryly. What was so different about this woman that he was denying all his natural urges, especially when he knew his advances would be welcome?

He was no fool. He knew an invitation when he saw one, even if Hilary wasn't aware she was sending off signals like a homing device. And she wasn't aware of it; he'd had enough experience to be sure of that.

And that was it, wasn't it? he told himself. She was too vulnerable. He couldn't bring himself to start something he wasn't prepared to pursue. Not with Hilary. She meant far too much to him to risk hurting her like that.

He lay still, examining that thought. He had a real problem. And he had better deal with it, he decided, before things got out of hand.

Just how he was going to do that was, for now, a mystery. He had too much else on his mind. Tomorrow night he would be settled into his cover, once he learned where the meeting would take place.

That shouldn't be too difficult, he figured, since the number of possible places for a border crossing was limited. The smugglers usually used the same trails over and over again.

Then he would follow Hal and Jerry back to Chambers's headquarters and take it from there.

Simon turned onto his side, feeling a surge of guilt at the thought of leaving Hilary in the village on her own. It could be days before he got everything wrapped up and could come back for her. She would be furious with him, he knew, but she would be safe.

He comforted himself with a decision to ask one of the women to keep her company in this house until he got back. Hilary would be safe enough here; the bandits rarely came into a village, especially one like this, since there was so little to steal.

He lay for a long time, listening to the forest's night sounds, which easily filtered through the bamboo walls. It always seemed so much noisier at night, all that croaking, hooting and whistling.

He could hear the faint grunts from the pigs, asleep under the houses in the main part of the village, and his stomach clenched as he heard the distant tinkle of a cow bell. It reminded him of the bell Hilary had given him. He'd tucked it into his backpack before he left Chiang Mai, unable to leave it behind.

He threw an arm over his eyes in a gesture of despair. He was getting sentimental. Much more of this and he'd be a basket case. At least after tomorrow he could forget about her while he concentrated on his job.

He shut his eyes in a determined effort to go to sleep, and opened them again a couple of hours later to the beat of the village women husking rice on their foot-treadle mortars.

He lay quiet, trying not to think of the woman who slept so close to him, until the chattering sounds fading into the distance told him the villagers were on their way to the fields.

Moving carefully, he slid his legs to the floor and reached for his shorts. The sun was already high enough to send slim rays of light through the walls. It would be good to feel the chill of the water against his burning skin, he thought as he slowly opened the door.

Striding through the tall palms and swaying bamboo, he drew in deep breaths of the warm, moist air. A faint mist still hung in the branches, sending rays of sunlight to the forest floor.

He reached the edge of the rushing waterfall and looked down into the clear blue pool below. That's what he needed—cold, clean water to wash away the ache that had left him restless and woolly-headed. He needed a clear mind for what he had to do tonight. He couldn't afford this distraction. He laid his towel on the ground, then slid his watch off and slipped it inside the folds of the towel.

He tugged at the button of his cutoffs and pushed the zipper down. He would see that Hilary was occupied today. He'd have the elder women show her how they make their various handcrafts. That should keep her mind off things while he was gone.

He dropped his shorts onto the towel, raised his hands above his head, paused for a few seconds, then dived into the chilling, exhilarating depths of the pool.

Back inside the house, Hilary scrambled into her clothes before Simon could return and find her undressed. She'd heard him leave and guessed he'd gone to the waterfall.

She decided to take her own bath later, after he'd gone to scout around for the smugglers' meeting place. In the meantime, if she hurried she could make use of the privacy of the forest before he came back.

The beauty of the morning took her breath away. The air, already warm, was filled with the exotic perfumes of the jungle, and she watched in delight as two colorful parrots sat high in the branches of a palm tree, chattering quietly, nodding as they nudged each other with their beaks.

The display of intimacy brought a fresh ache to her body, and she moved away, determined not to dwell on what might have been. Maybe soon she'd have the scorpion back and could then go home and try to forget this Shangri-la and its bittersweet memories.

* * *

Simon broke through the surface of the water, gasping as his body recovered from the chilling impact. He tossed his head, flinging the water out of his hair, and as he did so, he caught a movement from the trees at the edge of the pool.

He stared in disbelief as the ragged figure reached for the towel and grabbed it with the cutoffs rolled up inside. Letting out a roar of outrage, Simon took three powerful strokes and reached the bank.

Even as he hauled himself out of the pool, he knew he was too late. The bandit, far faster on the callused soles of his feet than Simon could ever be, was long gone.

Cursing over the loss of his watch, Simon stood with water dripping from him and stared into the thick forest. He would have to ask Hilary to lend him her watch.

Hilary. His skin tingled as it dawned on him that he had nothing to cover himself with. Everything he had was back at the house. With Hilary.

He grabbed a handful of foliage from a broad-leaved plant, dried himself as best he could, then eyed the leaves thoughtfully. They weren't much, he thought but they would cover the essentials.

At least he wouldn't have to walk through the village like this, he mused with a wry smile, though the villagers probably wouldn't give him a second look.

Hilary was another matter. He would just have to slip into his room without her noticing. With any luck, he told himself as he stepped carefully back to the house, she would still be asleep.

Hilary was intent on watching the incredibly beautiful markings of a large butterfly when she heard the sharp snap of a twig.

It was close by—too close. She straightened quickly, her mind full of Simon's warnings about bandits. She'd taken no more than three steps when she saw Simon step out into the clearing.

She slapped her hand over her mouth to stop the gasp. He was within a few feet of her and apparently hadn't seen her there beside a thick stand of bamboo.

He was stark naked except for a bunch of leaves he held against his belly.

What had happened to his clothes? she thought wildly. Surely he hadn't gone out like that. Her question was answered when he moved gingerly toward the house as if worried about making a noise.

Someone must have taken his clothes, she realized. A bandit? She pressed her hand harder against her mouth as she took in every detail of his incredible body.

She'd been stunned by the sight of him the day before, she thought, but it was nothing to what she was experiencing now. Fighting back a moan, she watched him take another step.

There was grace and beauty in every line of his strong, tanned body. The muscles in his long legs, his smooth back and powerful shoulders rippled in the sun as he moved slowly forward.

He wasn't the first naked man she'd ever seen, but he was the first to have affected her like this. She couldn't think, or even breathe; she could only marvel at the magnificent form of the man in front of her.

He moved out of sight, and, anxious to keep him in view for as long as possible, she stepped forward. Her foot collided with an exposed root, and she stumbled into the bamboo with a crash that went on echoing in the shaking branches.

Simon swung around and met her confused gaze head-on. For a moment he stood frozen, looking like a bronze statue of David. Then he moved his shoulders in a shrug.

"Oh, what the hell," he muttered, and threw down the leaves before turning on his heel to stride to the house.

She watched him every step of the way in silence, her breath coming out in a rush when he closed the door behind him. Only Simon King, she acknowledged with a sigh of resignation, could have carried that moment off with such poise.

Her mouth twisted wryly when she remembered wishing she could disconcert him. Even with this, he'd turned the tables on her. It was her face that was red, not his.

Oh, how she envied him that self-assurance. And how she hated the fact that the encounter hadn't appeared to faze him one bit, while she'd been reduced to a stunned silence.

Now, she realized, she was going to have to face him with the knowledge between them that she had deliberately stood and stared at his naked body.

How she was going to carry that off without wearing a constant flush on her cheeks, she had no idea. Squaring her shoulders, she moved reluctantly toward the house. The sooner she got it over with, the better.

Inside the house, Simon sat on the edge of the cot, his face buried in his hands. He couldn't handle this, he thought desperately. One second longer out there and it would have all been over.

He couldn't take much more of that look in Hilary's eyes without doing something about it. He had to get some breathing space. They wouldn't be able to look at each other now without remembering that moment when he'd turned and found her staring at him.

He groaned softly. The need to answer the urgent demands of his body was becoming unbearable. How he'd found the strength to walk away just now was nothing short of a miracle.

Swearing quietly and viciously, he stood, dragging his shirt on. He would have to leave now, before his body got the better of his mind.

He pulled his camera from his backpack and checked it. He was tightening the straps of his pack when he felt, rather than heard, Hilary enter the house from the other door.

He could feel the prickling sensation all the way down his spine as she walked into her room. It was one of the hardest things he'd ever done to say casually, "I'm going to take a look at the border now. I'll walk you into the village first and introduce you to some of the elders. They'll be happy to show you their craft work. You'll probably enjoy seeing how it's done."

Hilary gave him a tight nod. She longed to ask him what had happened out there but couldn't bring herself to say the words.

"Will you be long?" she said, then cursed herself for sounding too anxious.

"It depends—" Simon hauled the backpack onto his shoulders and looked at her over the top of the partition. "—on how long it takes me to find the location."

Hilary nodded, avoiding his gaze. She pretended to straighten the blanket on her bed. "You will come back—before tonight?" *Please,* she prayed silently. *Please come back for me.*

"If I have time. And speaking of time, I'd like to borrow your watch."

Guessing that whoever had taken his watch had also taken his clothes, she handed it over without a word. "And if you don't have time?" She managed to lift her head and look at him, though her stomach clenched when she met his steady blue gaze. She felt as if she were looking through a force field of high-voltage electricity.

"I'll come back for you, Hilary."

It wasn't until she had followed him outside into the sun, dispersing the tension between them, that she realized he hadn't mentioned a time, or even a day.

In spite of the cold, heavy feeling in her stomach, she accepted the fruit and sweet-tasting bread the women offered them in the village.

Simon ate quickly, in an obvious hurry to be off, and she was proud of herself for managing a smile when he lifted his hand in a cheerful salute.

"Don't go any farther than the main village and the house," he told her, his eyes belying the casual tone of his voice. "Lin Suk will keep you company till I get back."

The older woman nodded vigorously as he said something to her in Thai.

Hilary pushed back the resentment at being made to have a guard. He was worried about her safety. That, at least, was something. "Take care," she said, trying desperately to read some sign of reassurance in his expression, "and promise me, Simon, you won't go chasing after Chambers without me. You know how important this is to me."

"I know."

To her amazement and utter confusion, he took the two steps that separated them, clamped an arm around her shoulders and gave her a swift, hard kiss. "Be careful," he said, his eyes burning into hers. "Don't step on any snakes."

He was out of sight before she remembered that he'd left without promising her anything about when he'd be back.

Hilary tried to be enthusiastic about the beadwork and delicate embroidery that the women worked on throughout the long morning. Any other time, she would have been enchanted with the beautiful handcrafts, but her mind insisted on drifting to the image of a proud, naked Simon striding across the coarse grass and to the still-potent memory of the touch of his mouth on hers.

By the middle of the afternoon her body felt listless, almost lifeless. Sitting in the shade of the stately teak and whispering bamboo, she watched the busy hands of the women while they chatted quietly to one another.

Every now and then one of them nodded in her direction, and she had to make an effort to respond. Finally she could stand it no longer.

She jumped up, startling the women. She had to be alone, to sort out her chaotic thoughts. Simon had gone, and he didn't intend to come back for her until he'd accomplished his mission.

She'd read it in his face and had been unable to accept it until now. She felt resentment, anger and frustration. He'd known how important it was to her, yet he'd deliberately walked off and left her to sit it out, maybe for days, until he was ready to come back to her.

If he came back. Her insides tangled together in knots as for the first time she faced her real fears. What Simon was attempting to do was dangerous. Extremely dangerous. Of course he'd left her behind; he wouldn't take her into that kind of situation, and she'd known it all along.

Lin Suk put her needlework down and began to climb to her feet. Hilary laid a gentle hand on her arm.

"No, it's all right. I'm tired. I'm going to have a nap."

The old woman looked back at her blankly.

"Nap," Hilary repeated. "Sleep." She placed her palms together and put them against her ear, tilting her head.

Lin Suk's face broke into a smile. She pointed to herself, and Hilary shook her head. Patting the leathery hands, she gestured at the needlework, and to her relief Lin Suk sank back on her cushion.

Smiling and waving, Hilary escaped down the wide path to the house. She had to have time to think, to decide what she was going to do.

She couldn't give up on the scorpion. She owed it to her father, whom she'd neglected because she was too weak to oppose her mother. This was her last chance to make things right, to do something important for him to make up for the years she'd failed him.

If only she had some idea where Simon could have gone. There was no point in even thinking of following him.

Her mind whirled with his warnings of snakes, bandits and Chambers's men. The thought of wandering in these hills alone terrified her. What she needed was a swim, a cool, relaxing swim to clear her mind. Maybe then she could decide what to do next.

One thing she was certain of; she was not going to sit here and wait for him. If she had to go back to Chiang Mai and start the hunt from there again, she would do it. Anything was better than spending the days here alone.

She stopped in the house long enough to find her soap and a towel, then hurried along the path to the pool. It was small as waterfalls go, she thought, looking around carefully to make sure she was alone.

Small but beautiful. The three jagged rocks that formed the steps were no more than twenty feet high altogether, but the stream rushed down fast enough to make a satisfying series of noisy splashes as it tumbled into the pool below.

She stepped out of her clothes and, remembering Simon's experience, hid them with her towel in a patch of thick undergrowth.

Sliding into the chill water, she gasped when the cold gripped her body, then gradually relaxed as she became accustomed to the temperature.

After exhausting herself with a series of dives and energetic races across the pool, she soaped her body and hair and rinsed off beneath the tingling force of the tumbling water.

She would not think about Simon now, she told herself. She would give herself a little time to concentrate on the sky and the quiet trees and the cool caress of the water.

It took Simon no more than two hours to find the location he was looking for. He'd expected it to take him the better part of the day, and his search was surprisingly easy and uneventful.

Although he spotted one small group of bandits on a bluff high above his head, they didn't notice him moving silently in the shadows of the trees.

He had one bad moment when he saw the distinctive markings of a hooded cobra slithering across the ground ahead of him, but it was interested more in reaching the safety of the long grass than in doing battle with him.

He'd learned long ago that most inhabitants of the wild would rarely attack unless threatened. It was man that was by far the most dangerous animal on earth.

Using his calculations from what May Song had told him, he kept to the main trails. A vehicle would be useless in this terrain; anyone coming to or from the border would follow one of the foot trails.

Much sooner than he'd expected to, in the thick of the jungle area that covered the border hills, he found it—evidence of recent mule trains, a discarded torn sack, spent ammunition from an apparent skirmish, probably with the bandits who attacked the caravans from time to time.

Although the Army Rangers patrolled the borders, Simon knew they rarely bothered to make more than a token appearance. Jade smuggling was taken for granted as much as the vast opium fields, and the rangers had bigger problems to contend with in their efforts to control the drug trafficking that was a constant source of irritation.

The jade smugglers used the same trails over and over, regarding the occasional fight with bandits as one of the risks worth taking.

Satisfied that he'd found the right place, Simon spent some time deciding on his cover. It would have to be somewhere that would give him a clear view of the trail and close enough that he would be able to follow Hal and Jerry through the forest in the dawn shadows.

He finally found it, in a hollow created by the gnarled stalks of some dying bamboo. After making sure that it wasn't already occupied by an irritable reptile, he decided to walk back down the trail and check out a path he'd seen forking out from it a few yards back.

It didn't take him long to discover that the path led to another access trail to the road. A much shorter one than the one close by the village where he'd left his car.

He had no doubt that Hal and Jerry also knew about this shorter route. If he hoped to follow them, he wasn't going to do it with his car stuck down by the village.

He swore. He would have to go back for the car, bring it up this new trail and hide it somewhere close by. He pulled Hilary's watch from his pocket and looked at it. He had plenty of time. Too much time.

It would take him no more than an hour to get back to the village. Since he'd be that close to the house, there was no reason why he shouldn't stay there in comparative comfort until it was time to move his car and get settled in his cover.

Except for one very good reason. Hilary. He shook his head. What was the matter with him? he asked himself irritably. He was acting like a kid with his first crush.

He was a grown man, and if he didn't know how to handle a woman by now, he never would. He'd go back and get some sleep, he decided. He could certainly use it if he was going to be on his toes that night.

He'd fended Hilary's questions off once; he could do it again. As for this physical attraction thing, he simply didn't have time for that right now. He had too much on his mind.

He shifted his pack, settling it more comfortably on his shoulders, and strode purposefully back toward the village.

He tried to ignore the twisting sensation low in his stomach as he neared the houses. Hilary was probably still with the women, he thought. He would let her know he was back and tell her he needed sleep. Maybe she'd take the hint and leave him alone long enough to do just that.

Lin Suk looked up as he reached her, a smile baring her toothless gums. She shook her head when he asked where Hilary was, then tilted her head onto her joined palms.

"Asleep?" Simon uttered a silent curse. "How long?"

Lin Suk shrugged and glanced up at the sun.

"Never mind," Simon said irritably. "I'll talk to her later." When he quietly opened the door of the house, he felt his stomach churning.

He prayed she'd be asleep and he could slide onto his bed without disturbing her. He stepped inside his room, pausing as his eyes became accustomed to the shadows.

There was no sign of movement. No sound. He crept forward and peered over the partition. Her bed was empty. He wasn't sure whether he was relieved or disappointed. Cursing at himself, he stretched out on the bed. She had most likely gone to the bathroom. By the time she came back he could pretend he was asleep, since it was unlikely that he was going to manage more than a doze.

The combination of heat and the soothing sounds of the forest relaxed him. He opened his eyes with a start to realize he'd drifted off to sleep after all.

He sat up and reached for the watch in his pocket. Over thirty minutes, and she still hadn't returned. How long had she been gone before that?

He tried to calm himself, to halt his flying imagination as it pounced on one horror after another. She had to be around somewhere. He'd told her not to go away from the village, but she'd ignored much of what he'd told her so far.

He took a deep, steadying breath and let it out slowly. Maybe she'd gone to the pool. He gritted his teeth. If she had despite his warnings, he'd give her a piece of his mind she wouldn't forget in a hurry.

He stormed from the house and, ignoring his good intentions, raced along the path to the pool. He reached the edge of the trees just in time to see her rise like a mermaid in the water to rinse her hair under the falls.

His breath slammed into his throat, cutting off his air as he saw her tilt her head back, her small, firm breasts jutting proudly toward the sky.

Just below the falls, the pool was shallow enough to stand, and the water reached to her waist. He wanted to see the rest of her, and in the worst way.

He fought it with every atom of energy in his body. He ordered himself to turn around and run back to the house before she saw him. Before it was too late.

He actually managed the turn and had taken several steps into the trees before his control snapped. He let out an agonized groan and lifted his face to the sky.

He was only human. A flesh-and-blood healthy male with all the pertinent sensations tearing at his body. There was only so much he could take, and he'd just reached his limit.

Before he'd fully realized his intention, he was tearing his clothes off, and with his bare foot kicked them impatiently into a bush.

His knees felt rubbery as he walked to the pool, and although his entire body burned with a smoldering heat, he could feel tiny shivers cascading down his back.

She was floating on her back, water washing gently over her exposed breasts and smooth belly. The ache in his groin intensified, and air hissed out of his mouth as his lungs contracted.

He shut his eyes, pulled in a long, deep breath and dived cleanly into the water.

Chapter 7

Hilary was staring at the sky, her mind deliberately closed against thought, when she heard the splash a few yards away.

The shock caused her to jackknife, and she went under, panic clutching at her as she caught sight of the dark shape coming at her through the water.

The second his body grazed hers she knew him. She felt her own body explode in a myriad of stinging sensations when he dragged her against him. She was conscious of coolness and warmth, rough hair and smooth skin, hard flesh and muscle.

She and Simon broke through the surface together, and then his mouth was on hers, hard and bruising, before they sank into the cool depths again.

She felt him flip onto his back, towing her with him, kicking with powerful thrusts of his legs. When he reached the shallows, he let her go long enough for them to gain their footing before he hauled her into his arms again.

A soaring, triumphant feeling of power thundered through her when she felt him throbbing against her belly. His mouth found hers, and the intensity of his demands shattered her last coherent thought.

This was not the gentle pressure of his first kiss, nor even the sweet, hard kiss he'd given her that morning. This was the demanding urgency of a need long denied, a frustration unappeased, a man claiming his woman in the final moments of conquest.

She opened her mouth to him, tangling her fingers in his wet hair, and something deep inside her began to form a tight band as his tongue mated with hers.

He slid his hands down the length of her back and cupped her behind, pulling her tighter into his throbbing heat.

She answered with a thrust of her breasts against his chest and pulled her hands across his shoulders, then down his back to his hips, her fingers memorizing his skin.

He lifted his head, and she heard his shuddering breath as his gaze burned deep into her soul.

"Hilary."

It was a hoarse, husky whisper, but it seemed to her that he'd shouted it from the hills. She wanted to cry and laugh all at the same time. She wanted everyone in the world to hear the emotion that had gone into that one word.

He pulled back, his gaze traveling down to her breasts. Reaching out, he gently took them in his hands, raising them slightly to bring her nipples clear of the water.

The band inside her cinched tighter as he lowered his head and she felt the rasp of his tongue lift drops of water from each swollen peak. A moan built in her throat and escaped through her parted lips. She moved her hands over his hips to the solid muscle of his thighs.

He straightened, his nostrils flaring, his eyes burning with blue fire.

Shaken, she held that fierce gaze, awed by the naked need on his face. She wondered if her own expression could possibly convey the tumult of sensations tearing at her loins.

Her heart hammering in her throat, she drew one hand across his belly to touch him.

His breath hissed out, and he grabbed her hand. "Not now," he said, his voice still hoarse, "not here. In the house. I want privacy."

Unable to speak, she nodded, and, pushing away from him onto her back, she flipped over and swam to the bank.

Simon found it impossible to move. He used these few seconds to regain some kind of control, enough to get them both back to the house. He felt tiny explosions like a hundred miniature fireworks going off in his body, and cursed his rampant emotions.

He could handle her, he'd told himself. Hell, he couldn't even handle himself. He watched her pull her smooth, slim body from the water and walk the few steps to where she'd hidden her clothes.

His groan seemed to start somewhere between his thighs and traveled all the way up to his throat. His teeth clenched as he strove for the control he needed to make this all it could be.

This was likely to be the one and only time. It had better be the one and only time, he warned himself. He wanted it to be as damn near perfect as he could make it. For both of them.

Gathering the remnants of his scattered strength, he pushed his arms forward and glided to the bank. When he hauled his body ashore, she'd wrapped her towel around her and knotted it between her breasts.

He knew she was watching him—he could feel her gaze searing his skin—but he dared not look at her until he'd pulled his pants over his hips.

She hadn't said a thing since he'd returned, he realized, and she didn't speak now. She stood, her clothes clutched to her chest, and waited while he gathered up the rest of his, then she put her hand in his outstretched palm and walked with him wordlessly back to the house.

He stole into his room. The shadows shifted and were still. He dropped the rest of his clothes onto the end of the bed and waited.

Had she changed her mind? he wondered in a rush of uncertainty. What would he do if she rejected him now?

Again he cursed his tortured thoughts. He hadn't felt so unsure of himself since he was an adolescent and it was all new.

In a way it *was* all new. This was the first time in his life when it really mattered to him. Not just physically but on a deep emotional level that he hadn't been aware of before. It thrilled him, and it terrified him.

Hilary placed her clothes carefully next to his, wishing she could find something to say. Something sophisticated and clever, the kind of thing Andrea was so good at.

All the way back to the house, she'd tried desperately to think of something, but her mind could only accept one thing. He wanted her. And she wanted him. Her whole body ached with wanting him.

She looked up at his face, and the quivering heat in her belly winged down to her thighs. There was no mistaking his intention; it burned in his intense gaze.

His strength unnerved her. She felt overpowered by his masculine confidence, his undeniable sensuality. She moved her tongue over her dry lips and felt her insides trembling when his eyes followed the movement.

She couldn't stop herself from flinching when he laid his hands on her bare shoulders and drew her toward him.

His expression told her he'd noticed her movement. "If you don't want this," he said, his voice whisper soft, "you'd better tell me now."

She swallowed. Still the words wouldn't come. She'd had only one lover, and that was a long time ago. It had been nothing like this. Nothing had prepared her for the smoldering tension that crackled between them, the almost unbearable anticipation of touching his superb body again.

Back there at the pool, in the heat of the moment, it had seemed so natural. Now, with the few minutes of respite she'd had to regain her senses, with time to actually think, it seemed so much more provocative.

"Hilary?"

The question burned in his eyes, commanded in his voice, and the tug inside her was a sweet pain. She found she didn't need the words, after all.

Simon watched, mesmerized, as she moved her fingers to the knot in her towel and loosened it. It fell in a heap at her feet, but he saw nothing but the exquisite beauty of her body. It surpassed even his vivid imagination. Her small, firm breasts, gently flared hips and long, smooth legs seemed to fill his mind, his soul and every pore of his skin.

His gaze roamed over her, and he felt a trembling, aching enjoyment in just looking at her. He was almost afraid to touch her, sensing her nervousness. A thought hit him, and he almost choked on his question. "You're not a virgin, are you?"

"No." She looked at him with anxious eyes. "I don't—I haven't—"

"I know." He ran a finger gently over the slope of her shoulder. "I can tell." He smiled, wanting to reassure her that her lack of experience excited him far more. "I'll take it slowly."

He tugged at the zipper of his pants and let them fall, stepping out of them without taking his eyes from her face.

To Hilary it seemed as if she'd been waiting all her life for this moment. She didn't know or care why he'd changed his mind, why he'd come back. The only thing that mattered was that he was standing in front of her, magnificently naked and, incredible though it seemed, wanting her.

Shyly at first, she let her gaze drift over him, then she forgot everything as the sheer perfection of his body incited a thundering response in hers. Her brief glimpse of him that morning had ignited only a spark compared to the heat raging in her now.

He stood, seemingly passive under her scrutiny, but when she lifted her bemused gaze to his face, she saw that his jaw was tense.

When he didn't move, she laid her hand on his chest and felt the thunder of his heartbeat beneath her palm.

He let out his breath as if he'd been holding it a long time. He rested his hands on her shoulders again, gently, as if he were afraid she might break.

She smiled, the last of her reservations melting at his touch. "I'm glad you came back," she said softly.

"So am I." He leaned forward and touched her lips with his.

She slid her hands to the back of his neck, bringing the tips of her breasts in contact with his chest. She felt the shudder travel all the way to his feet as he opened his mouth over hers and dragged her up against his burning flesh.

"You're so beautiful," he muttered, and lowered her gently onto the bed, crowding her with his body in the narrow space.

She turned on her side to face him, molding herself to him in her need to feel as much of him as possible against her. He wrapped strong arms around her, his mouth hungry on hers.

She answered the urgent demands of his long, hard kiss, returning it with a fierce need of her own. His tongue was a warrior, battling for supremacy over her reeling emotions. She was trembling when he finally lifted his head.

He pushed her onto her back, and she closed her eyes, a soft moan escaping from her as his fingers gently traced her throat, then splayed across the swell of her breasts.

She waited in an agony of anticipation as he explored the soft curves, teasing the sensitive skin below the aching peaks.

He took his time, ignoring the thrust of her breasts as he branded her belly with his touch. When he brushed her nipple with his thumb, she whimpered, her body squirming in a plea for release.

He obliged her, lowering his mouth to the swollen buds. She cried out, tangling her fingers in his hair while his tongue created unbearable spasms of pleasure, and sent them radiating throughout her body.

He spread his palm flat on her belly, and she felt the heat of it as he moved it down to her thighs. She heard her own voice again, hardly recognizing it, when his fingers found the source of a seething, raging torment and drove her to an agonizing new height of passion.

She strained against his hand, seeking release, but he would not give it to her yet. In desperation she reached for him, her body vibrating with pleasure when she heard his groan as she closed her fingers around him.

Simon clenched his teeth as he bore the exquisite torture of her fingers. When he could bear it no more, he gently pushed her hand away and lifted himself to kneel astride her. He stared down at her flushed face, at her half-closed eyes and parted lips, and knew he had never seen anything more beautiful in all his life.

Hilary, looking up into the heat of his gaze, felt a moment of fear. Once she knew this man, there would be no going back. She placed her hands on his thighs and watched the flame leap in his eyes.

She heard his ragged breathing, saw his chest rise and fall, then lowered her gaze to linger on his potent masculinity, knowing that these precious moments might be all she would ever have of him.

He braced his arms on either side of her and lowered his hips until he was touching her. At the contact she moaned his name and slid her hands over his back.

"Now," he said in a husky whisper. With his knee he nudged her thighs apart and knelt between them.

"Yes—now." Feeling the heat of him touch her, she opened to meet him. Her low moan mingled with his as he entered her, slowly filling her with his throbbing heat.

She tensed as her body reacted to the unfamiliar sensations.

Immediately he was still. "Relax," he said softly. "I'll take it easy."

"I'm sorry," she whispered. "It's just that it's been a long time...."

"I know." He leaned forward and gently brushed her lips with his, grazing her mouth with his mustache.

When he withdrew and carefully reentered, she willed herself to relax, then arched her back, her body exploding with new sensations that seared her mind.

In her effort to take him deeper, she held him with muscles she never knew she had. She dug her fingers into the smooth skin of his back, and when that didn't bring him close enough, she lowered her hands to his hard buttocks and gripped the firm flesh.

He moved inside her in slow, deep thrusts, his arms still bracing his upper body so that he could see her face. She turned her head, making little noises of pleasure deep in her throat, her eyes shut tight.

His own surge of passion took him by surprise, and he forced his hips to still. She opened her eyes and looked at him, and he was shaken by the force of the need blazing in her gaze. He wanted to make it go on forever yet knew he couldn't last another minute.

He lifted his hips and drove more deeply into her, excitement drumming through him as she thrashed her head from side to side.

She cried out, feeling the pressure build until she could bear it no longer. She felt him bury himself inside her again and again, each violent movement of his hips bringing her fresh torment.

She heard his strangled cry, felt the powerful shudder of his body and met him headlong, soaring into the glorious explosion of release at the same time he erupted inside her.

Inexplicably, she felt tears rolling down her face. It had never made her cry before. Not even that first time, when she'd thought she'd been in love. She'd been mistaken.

This was what it was like to really love a man. Physically, spiritually, emotionally, with every particle of her being. To become part of him, joined to him in such a way that if they never saw each other again he would remain a part of her for the rest of her life.

She would not allow herself to think about that now. She let her senses take over, concentrating on the weight of his damp body on hers, his face buried against her shoulder, the rhythm of his breathing, the male, musky smell of him and the joy of him being still inside her.

She loved him. And for the moment that was enough.

When he stirred and rolled onto his side, she felt a deep, tearing sense of loss. She moved over to give him room on the narrow bed, and he shifted closer to her, resting a hand on her hip to balance himself.

He propped his head on his other hand and smiled at her. "Hi."

"Hi." Her voice trembled, and she saw his expression change.

He lifted his hand from her hip and brushed at her cheek with his thumb. "Did I hurt you?"

"No." She laid her fingers against his lips, then traced his mustache, gently smoothing the soft hairs.

He caught her fingers in his mouth and scraped the ends of them with his teeth.

It was an erotic sensation, and to her surprise she felt a strong tug of desire again, deep in her belly.

He let her go, his eyes still looking anxious. "Why are you crying?"

"Beautiful things always make me cry."

"You think I'm a beautiful thing?" He raised his eyebrows in a comical expression, and a laugh gurgled in her throat.

"I think you're pretty," she said, and laughed again at his expression.

"I think I prefer beautiful." He let his hand trail down her throat. "Like you."

It was the second time he'd called her beautiful, she realized. Did he really think that? Or was it just something men said at times like this?

"Why did you come back?" she asked suddenly.

His hand stilled, and she wished she could take the words back. Somehow she knew she wasn't going to like what he had to say.

"Does it matter?" he said lightly, avoiding her eyes. "Isn't it enough that I came back?"

"You didn't intend to when you left here." She couldn't seem to stop it now that it was begun. She knew she was destroying what little time they had left alone, and she hated herself for her insecurity. Why couldn't she just accept the fact that he was here, and let it go at that?

She heard him sigh, and he shifted onto his back, his hands behind his head. "I came back because I had to move my car," he said, his voice expressionless. "I had some time, so I was going to get some sleep. Then I couldn't find you and I thought—I went to the falls to see if you were there, and you were."

She stared at his profile, wondering why his words hurt her so much, when it was what she'd expected to hear. She'd known all along that for him this had been nothing more than a spontaneous response.

She'd been there, ready and willing, and he'd reacted the only way a healthy male could have. She'd let her own emotions fool her for a moment, putting too much into that one husky whisper of her name, but deep down she'd known.

And, knowing, had still fallen in love with him.

She let her gaze wander down his body, aware that this would probably be the last time she ever looked at him like this.

And in that moment she knew that she could not just walk meekly away. All her life she'd suppressed her own needs and feelings for the sake of everyone else's.

She'd let her mother and sister shut her out of their lives because of her sister's career. She'd stayed out of her father's life because she hadn't wanted to upset her mother. Every decision she'd ever made had been for someone else.

Now, she vowed silently, it was her turn. She would stay with him as long as she possibly could. She might never have his love, but it wouldn't be because she hadn't given it every opportunity. And if she still lost, so be it. She could live a long time on memories.

The best way to handle it, she decided, was attack. "That's twice you broke your promise to me," she said, propping her head on her hand to look at him.

He turned his head, and she wished she could read the expression in his cool blue eyes. "I never break a promise," he said quietly. "I never made you any promises."

He hadn't, she realized. Except for the one assurance that he would come back for her—eventually—he'd been very careful not to promise anything.

"Well, not in so many words," she allowed. "But I felt we had an agreement. You said we would find Chambers together."

"I changed my mind." He looked back at the roof, his mouth hard. "When I thought about the danger I'd be putting you in, I decided it was too big a risk."

"*You* decided?" She felt a twist of pain as she watched him swing his legs off the bed and reach for his pants. "What about me? Don't I have a say in this?"

"Not as far as I'm concerned." He stood and pushed each foot into the legs of his pants. "It's my job to hunt Chambers down, and it's my job to accomplish that without endangering innocent people. If anything happened to you, I would be responsible."

"Your job." She swallowed the bitterness that rose in her throat. "My feelings don't count in this, do they?" She watched him tug his pants over his hips and pull up the zipper.

He looked at her then, and she wanted to cry at the expression on his face. "I can't let feelings count, Hilary. It could cost us both our lives."

She sat up, pulling the light blanket up over her to cover her breasts. "It's my life, Simon. If I want to risk it, then I have that right."

He ran a hand through his hair in exasperation. "Dammit, Hilary, you don't understand. You don't know what it's like out there."

"It can't be that bad," she said shortly, "if you love it enough to give up *your* life for it."

He stared at her, wondering why he couldn't tell her. Why he couldn't say that he hated it, that he'd had enough. That he'd left the agency two years ago and had agreed to come out of retirement and do this last job only because he had a personal stake in it. That he wanted to finish what he'd begun two years ago, and that he couldn't write the final episode to that phase of his life until he had finished it.

And what then? That's why he couldn't tell her, he realized. He couldn't let her think there might be a chance for them, because he was afraid he might start believing it himself. And he wasn't at all sure he could give her that commitment.

He wasn't sure that he could control the wanderlust in him. He had kept himself free, unencumbered from all the trappings that until now he'd regarded as little short of imprisonment.

Until now. He pushed the thought away before he weakened. "It's different for a man," he said curtly. He knew as soon as he looked at her face that he'd said the worst possible thing. "Oh, come on, Hilary." He held up his hands in a placating gesture. "You're not going to give me that feminist stuff, are you?"

"I certainly am." She tugged at the blanket until she could wrap it securely under her arms, and slid off the bed. He'd just given her the ammunition she needed.

"You are a lot of things, Simon, but I never suspected you of being a chauvinist." She pulled herself up to her full height, trying to maintain an air of dignity. "Discrimination, if I might remind you, is illegal. I have a job to do, too. I've been appointed to deliver a valuable antique to the United States."

She saw the flicker of uncertainty in his eyes and pressed her point. "I'm responsible for that antique, and as such I have a moral and a legal obligation to do whatever it takes to retrieve it from whoever stole it. Any interference in that respect—particularly for the reasons you've expressed—has to be construed as an obstruction of duty and a clear case of discrimination."

She saw his mustache twitch, and hope bounded in her.

"You do know, of course," he murmured, "that not one word of that would hold up in court."

She grinned. "Maybe not, but I'll do my damnedest to make it stick. You might as well accept this, Simon. I am coming with you. And this time, Mr. Chauvinist King, you won't give me the slip. Wherever you go, I'll be right behind you."

"That could be embarrassing."

"To whom?" she said, smiling sweetly.

He sighed. "You remind me," he said slowly, "of someone I know."

"Oh?" She tried not to let her spasm of jealousy show in her face. "Do you know her well?"

His grin made her wonder if he'd detected her feelings for him.

"Very well. She's my sister." Simon watched the relief flash in her eyes and felt a moment of helplessness.

He'd known from the moment he'd walked into the village earlier that this was going to happen. All of it, from his giving in to his need for her, to this, his inability to leave her behind again.

He knew she meant what she said. He knew, as he'd known all along, that she wouldn't give up. That if he didn't take her to Chambers, she'd find a way to follow him. It was the only way he could justify his decision—by telling himself she was safer with him than on her own.

"All right." He held up his hands as she took a delighted step forward. "I must insist on a compromise, though."

Her smile faded. "What kind of compromise?"

"You stay in the car tonight while I go to the border. I'll have to come back for the car to follow Hal and Jerry, so you will be with me, all the way from there. Agreed?"

In answer she stepped forward, slid her arms around his neck and pressed her warm mouth to his. "Agreed," she said softly, and smiled up into his face.

He held her with one arm while he fished in the pocket of his pants. He pulled out her watch, looked at it solemnly and tucked it back in his pocket.

"I think there's time," he murmured. He loved the way her eyes sparkled when she looked at him.

"Time for what?" she asked innocently.

He leaned back and, with fingers that were surprisingly uncoordinated, tugged at the blanket that hid her breasts. "For this." He tossed the blanket on the floor and pulled her against his bared chest.

He felt her mouth open under his, and the throbbing began again deep in his groin and spread swiftly through his body. He contracted his stomach as he felt her fingers at his waistband, and he shivered when she tugged carefully at the zipper.

He stood, motionless, while she slid his pants down over his hips to his ankles, and then he lifted his feet one at a time to free them.

He bit back a groan as she ran her fingers up the backs of his legs, and then released it when her mouth traveled up his thigh.

Seconds later he reached for her, lowered her onto the bed and covered her with his body in one swift movement. She destroyed his control as easily as a flame destroys a moth. When he was with her like this, he could think of nothing else but the heat tormenting his body and the soft, warm haven waiting to ease his raging hunger.

When he finally entered her, it was with a fierce desperation he had never known before that left him shaken and more than a little afraid.

The jungle could be extremely noisy at night, Hilary discovered several hours later. The time until now had passed quickly. She and Simon had eaten with the villagers before leaving, and the children had accompanied them to the edge of the hill, then quietly disappeared back to their homes.

The climb down had seemed easier, and Hilary was tense with the knowledge that she and Simon were drawing close to their objective.

When they'd reached their new position, Simon had hidden the car in a thicket of tropical foliage. After extracting a promise from her not to leave the car under any circumstances, he'd left, melting into the darkness like the shadows that surrounded her.

Sleep, she found, was impossible. The sounds of the jungle whispered, shuffled and called all around her. The moist night air touched her skin with chilling fingers, and she drew her sweater on, glad that she'd taken Simon's advice about bringing it.

She spent her time thinking about her father and the years she had wasted by allowing herself to be manipulated.

Whatever the future held, she decided, she would never do that again. She would be her own person, in control of her own life. Her only regret was that she'd waited until her father's death to discover who she really was.

She pushed her thoughts away from her father and let them dwell on Simon. In one afternoon she'd come to know him far more intimately than any man she'd ever met.

Yet she still didn't know him. Not the side of him he took such pains to hide. She couldn't help sensing the deep emotions he buried behind that facade of casualness. Why was he fighting those feelings? Who was he saving them for? Not for her; that much was obvious. She sighed. There was still time. She would not admit defeat until every door had been closed.

She was drifting into sleep when a flurry of snarls and growls nearby brought her upright on the seat, her heart pounding furiously.

The fight gradually faded away in the distance, but she didn't sleep again. Soon after that another sound brought her up in her seat, then, remembering Simon's instructions, she slid to the floor.

She could hear a car engine—more than one vehicle, by the sound of it. She waited, her skin prickling and her heart once more beating a tattoo, as at least five vehicles slowly passed by her not more than ten yards from where Simon had run the car behind a clump of broad-leaved tropical plants.

Wondering if one of the cars belonged to Hal and Jerry, she had to fight the temptation to look out the window. She waited until long after the silence had closed in on her again, then she carefully raised her head, letting out a sigh of relief when she realized she was alone.

She lay slumped in her seat, barely moving, until a finger of pale light spread out behind the hills, announcing dawn.

Her pulse quickened as she watched the pink and cream rivulets seep across the sky and then widen into a pastel blue as the sun took over.

What was Simon doing? Were the smugglers at the border? Had he seen Hal and Jerry? Was he in the right place? Questions bombarded her mind as she waited, wishing passionately that Simon had let her go with him.

She rolled down the window as the sun warmed the car's interior. The mist had draped filmy cloaks over the trees, and the pale sun glistened on the dew that clung to the long grass.

The morning smelled fresh and clean and faintly exotic, like the expensive perfume of some of her glamorous clients. Hilary smiled. She was a long way from Los Angeles. What

would her mother say if she could see her now? If she'd seen
her yesterday afternoon—cavorting naked in a waterfall
with a man?

Something deep in her belly twisted in a knot as she
thought of Simon. She looked around at the lush greenery,
the tall palm trees and spindly bamboo. Where was he?

Simon was crouched on aching legs as the smugglers
haggled over the prices of their merchandise. From his
cramped hideout he couldn't hear what they were saying,
but through the zoom lens of his camera he could clearly see
Hal and Jerry and the short, bowed figure of the man who
stood between them.

That had to be Chen, Simon realized. There were several
other dealers there, emptying the heavy sacks onto the
ground. The large brown objects, which looked like a cross
between coconuts and smooth boulders, were, Simon knew,
the freshly mined jade.

Chen was examining each one, stopping now and again
to cut a "window" in the shell of a boulder with a sharp tool
to get an idea of the colors hidden within. Several yards
away, Simon's camera clicked busily.

Burmese jade—or jadeite, as it was officially called, Simon had learned—could be varying shades of lavender,
peach and yellow white, or anything in between. But the
bright green imperial jade was the most valuable and would
be essential if Chen's carvings were going to fool the ex-
perts.

Even then they were taking a chance, Simon thought, as
Hilary's discovery had proved. But then, unless anyone examined them closely, it was unlikely that the switches would
be noticed. Objects that are seen constantly become taken
for granted.

Chambers probably reckoned that by the time the operation was discovered, he would have acquired enough antiques to make the risks well worth his while.

Simon wondered briefly just how many antiques Chambers had successfully transposed into hard cash from grateful collectors. He fervently hoped that the scorpion was not among them. It would devastate Hilary if she'd gone through all this, only to find that the carving had been sold and could be hidden anywhere in the world.

If it was the last thing he did, Simon vowed silently, he would make Chambers tell him where that piece was, even if they lost the rest. Always provided, of course, that Simon's own mission was carried out successfully.

He eased his aching muscles into a new position, wincing as a cramp knotted the back of his thigh. If they didn't make a move soon, he thought grimly, he would have to stand up.

To his intense relief, he saw Chen swing a bulky sack over his shoulder, his knees sagging with the weight. Shoving the camera into his backpack, Simon waited, praying the other dealers stayed where they were until he had a chance to slip out of hiding.

He watched Hal and Jerry pass within a few feet of him, Chen lagging behind. He felt sorry for the old man, who looked bone weary and scared. Simon thought about May Song, alone and frightened, and gritted his teeth. Chambers had a lot to answer for.

Simon sat still long enough for the three men to move a safe distance ahead, then he eased his way out of the bamboo shelter. The rest of the dealers were still intent on their bargaining, and he trod silently across the long grass, hoping he didn't step on an unsuspecting snake.

Once he was out of sight of the dealers, he joined the trail and had gone only a few yards when he heard the splutter of a car engine disturb the quietly chattering forest.

Doubling over, he sprinted forward just in time to see Jerry's white car lurching down the trail to the road. His own car, he knew, was somewhere up ahead. But where? he felt disoriented as he crashed through the trees.

He'd covered the car tracks well, so that they wouldn't be seen by Hal and Jerry. Too well, he thought, swearing to himself. The trees and shrubs all looked the same.

For a moment he felt a surge of panic as he heard the white car roaring down the trail, then, to his right, came the cough of an engine, then a rumbling growl as it caught and held.

He spun around and raced toward the sound, reaching the car door just as a white-faced Hilary slammed into gear. He wrenched the door open, issued a sharp command for her to move over, and flung himself into the seat.

The car was already rolling forward, and he was busy concentrating on hitting the trail as quickly as possible. It was some time before he could take a look at the silent woman at his side.

When he did, his stomach muscles contracted. She was hunched in her seat, her mouth drawn tight, her arms hugging her body.

"Are you all right?" Snatching his gaze away again to watch the bumpy trail, he barely heard her quiet answer.

"I'm fine."

"You don't look fine." When she didn't answer, he shot her another worried glance. "What's wrong?"

"Nothing. I thought— You took so long to come back, I thought they'd found you."

He swore. "You were going after them by yourself, weren't you?"

"No. I was coming to look for you. I was going to take the car as close as I could in case you were hurt and I had to help you."

It dawned on him then how much she would have cared if something had happened to him. This was what he'd been afraid of. This was why he'd fought so hard.

As soon as he got the chance, he told himself, he would have to explain a few things to her. Somehow he would have to make her understand that what had happened between them didn't change things. That it couldn't happen again.

That he couldn't make her happy—no matter how badly he wanted to.

But for now all that would have to wait. He'd made up time on sharp curves, taking chances that he knew were terrifying Hilary. He hated that, but he couldn't afford to let Hal and Jerry out of his sight now.

Hilary's discovery of the theft could trigger off an investigation at the museum, and Chambers would probably shut down this particular operation. He was running out of opportunities to pick up Chambers's trail. This time he had to stay with them.

He saw them turn onto the road several yards below him, and he lifted his foot from the accelerator, letting the car coast around the last curve. By the time he reached the road, they were well ahead of him.

He settled in behind them, leaving enough distance so they couldn't identify the driver of the vehicle in their rearview mirror.

He felt Hilary stir at his side and heard her trembling sigh. His quick glance at her reassured him. Her color had returned, and she looked more relaxed.

"Sorry about the rough ride," he said, forcing a casual note into his voice, "but it was necessary."

"I know." Hilary stared at the white car up ahead, willing her body to stop trembling. "I'm just glad you're all right."

Glad, she thought ruefully. What a stupid little word to describe how she'd felt when she'd seen him charging toward the car.

She shuddered, remembering how she'd heard the engine of the white car roar to life, had heard it pass by and had waited forever for Simon to appear. When he didn't, she'd been so sure he'd been hurt by those two thugs.

She'd been frantic, scrambling over the front seat in her hurry to start the car and get as far as she could up the trail.

When she'd seen him racing toward her, she'd felt the strength flow from her body with the force of her relief.

Close on that had come the stark realization of the kind of pain she would feel at losing him.

Luckily, his reckless drive down the trail had wiped all other thought from her mind, and, she decided, she would not dwell on it now. There would be more than enough time for that later.

"Did you see Chen?" she said, her stomach jolting when she saw the expression on Simon's face.

"I saw him. He looked scared to death. He's in the car with them."

"Poor Chen," Hilary said quietly. "And poor May Song. It must be awful for both of them."

"Well, let's hope it won't be for much longer." He leaned forward then, his face creased in a frown.

"What is it?" She followed his gaze, but the white car was still moving at a steady pace ahead of them.

"I expected them to turn off before now," Simon muttered. "If they're going into the hills, they should have turned up one of the trails back there. If they stay on this highway now, they'll end up in Chiang Mai again."

"Do you think they're going back to May Song's house?" She gave him an anxious look. "Maybe the house is Chambers's headquarters, after all. Maybe he was there the whole time."

Simon shook his head. "No. I searched the place pretty thoroughly. I didn't find anything. I doubt he's ever even been there. I think Hal and Jerry go there to pick up Chen whenever they have a new project for him."

He stretched his back to relieve his cramped muscles. "They must have a big project in mind this time, judging by the amount of jade Chen was carrying. He picked out the largest boulders he could find."

Hilary caught her breath. "You think they're planning to steal another carving? Can't we warn the arts department? They can keep watch on the museum and catch them at it."

Simon shook his head. "Chambers is clever. He'd know if the museum was being watched. Besides, they might catch whoever was stealing the antiques for him, but you can bet they'd never catch up with him. I know only too well how slippery he can be.''

There it was again, thought Hilary. That hard, dangerous note in his voice that scared her. She'd hate to be standing in his way if that lethal power was ever unleashed.

She started when Simon cursed heavily and stamped on the brake. They'd just rounded a bend, and she followed his gaze, her heart skipping when she saw the stretch of road ahead.

It lay in front of them, a straight gray ribbon dividing the flat pastures on either side for at least a mile. Going into the curve, the white car had been no more than fifty yards ahead of them.

Now the road was empty, except for a dust-covered scarred bus lumbering toward them in the opposite lane. The white car had vanished.

Chapter 8

Hilary's cry of dismay echoed Simon's curse as he guided the car onto the grassy verge and brought it to a halt. "Where could they have gone?" she said, looking around in bewilderment. The area seemed deserted.

On one side, the flat fields of wild grass stretched lazily out to the foot of the hills, which were covered in the dense foliage of the jungle. Across the road, the pastures rose into gentle slopes of grass and shrubs and would, Hilary knew, eventually run into the vast paddies of the lowlands.

Nothing moved in that lush green landscape except for the low-hanging branches of broad oak trees gently stirred by the warm breeze.

"Back there," Simon said, his sharp tone startling her.

She followed his gaze through the rear window and saw a faint, thin trail of dust just visible above the trees in the curve of the road.

"Where the hell—" Simon muttered, and stepped on the accelerator, spinning the car around on two wheels in the middle of the road before racing back in the direction they'd come.

Hilary stifled a gasp as they hurtled around the bend and swerved to avoid the bus that was now ahead of them.

She held her breath when Simon pulled around the swaying vehicle and darted ahead of it, his eyes glued on the wisp of dust. As they swept closer she could see the gray cloud angling perpendicular to the road.

Again Simon slammed on the brakes, bringing a protesting blast from the horn of the bus behind him. The tires squealed as he thrust the wheel over, sending the car plunging into a gap that until now had been hidden from view.

Hilary braced her hands on the dashboard and shut her eyes as bushes on either side scraped the doors. Then the car was through and bouncing up a rough, rutted path toward the hills.

"Where are they going?" Simon muttered more to himself than to Hilary. "There's nothing up there but jungle."

She leaned forward, peering through the haze of dusty sunlight. "I can't see the car. Do you think they saw us following and are hiding till we go by?"

"I don't know." He touched the brake, gradually slowing the car to a crawl. "Whatever's going on, I don't like it."

His voice, more than his words, made her flesh creep, and she rubbed at her bare arms. "Do you think they're waiting for us in there?" She nodded to where the dense shrubbery skirted the hills.

"If they are," Simon said grimly, "they have the advantage. We're sitting ducks out here." He shifted his foot onto the accelerator. "We might as well go all the way in now and find out what they're up to."

Hilary's body ached with the tension as the car crept steadily forward. They could be anywhere, hidden behind the huge leaves of the jungle plants or lying beneath the green foliage that spread thickly over the lower slopes.

Did they have guns trained on her and Simon, she wondered, ready to shoot them the minute they emerged from the car? Her stomach clenched at the thought.

She was on the point of asking him if he was wearing his revolver, when she heard him let out his breath with a hiss.

"There it is," he said in a low, tense voice.

She saw it, too, as soon as she turned her head. The white car sat placidly beneath the low branches of a graceful teak several yards ahead of them.

"It's empty," she said in relief.

"It *looks* empty," Simon corrected her quietly. He stopped the car. "Get out."

"I will not." She gave him a mutinous glare.

"I don't have time to argue, Hilary. Get out—now."

"I'll get down," she said firmly, "but I'm not getting out."

He gave her one hard stare, then looked back at the car. "Then keep your head down if you don't want it shot off."

She dropped to the floor before he finished speaking. Beads of perspiration ran down her forehead as she crouched next to his legs in the small space in front of the seat.

She could feel the tires rumbling over the rutted path, and the roar of the engine sounded deafening in her ears. She kept her gaze on Simon's face, watching his narrowed eyes as he edged the car forward.

Her stomach rolled uncomfortably as she saw him ease a hand inside his shirt, and although she'd been expecting it, she couldn't help the twinge of fear when she saw the revolver gleaming in the sun.

He brought the car to a gentle halt and spoke without looking at her, his lips barely moving. "You stay down, Hilary, or you're dead."

The terse words frightened her, and she whispered, "Don't worry—I will."

She wanted to touch him, to beg him to be careful. Knowing that any movement on her part would wreck his concentration, she kept her arms clamped around her knees.

The door on his side opened without a sound, and she held her breath as he lowered one foot to the ground and hesitated. Then, with a speed that shocked her, he flung himself out of the car.

She saw him drop to the ground, and then he rolled out of her sight. She found herself chanting over and over in a silent whisper, "Please be careful, oh, please be careful."

She realized her hands were over her ears, and she jerked them away, terrified that she would hear shots and just as terrified that she wouldn't hear them if they came.

She waited as, through the open door of the car, she heard animals of the forest twitter and shriek.

Her heart lurched as the door next to her swung open, then she was tumbling out, almost crying in relief as Simon looked down at her, his face tense.

"You were right," he said, making an effort to smile. "It was empty."

Her relief was tempered with dismay. "They got away?"

"Yeah. Come and look." He led her past the white car to what at first appeared to be a cave.

As she stepped into its opening, Hilary discovered that it was actually a narrow gorge that angled in between the hills, invisible from the road.

Holding on to Simon's hand, she followed him through the narrow passage and heard the rush of water as they approached the other side.

The gorge opened up onto the riverbank, and Hilary caught her breath when she saw two flat-bottom boats moored to a rough landing that consisted of bamboo poles lashed together.

The boats had straw canopies, but no engines, and were apparently propelled by the long poles she could see propped against the narrow benches.

"River rafts," Simon said. "They must use them all the time. This has to be the closest point to where they can leave the car. No wonder I couldn't pin them down. I never thought of the river. It's the perfect hideout for them. Winding through the hills like this, they could stay out of sight forever."

"But you still don't know where," Hilary said, looking at where the water disappeared around a bend on either side of her. "They could be anywhere."

"Not quite." Simon pointed past her. "See that line of boulders across the water? There's no way they could maneuver a raft through that. Which means they had to go downstream, this way."

Hilary eyed the rippling water, and then looked at the rafts. "So if we follow them down, eventually we'll see their raft."

Simon cleared his throat. "I don't suppose there's a chance that you'll stay with the car till I get back."

Hilary grinned. "Not on your life."

To her surprise he merely nodded. "All right. But first I'm going to hide the car. I don't want any surprises from the rear."

When she hauled her bag from the back seat, she could see the objection forming on his face. "I'm not going without it," she said firmly.

He shook his head but said nothing, and she watched him take his backpack from the car and place it on the grass. She waited for him to run the car into the undergrowth, fighting tremors of apprehension. So far they had been lucky. How long would their luck hold out before they eventually ran into Chambers and his men?

She thought of Simon's gun, which was now apparently tucked back into his holster. How would she feel, she wondered, if she saw him use it? She had glimpsed that dark side of him only now and again, that lethal power that frightened her.

Would it change how she felt about him if she witnessed the deadly force she knew he must be capable of? Even before her mind had formed the question, she knew the answer. Nothing could change the way she felt about him. It was that strong, that binding; she would never escape it, no matter what happened.

The thought sobered her, and she followed him back through the gorge, her heart already aching with the knowledge that the memories might be all she would ever have.

The river brought a small measure of peace, in spite of the dangers that lay ahead. It was impossible not to be tranquilized by the slow-running water, Hilary thought as they boarded the raft and began to glide silently downstream.

The current helped their progress, making it unnecessary for Simon to use the pole for more than just a guidance for the raft.

Hilary sat in the shade of the canopy, watching the forest slip by. Thick ropes of green vines hung from twisted branches and dangled into the water. Luxuriant ferns and plants with leaves as big as surfboards lined the banks, while beneath them water tumbled over rocks and lapped gently at the muddy shore.

And in the midst of it all, the teeming wildlife flitted and slithered through the vegetation, heedless of the raft slipping by below.

"It's seems so peaceful," Hilary remarked as she leaned over and trailed a hand in the water. "It's hard to imagine there's cruelty and evil in such a paradise."

"You might find it sooner than you think if a crocodile gets that hand," Simon said mildly.

She yanked her hand from the water with a little shriek. "I haven't seen any," she said accusingly when she'd recovered.

He shrugged. "Just because you haven't seen any doesn't mean there aren't any. That's a fact well worth remembering if you want to stay alive."

She shifted uneasily, knowing he wasn't only talking about crocodiles. "What are you planning to do if you find Chambers's hideout?" she said, her tension returning as she stared at his set face.

"That depends." He jabbed the pole deep into the riverbed to keep the raft midstream. "I'm not taking him on single-handedly, if that's what you're asking. If Chambers gets his hands on me again, he won't be playing games. Not this time."

Hilary swallowed. She was beginning to feel very glad that Simon was carrying a gun.

"I'm hoping we'll find something to hang on him," he went on, "enough to bring him in for questioning. Then I can interest the Thai government in giving me a hand."

"Like the scorpion?" Hilary said, feeling a twist of excitement at the thought of being so close to recovering the carving.

"Hilary, don't put too much hope into finding it."

He sounded concerned, and she looked at him sharply. "But you said you thought Chambers had it."

"I said I thought he was responsible for the theft." Simon shifted his gaze long enough to give her a brief glance. "He's probably sold it by now."

"No," Hilary said, her brows meeting in a stubborn frown. "I can't believe that. He still has it. I just know it."

"How do you know it?" Simon said gently. "Chambers isn't the type to hang on to something for sentimental value. He deals in hard cash."

"Well, maybe he hasn't found a buyer for it yet." She knew she was being unrealistic, but she couldn't bear the thought of having come this far and being so close, only to fail now. "I'm not giving up on it, not until we know for sure."

She looked at him, trying to keep her voice steady. "Why did you let me come with you if you thought Chambers had sold the scorpion?"

"I *didn't* intend for you to come with me, remember?" He kept his gaze on the river ahead, searching the banks. "Not until I figured you'd get yourself into more trouble if I left you behind."

His sigh of exasperation irritated her, but she kept silent.

He looked at her then, his eyes pleading with her. "Hilary, even if Chambers still has the scorpion, we can't take it. The minute he discovers it's missing, he'll know we're on to him. He'll be gone before we have time to blink."

"He won't know it's missing," Hilary said, unable to disguise her satisfaction. "We'll do what he did."

Simon gave her a blank look. With a smile of triumph she drew an oblong box out of her bag and opened it. She held it out to him.

He sucked in his breath. "The fake scorpion." He shook his head. "So that's why you wanted to drag that bag along. You figured on another switch. There's hope for you yet."

"Thank you. I'm glad you approve."

"Oh, I approve."

His tone told her more than the words did, and she tucked the scorpion back in her bag, feeling the special warmth only he could give her.

A second later her head jerked up when she heard his hiss of breath. She gripped her bag with sudden tension as she caught sight of a raft just beyond the curve in the river ahead. It was pulled onto the bank, almost hidden beneath a clump of trailing ferns.

Simon put his weight on the pole, bowing the wood to near breaking point in his effort to slow the raft. It swung around in a violent arc and headed for the bank.

Hilary closed her eyes, expecting more than the light bump that signaled they'd run aground. Simon had jumped out and was already splashing ashore before she opened them again.

He held out his hand and she took it, leaping to the ground at the edge of the water.

"Get behind those bushes," Simon whispered, "and stay down."

Praying she didn't sit on a snake, she crouched and waited for him. He joined her a couple of seconds later and lowered her bag and his backpack at her feet.

"Are we going to take a look?" she murmured. "Are you sure that's the raft they took?"

"No, I'm not sure." He opened his pack and took out his camera, then found two rolls of film, which he tucked in his pocket. "But I'm going to find out. You stay here with the bags."

She glared at him, and he raised his hands helplessly. "All right," he muttered, "I knew you wouldn't listen, but I had to try." He picked up his camera and stood, looking cautiously through the bushes.

"Can you see anything?" Hilary said in a loud whisper. Her nerves were stretched so tight her throat hurt.

"No." He squatted beside her again. "Now, listen to me, Hilary. I've left the raft loose. If they see it, they'll hopefully assume it just broke free. We're going to go in slowly, and I want you to give me your solemn promise that at the first sight of trouble, you will get the hell out of here as fast as you can make it."

His eyes looked at her, intense, almost colorless, and gleaming with a cold, deadly purpose that terrified her. She watched him slip his fingers into his back pocket and bring out a laminated card.

"If I don't make it back," he said in a chilling matter-of-fact tone, "get back to the car. I left the keys in the ignition. Call the American Embassy in Bangkok and give them the information on this card. Tell them everything. They'll know what to do."

Her fingers trembled so much she could barely take the card from him. Until this moment she'd never really considered the fact that he could be killed. That they could both be killed. Even when she'd thought he was hurt at the border, she hadn't allowed herself to think beyond that.

She glanced down at the card in her shaking hand. It was an ID card that stated that the holder was a United States government agent, and it bore a smudged portrait of a solemn Simon. She noticed, with a small part of her mind, that he was thirty-two years old. She'd thought he was older.

Her stomach churned when she read his next of kin. It was his father, listed as Jonathan King, and she prayed no one would ever have to contact him with bad news. She forgot about it when he grasped her wrist.

"Promise me, Hilary."

She looked into his cool eyes and pulled in a shaky breath. "I promise."

He held her gaze for a moment longer, then straightened. "Stay behind me, and keep on your toes."

He didn't need to tell her that, she thought. Every nerve in her body felt stretched tight. She felt as if she were walking on a tightrope—one false step and she would overbalance and fall.

Simon moved carefully through the undergrowth pausing every few steps to listen. When he stopped for the third time and stood motionless, Hilary felt hairs prickling on the back of her neck.

"What is it?" she whispered, then clamped her mouth shut when he raised a hand sharply in a movement of warning.

"Can you hear it?" he said quietly, just when she thought she'd explode from holding her breath.

She strained her ears for several seconds, but all she could hear was the tumult of wildlife all around her. She shook her head, and he frowned.

"A hum," he said, bending closer so she could hear his soft voice. "Concentrate and you'll hear it."

She shut her eyes, then opened them when she detected the low buzzing sound. "What is it?"

"Generator. More than one, by the sound of it." His eyes gleamed down at her, revealing his excitement. "I think we've found him."

Her stomach lurched. Her lips formed the words, though no sound came out. "Chambers?"

Simon's mouth lifted in a triumphant smile. "Let's go and see. And be careful."

The hum grew louder as she followed Simon's solid figure through the tropical foliage of the forest. She saw it at the same moment he did, dead ahead of them on the banks of the river, hidden until now by the sharp bend.

It looked very like the village they'd left the night before, except for the impressive two-story house that had been built in the center of several smaller ones.

Simon pulled her down behind a cluster of coarse ferns and slid his pack off. She saw him drape the strap of his camera around his neck, and her stomach somersaulted when he reached inside his shirt for his gun.

"I'm going to try to get a closer look—" His whisper broke off as two men emerged from a house on the edge of the village.

Hilary gulped as she recognized the two figures, one tall and lanky, the other short and squat. Hal and Jerry. She was close enough to feel Simon's body tense, and she glanced up at him. His eyes were like two chips of ice, and the angle of his jaw looked murderous.

Shaken, she looked back at the men and saw them march across to the large house and climb the steps to the veranda. Their sharp rap on the door was answered almost immediately. Whoever opened it remained invisible as both men disappeared inside.

"Bingo," Simon said softly.

"You think he's in there?" she asked, her voice shaking.

"I know he is." His gaze shifted to the smaller house that Hal and Jerry had just left. "He'll keep for the moment. I'm more interested in who's in there."

Hilary's pulse jumped. "Chen!" She'd almost forgotten about him. "How can you be sure?"

"Don't worry. I'll make sure." Simon nodded toward the house. "We'll circle around behind it, and you can stay put while I check. If he's in there, we can get in without being seen by the big boys.''

He backed out of the ferns, pulling Hilary with him. He thrust her bag at her and swung his pack up by the strap. "Just be ready to make a run for it if we have to," he reminded her, and without waiting for her answer pushed his way carefully through the undergrowth.

The back door of the house was standing ajar as they drew level with it, Hilary saw with relief. At least Simon should be able to see in without alerting the occupants.

Even so, she felt the familiar hollow feeling in her stomach as he crept forward, his body bent double. She watched him edge up to the door, the sun glinting on the gun in his upraised hand. Slowly he moved his head until he could see inside.

She felt light-headed with relief when he gave her an urgent signal with his hand, and she raced across the few yards separating them, clenching her bag.

Simon pulled her inside and closed the door, and behind them a startled voice spoke sharply in Thai. Simon answered, also in Thai, while Hilary blinked in an effort to see the shadow figure who stood at the other end of the simple house.

"You speak English, Chen?" Simon asked quietly when the old man stared at him in silence. "My name is Simon, and I'm a friend of May Song. This is Hilary, and she's a friend, too." He tucked the gun back inside his shirt and drew her forward.

"May Song sent you?"

Though his tone was still sharp, Chen's English was surprisingly good, Hilary thought with relief. At least she would be able to understand what was being said.

"Yes." Simon took a couple of steps toward the old man. "She told us Chambers was forcing you to work for him."

It was similar to the house they'd stayed in at the village, Hilary realized, except it only had one partition, which reached halfway across the center.

Simon stopped at the partition.

"Why would she tell you such a thing?" Chen said, his voice heavy with suspicion.

It wasn't surprising, Simon thought. They could easily be Chambers's cronies checking up on the old man to make sure he was toeing the line.

"Give me my card," he said to Hilary, holding out his hand, and she fumbled for it in the front pocket of her bag. He took it from her, giving her a reassuring wink when he saw her tense face.

He handed the card to Chen, who studied it gravely. "So. You are American government man," he said, handing it back to Simon. "What do you want with me?"

"I need your help. In return, I want to help you."

Chen shook his head and moved forward into a beam of light. "No one can help me," he said distinctly.

Hilary bit back a gasp. Chen's voice had sounded strong, so strong that she had forgotten for the moment that he was an old man. His bowed back and heavily lined face were a shocking contrast to the vibrancy of his voice.

"How long do we have before they come back?" Simon said, gesturing at the far door.

"They will not disturb me until sundown, when it is time to eat again. Today is a day of rest." He looked at Hilary for the first time, his dark eyes bright in his pale face. "If you are a government man," he said quietly, "you and this lady are in great danger."

Hilary's stomach, which had reacted at the mention of food, promptly rejected the hunger pangs.

"I know," Simon said urgently. "That's why I have to talk to you—now. It's the only chance we have."

Chen stared at his face for several seconds, then moved behind the partition. "We will sit here. It will be safe for a while."

A narrow mattress lay on the floor, and Chen waited for them to sit down. "I have fruit if you would care for some," he said, addressing Hilary.

She looked up and smiled, anxious not to offend him. "That would be lovely. Thank you."

The old man nodded and shuffled behind the partition. He reappeared almost at once with a large wooden bowl filled with stubby bananas, quartered pineapple and slices of papaya.

He set the bowl on the floor in front of Hilary, then lowered his frail body to sit cross-legged, next to Simon, on the end of the mattress.

"Now," he said, his dark eyes fixed on Simon's face, "how can I help you?"

"Tell me everything you know about Chambers and what he's doing here," Simon answered.

Chen released his breath in a drawn-out sigh. "You know I cannot do that," he said softly. "I would be putting not only my life in danger but also the lives of my family."

"Not if I can get Chambers and his men back to the States and put them away," Simon assured him. "That's why I'm here. But I need some kind of proof to get the help I need to do that." He leaned forward. "Chambers is cooking heroin, isn't he? Tell me where his refinery is. That's all you have to do. I'll do the rest."

The old man studied him. "And if you do manage to capture Chambers before he finds out who betrayed him, will I not also be taken?"

"You have nothing to do with the refinery, do you?" Simon touched his arm. "We know why you're here, Chen. May Song told us."

Chen's eyes flashed. "May Song should not have done that. She has put us all in danger."

Hilary could keep quiet no longer. "She told us because she trusted us. And she was worried about you. She wanted to help you." She peered around Simon at the expressionless eyes, which had shifted to her face. "Simon can help you," she said firmly, "if you let him."

The old man was silent, and Hilary stretched out a hand for her bag. Pulling it toward her she opened it and drew out the flat box. The scorpion glowed with a dull light as she lifted it out. "Have you seen this before?" she demanded.

Chen took the piece from her and turned it over in his hands. "Where did you get this?" he said sharply.

Hilary told him, barely stopping for breath until she was finished.

In the silence that followed, Chen handed the carving back to her.

"This is part of your culture," she said desperately. "Those men have desecrated these ancient carvings, taken them from their rightful place and sold them for profit. How can you ever rest peacefully, knowing you are part of that?"

Chen's eyes once again flashed with anger. "I do not do it willingly," he said, folding his arms. "If I do not do this thing, Chambers has promised to take my grandchildren to work in his refineries."

Hilary's gasp echoed in the shocked silence.

"So he does have refineries," Simon said in quiet satisfaction.

Chen, apparently aware that he'd said more than he intended to, nodded reluctantly. "Three of them."

"And a nice little operation robbing museums on the side," Simon muttered. "That bastard never knows where to stop."

Hilary leaned across Simon and laid her hand on Chen's arm. "What happened to the real scorpion?" she said hopefully, half-afraid to hear his answer.

"He has it, in his house," Chen said dully. "It was part of a deal that did not work out. The buyer could not find the money. There were three pieces in the deal. The scorpion is one of them."

"How many carvings have been stolen?" Hilary demanded, holding down on her surge of excitement at his disclosure.

"Eleven. I carved eleven copies so far." Chen stared at her. "I had no choice. Chambers will destroy my family. If you tell anyone of this, he will do it—"

"How did you get mixed up in this?" Simon interrupted. "Where did Chambers find you?"

Again Chen uttered a long sigh. "I grew up in China," he said quietly. "I made good money carving jade. My two daughters were born in China. When my elder daughter was grown, she met a man from Cambodia. She married him and went with him to his country. My younger daughter visited them and also met a man. When our grandchildren were born, we left China and went to live in Cambodia, to be near our family."

He paused, and Hilary felt sick, knowing what had to come next.

"When the Khmer Rouge took over Cambodia, they separated families and sent them to different slave labor camps to destroy family loyalties." The shudder that shook his body seemed to vibrate in the shadows around him.

"It took us a long time to reach the safety of Thailand. And an even longer time to find a way out of refugee camps. I searched for my daughters and their families. I needed money to help the search. I carved jade in a factory."

His pause was longer this time, and Hilary stirred uneasily.

"I found my two daughters," he went on, "but their husbands were dead. And two of my grandchildren."

Hilary gave a sharp cry, and Simon sent her a quick glance of concern.

"The rest of us tried to forget," Chen went on tonelessly. "I had much experience with jade carving, and word of my work grew. Chambers also heard the word and knew where my weakness lay."

He raised his eyes to Simon's, his wrinkled face empty of expression. "My daughters and my wife. They have been through so much. How could I risk the lives of my grandchildren? I did what he asked. Without question."

"But what about the police?" Hilary cried. "They wouldn't have let something like that happen."

Chen shook his head. "Children disappear every day. I have been told that in Thailand there are two million children who work, many of them locked in factories and forced to labor long hours under terrible conditions. Four thousand of them, all under fourteen years old, are in brothels. My grandchildren would be just three more."

Stunned, Hilary could only stare.

"Chen, tell me where the refineries are. I'll take pictures of them and show them to the people who will help me. We'll come back together and round up everyone. There'll be no one left to hurt you or your family. I'm sure that if you testify against Chambers, once they know you were forced to work for him, they'll drop any charges against you. I'll do my best to see that they do."

Chen hesitated for several heart-stopping seconds, then slowly nodded. "I will help you," he said quietly. "For the sake of the children."

"Your grandchildren will be safe," Simon assured him. "There will be no word of your involvement in this until all Chambers's men are in custody. I'll get word to you before the raid when it's to be. All you'll have to do is stay low until we can pick you up."

Chen smiled. "Thank you, my friend. But I meant the children who work here. In the refineries."

"No!" Hilary grasped the old man's arm. "You don't mean he actually has children working for him now?"

Chen nodded. "Sixteen, the last time I counted. Some of them very young."

Simon swore. "That could make things difficult." He climbed to his feet, his face grim. "All right, Chen. The refineries."

Chen rose slowly, his bones creaking as he moved. "They are farther down the river. You will hear the generators. They look like big houses, like the one out there—" he waved his arm at the door "—but inside they are factories."

Simon gave him a brief nod. "I'll find them. Hilary—"

"I know," Hilary said wearily. "Stay here."

"You got it. It's still a few hours till sundown. You'll be safe enough here. I'll be back as soon as I've got enough pictures."

She scrambled to her feet and looked up at him. "You *will* be careful, won't you?"

He grinned at her. "Aren't I always?" He lightly brushed her cheek. "I won't be long," he said softly, and, with another brief nod at Chen, turned and slipped out the door.

Hilary managed to give Chen a smile before she busied herself with packing the scorpion back into her bag. She was startled when she heard him say quietly, "You worried about Mr. King?"

"Not really." She lifted her shoulders in a shrug. "I think Mr. King can take care of himself."

Chen nodded. "I think he is a man to be trusted."

She met his dark eyes steadily. "You can trust Simon to do the very best he can. He's a good man."

"You also work for government?"

"No," she said with a light laugh, "I just happened to be in the wrong place at the wrong time."

"Then you and Mr. King are not partners?"

"Mr. King and I are not anything," Hilary said dryly.

"But you love him."

It was a statement, made quietly, and she felt the familiar blush sweeping across her cheeks. "I didn't think it was that obvious."

"Only to an old man." Chen nodded, smiling. "Mr. King, he doesn't know how you feel?"

She sighed. "Oh, I think he knows. He just doesn't care enough for it to matter."

"Ah." Chen folded his arms. "It is easy to hear the lion's roar and to witness his bravery. It is the heart of the lion that is difficult to see."

"I'm not terribly sure this lion has a heart," Hilary said sadly.

"He has one." Chen leaned over and patted her hand. "You just have to look for it. One thing you can be certain of. A lion does not give his heart easily. When he does, it will be forever."

Hilary nodded wistfully. "I'll keep that in mind," she said, clasping the gnarled hand in hers and holding it a moment before letting it go. "How long have you and May Song been married?" she added brightly in an effort to change the subject.

Chen smiled. "Too many years to count. We have spent a lifetime together. A good lifetime."

"I'm glad." Again Hilary pressed his hand. "It will be even better now, once we get all this mess sorted out. It must have been so awful for May Song, worrying about you."

"Every time I go with Chambers's men, she thinks I might not come back. It has been hard for her."

"I know. She was very frightened when we talked to her." Hilary frowned. "One thing I find hard to understand... Chambers must be making a fortune with all this heroin. Why would he want to get involved in stealing jade antiques? Surely that's just adding to the risks, and he has so much to lose if he's caught."

"You have not met Chambers." Chen reached for a slice of papaya and handed it to Hilary. "If you had, you would know. It is the risks that interest him. He is a strange man— a very dangerous man. He enjoys—what is that American expression?—beating the odds."

Hilary bit into the papaya. "Like someone else I know."

Chen looked at her, his intelligent eyes half-closed. "Ah, but Mr. King satisfies his need for excitement by righting wrongs, not committing them."

Disturbed that he had read her mind so easily, Hilary sighed. It was that very need for excitement that stood between them. She could never hope to compete with his job and the life-style that went with it.

To Simon she was a pleasant diversion, nothing more. And wishing for anything more was simply chasing rainbows. So why did she still go on wishing? Because she was a fool, she answered herself wryly. And because she was too much in love to give up.

The minutes dragged by while Chen talked about his craft—trying to keep her mind off her anxieties, she suspected.

The Chinese valued jade beyond all gold and gems, he told her. It was their most precious possession. They believed it was the link between earth and heaven—the bridge between life and immortality. A Chinese gentleman paced his life by altering his gait to make the jades dangling from his belt tinkle to a measured beat.

No price was too high, no effort too large and no praise too great for a fine piece exquisitely carved. "It is said," Chen said, his voice reverent, "that one can put a price on gold, but jade is priceless."

He looked at Hilary gravely. "And that is why Chambers is willing to take such risks. There are men who would sell their soul to own such pieces as the scorpion—and very probably have."

He shook his head. "It is a great shame that such a beautiful stone, so full of mystery and magic, could cause such pain and evil."

Hilary opened her mouth to answer him, then snapped it shut as the door through which Simon had disappeared slammed open. He stood in the doorway, water dripping from his clothes and pooling at his feet.

Hilary gasped, shoving herself up from the mattress. "What happened?"

"Dogs," Simon said curtly. His eyes glittered at her, and her blood ran cold as she heard the distant baying.

"I hope you're a good runner," he added, his voice grating with tension. "They're right behind me."

Chapter 9

Y ou must go at once," Chen said urgently.

Hilary stared at Simon's wet clothes. He was soaked from the chest down.

"I've put them off for a little while." Simon looked over his shoulder. "I cut across the curve of the river, but it won't hold them for long."

"I haven't been near the refineries for days—I didn't know about the dogs." Chen picked up Simon's pack. "They must have brought them in recently. Go! Chambers could be here any minute. I will try to confuse them. Which way will you go?"

"Upstream," Simon said, catching the pack when Chen threw it to him. "Chambers and his boys are back at the refineries with the dogs. They must have gone over there while we were talking."

Hilary grabbed up her bag and hurried across to him. "Are you all right? Did they see you?" she asked anxiously.

"No. I'm hoping they'll just think it's a curious local wandering around." He grasped her arm. "I'll be in touch," he said to Chen, and thrust Hilary out the door.

She threw one last desperate glance over her shoulder. The real scorpion could be no more than a few yards away. So close and so undeniably out of reach.

She managed a mumbled "goodbye" to Chen, then raced with Simon across the few short yards to the shrubs.

"Keep down and keep moving," Simon ordered, and, bent double, led her at a fast pace toward the river.

"We'll have to wade upstream," he told her when they reached the riverbank.

Hilary glanced warily at the water. It had looked a lot more inviting to her when she'd floated down it on a raft. "What about crocodiles?" She held her bag up in front of her as if to shield them off.

Simon, already splashing through the water, looked back at her. "They're practically extinct. Those dogs, however, are very much alive."

And they sounded very close, she realized as the barking became more frenzied. They must have picked up the scent. Her fear of the dogs far surpassed the threat of practically extinct crocodiles, and she plunged in after Simon.

Terror kept her going as he waded ahead, staying close to the bank. She was up to her knees in the water and stumbled on the rocks that appeared under her feet without warning. She prayed she wouldn't overbalance, not sure she'd have the strength to get up again.

She hoped Simon's camera hadn't been damaged and wondered if he'd managed to take any pictures before he'd been chased off by the dogs. She wanted to ask him, but it took all her breath to keep up with him. He was practically running, stopping every now and then to make sure she was still behind him while she struggled in the knee-deep water in an effort to stay on her feet.

It was some time before she realized that the dreadful baying of the dogs had faded into the distance. Even then Simon didn't let up.

She was sobbing for breath by the time he paused and waited for her to catch up to him. "I think we can go ashore again now," he said when she reached him. "The dogs must have given up."

"Thank God." She gasped for air, certain her legs wouldn't hold up another minute.

Simon grasped her arm and helped her up the bank. "It'll be easier now," he said, steadying her while she caught her breath.

"How far is it to the car?" she asked him when she could talk again. "It seemed a long way coming down the river."

"It's not that far." He shunted a strap off one shoulder and swung the pack around in front of him. "We'll cut off some of the curves, and we'll be moving a lot faster." He opened the flap and pushed his camera inside. "Give me your bag," he said, and took it from her. "I'll carry it. Just watch out for snakes."

"Snakes," Hilary repeated wearily. "Of course. Dogs, guns, crocodiles and now snakes. And I thought the Los Angeles freeways were dangerous."

He flashed her a quick grin. "I'll take the snakes anytime."

She sighed. "To each his own." She trudged wearily behind him, too tired and depressed to care whether she saw a snake or not. She could have cried with relief when Simon halted ahead of her.

"There's the gorge. With luck we'll find the car and get out of here."

"With luck?" She stared at him, wondering how much more of this she could take.

"Never underestimate the enemy," Simon said lightly, which didn't do much for her peace of mind.

She followed him to the gorge and obeyed his order to stay hidden in the narrow passage between the hills until he checked out the car. He disappeared from view, and it seemed an eternity until he came back for her. When he gave her a shout and signaled for her to join him, relief gave her the strength to walk to the car.

Only then, when she collapsed onto the burning seat, did she realize how tightly strung her nerves had been.

She waited until they had bumped along the track and were once more speeding toward Chiang Mai before she allowed herself the luxury of relaxing.

"Tell me what happened," she said, slipping off her wet sandals. "Did you have time to get the pictures?"

"Enough. At least I'll have some solid help when I go back to pick up Chambers." He sent her a quick glance. "I'm sorry about the scorpion. I know how disappointed you must be."

"Disappointed, frustrated and miserable describes it better." She leaned over and rolled her wet pants up to her knees. "It means too much to me to give up on it, though."

She took a deep breath. She would have preferred to postpone this conversation until later, when Simon was feeling more comfortable. Sitting in those wet clothes had to be unpleasant, though he did look as if he was drying out above the knees, she decided when she looked at him.

She met Simon's uneasy glance and tried to look as if she weren't expecting a battle. "I'm coming with you when you go back."

"The hell you are." He switched his gaze back to the road. "This is one little adventure you're staying out of. I've got enough on my hands figuring out how I'm going to pull this deal off without any of those kids getting hurt."

"Oh, God." Hilary looked at him in dismay. "I'd forgotten about that. Chen was right, then. There are children in that place." She clenched her hands. "What kind of monster is this Chambers?"

"A dangerous one. He's mean and ruthless, and so far I haven't found his weak spot, if he has one." He leaned on the horn to warn the ox-drawn cart in front of him that he was about to pass. "The problem is that Chambers is intelligent, and that makes him all the harder to deal with. He's always one step ahead of me."

And that, thought Hilary, was what infuriated Simon the most. The fact that no matter how hard he tried, how close he came, Chambers had so far managed to elude him.

"This time," Simon said, his voice harsh with determination, "he won't get away. I'll make sure of that. He might be able to give the Thai government the slip, but I've got some help of my own."

"Agents?" Hilary said in surprise. "I thought you were here alone."

"I'm on this job alone." He pulled the car around the swaying cart and swung back into the lane. "The U.S. has DEA agents patrolling the borders. We've got a vested interest in the area, because a large percentage of drugs coming out of Asia end up in the States. That's how we got on to Chambers."

"A border patrol?"

"No. A stroke of luck." His laugh was bitter. "And we haven't had many of those."

"What happened?"

"A boat ran aground off the Oregon coast. It must have off-loaded from a larger boat out at sea. There'd been reports of an unidentified cargo ship, but when the Coast Guard went to investigate, it had disappeared.

"They picked the smaller boat off the rocks and found it loaded with heroin—hidden in bales of rubber from Thailand. The three men they dragged out of the sea all had connections with Chambers. One of them talked and gave the DEA enough information to send me out here looking for him."

"Because you knew him?"

"That, and the fact that I know the country. I once spent a year out here, courtesy of the United States government."

"So that's how you came to speak the language," Hilary said, nodding. "I wondered about that."

He sent her a fleeting smile. "It's strictly guidebook Thai. I don't recommend it if you want to hold an intelligent conversation."

"You seem to do all right with it," she observed, thinking of the dinner at the Akha village. Then she forgot about Chambers and everything else as the memory of the village brought back in vivid detail the moment Simon had dived into the pool—and the unforgettable moments that had followed.

"You're very quiet," Simon said suspiciously after several minutes of silence. "What are you cooking up in that scheming mind of yours?"

She flushed instantly, wondering what he would have said if he could have read her mind just then. She felt a deep, haunting pain when it occurred to her that her time was running out. She might never have those moments again, she thought, and was aching for his touch.

"Hilary?" He sent her a look of concern, and she made a pretense at being offended.

"Scheming? If anyone's scheming, it's you, Simon King. How many times did you try to sneak off without me?" She fixed a baleful eye on him. "Well, don't think you can get away with that again. Whether you like it or not, I'm going to be right behind you when you go back for Chambers."

The look he gave her warned her he was deadly serious. "No, Hilary, you are not. This is a government operation, and there'll be no civilians on it. And that's official."

She looked at him in desperation. "The scorpion, Simon. I have to get it back. I have to."

"I'll try to find it when we go in after him." He avoided her gaze and kept his eyes on the road. "But I can't promise anything, Hilary. I'm sorry."

She slumped back in her seat, sick with the knowledge that after all she'd been through she would have to accept defeat. "What about afterward?" she said without much hope. "If Chambers has valuable antiques belonging to the museum, surely the Thai government will give them back."

"If they're still there when it's over, they'll probably be impounded as evidence. Chambers must have some help on this operation. Local help. The Thais will want to deal with them themselves. Eventually you'll get it back, I guess."

She looked at him miserably. "You don't sound very sure."

"I just don't want you to expect too much. We'll have our hands full rounding up everyone and getting them back to town. Anything could happen in the meantime, before we can get back and clean up."

"What about Chen?" Hilary said, sitting up with renewed hope. "Do you think he could get it for me?"

"I don't know." He paused as if he was working out what to tell her. "I can't promise, Hilary. I can only say I'll do what I can."

And it *would* be the best he could do, Hilary acknowledged silently. She'd have to be satisfied with that.

The lights of Chiang Mai were flickering on when Simon drove through the town. Hilary looked wistfully into the sunset, remembering the warmth of his arm around her when they had danced under the stars. It seemed so long ago now.

The car came to a gentle halt in front of the inn, and she had to fight the urge to throw her arms around him. She wanted to hang on to him and never let go again.

It wouldn't do her any good, she told herself sadly. If this lion ever lost his heart, it would be to someone quite different from Hilary Barlow.

Even so, she couldn't stop the question that forced its way out. "Would you like to come in and clean up? They have a nice restaurant here. I…" Her voice trailed off as she saw the refusal in his eyes even before he said the words.

"I'm sorry, Hilary, but I have to get back to my room. I have a lot of phone calls to make. I'll need most of the night to take care of everything."

She nodded, pasting a smile on her cold lips. "Of course." She swallowed. "Will I see you tomorrow?"

"Yes." His eyes told her nothing when he looked at her. "There's a flight leaving for Bangkok in the morning. I'll take you to the airport."

"Thank you." The lump in her throat threatened to choke her. She had to get out of the car, she thought frantically, before she did something really stupid. "What time?" She groped for the handle, unable to look at him any longer.

"I'll pick you up at seven-thirty."

"I'll be ready." She got the door open at last and stumbled out. Recovering, she reached back for her bag and froze when he leaned forward and covered her hand with his.

"Get a good night's sleep, Hilary," he said quietly.

She saw something in his eyes then, something she couldn't read. She struggled with the dozens of words scrambling through her head, knowing she couldn't say any of them.

"You, too." She pulled her hand out from under his. "Good night, Simon."

He lifted his hand in a brief salute, and she watched him drive away, leaving a cold, empty place where her heart should have been.

Hunched in a corner of the busy restaurant, she ate dinner alone, picking listlessly at her meal. In spite of the fact she hadn't eaten more than a piece of fruit in almost twenty-four hours, everything she put in her mouth seemed tasteless, and she felt relieved when the smiling waitress cleared her dishes away.

She played with the idea of walking along the riverbank, but the thought of doing so alone only increased her melancholy, and she decided finally to take Simon's advice and try to get some sleep.

The bed felt soft and comfortable—a lot different from the narrow cot she'd slept on in the village, she thought wryly, and a vast improvement on the cramped back seat of the car.

Her last thought before she drifted off to sleep was that she would give everything she owned to be back on that narrow cot with Simon, or even waiting for him in the back seat of the car.

She came awake suddenly, her pulse fluttering wildly as she realized that an insistent tapping on her door had disturbed her sleep. She held her breath, then lifted her head off the pillow as she strained to hear it again.

When it came, her heart seemed to leap to her throat. She switched on the lamp by her bed and looked at her watch. It was a little before six. She stared at the door. It couldn't be Simon. It was way too early.

The tapping started again, becoming more insistent, and hope began to build. She slid her feet out of the bed, reaching for her silky peach robe, which had slipped to the floor.

Nervously she crossed the room. "Who is it?" she said in a fierce whisper.

"Open this damn door."

It was no more than a hoarse whisper, but she recognized it instantly. With a cry she flung open the door and pulled Simon inside.

"Aren't you a little early?" she asked unsteadily.

Her heart leaped when she saw his wide grin. "A little. I told the night clerk you were my sister and I had a family emergency."

"And he believed you?" She pulled her robe closer around her, remembering her brief nightgown. Simon was fully dressed in jeans and a black open-weave sweater. It put her at a distinct disadvantage, she discovered.

"No." He laid his lightweight jacket on the bed and pushed the sleeves of his sweater up his forearms. "But he took the money I offered him and pretended not to see me."

Hilary sat down quickly on the bed before her legs could give out. Simon in tight jeans, she'd noticed, made a very disturbing picture. She went back to her first question. "So what are you doing here?" Not that she cared. She was still trying to climb off the ceiling at the sight of him.

"I came to give you a present." His smile bared his teeth beneath the mustache, sending her blood racing.

"Couldn't it have waited?" she said faintly.

He shook his head. "Not this one."

Mystified, she watched him reach into the pocket of his jacket and draw out a familiar flat box.

He handed it to her, his light blue eyes sending her a message that filled her with precarious hope.

She raised the lid. Stunned, she stared down at it, unable to believe what she was holding.

Slowly she lifted it out of the box, her hands shaking. Light shimmered along the outstretched claws and glowed in the brilliant swirl of emerald green.

The swirl she knew so well—so very well. Her breath hovered in her throat, and she felt tears form on her lashes before spilling down her cheeks. There was no doubt. She was holding the scorpion. The real scorpion. The beautiful piece of jade carved for an emperor more than two hundred years ago.

She looked up at Simon, her vision blurred by her tears. "How?"

He sat down next to her, longing to touch her and knowing he couldn't. "I went back last night. I managed to get into Chambers's house and exchange it with the fake."

If she kept looking at him like that, he thought desperately, he wouldn't be responsible for what he did.

The peach robe parted at the neckline, giving him a glimpse of the soft curve of her breasts. He longed to caress those curves again and feel her excitement in the swollen peaks.

It would be so easy. He knew how little she was wearing under that silky material, which displayed the outline of her body so provocatively.

He had no idea why he'd come straight here, instead of doing the sensible thing and waiting until he took her to the airport. It was pure selfishness.

Knowing what the scorpion meant to her, he couldn't wait to see her expression when he handed it to her. Or maybe, deep down, he'd wanted a little more time than the rush to the airport would have given him. And now that he was with her, he wanted very badly to do something about it.

She was looking at him, her beautiful brown eyes wide with concern. "But how did you get the scorpion? Wasn't it in Chambers's house? What about the dogs?"

"I had a little help." He felt guilty, remembering how relatively easy it had been. So easy, it had been all he could do not to storm into Chambers's bedroom and take him prisoner right there and then.

Luckily his common sense had intervened. He wouldn't have reached the river before they were on to him. And he needed much more than Chambers. The operation involved dozens of men, contacts, dealers and buyers, not to mention the people who arranged the transportation of the drugs.

He had to be sure they rounded everyone up and confiscated all the information necessary to blow this thing apart once and for all.

And there were the children. He was going to need some special help to protect them in the final confrontation. He was glad he'd put in that call to the States two days ago. The men he had chosen were very special.

He realized Hilary was still waiting to hear his story. "I took an inflatable raft with me—that was one of the errands I had to run last night. It moves a lot faster than those clumsy river rafts, so it didn't take me long to paddle downstream."

He smiled. "The dogs were easy. A few pounds of doctored meat and they were dead to the world. By now they'll have slept it off and no one will be any the wiser."

"Except for a slight hangover."

Simon grinned. "They're not going to be frisky. Anyway, I woke Chen up, figuring he'd know his way around Chambers's house and could get me in. I couldn't believe it when he told me he had keys to the house. That's where he did his carving, in a room at the back."

He gave a dry laugh. "Apparently Chambers didn't trust his own people. He wanted Chen's work under his roof, where he could keep an eye on him. He had to trust Chen, but he knew Chen wouldn't double-cross him—he had too much to lose.

"Chen had the keys to everything, including the cabinet that held the jade, since he was working on pieces all the time. I just switched scorpions and got out of there."

Hilary stared at him. "How did you get out of there without anyone seeing you? Didn't they have guards posted?"

Simon nodded. "One. He shared a few cups of rice liquor with Chen." His mouth curved in another grin. "The dogs aren't going to be the only ones with a hangover. As for Chambers, luckily he's a heavy sleeper. And I'm not exactly inexperienced in these things."

"So I've gathered," Hilary murmured. "But when did you take the copy of the scorpion?"

"On the way back from the village. When I left you in the gorge while I checked out the car. I didn't say anything then because I didn't know if it was going to work out. I'm surprised you didn't miss it."

"I didn't even look in the bag after I left you." She'd been too miserable to look at anything that would remind her of the past few days. The realization of what Simon had done for her filled her with an overwhelming rush of gratitude.

Carefully she laid the scorpion back in the box and placed it on the night table. "You took a terrible risk," she said quietly. "I don't know how to thank you."

"You just did."

His smile looked strained, she noticed, and he was having a hard time meeting her gaze. He must care for her, she told herself, to have taken such a risk for a carving that meant nothing to him. Why didn't he say something? If she didn't make a move now, he would leave and she would never get another opportunity.

She touched his arm tentatively, her eyes willing him to respond. "I'll never forget what you did for me."

With a sigh of resignation, Simon gave up the struggle. He reached for her, his body responding immediately as he dragged her against him. His mouth found hers, and, impatient now, he pushed her robe from her shoulders.

Hilary whimpered as throbbing need tugged at her. She felt the fire of Simon's tongue as he traced her lips, then urged them apart. His hand moved to her breast and covered it, his thumb already beginning a sweet torture.

She tunneled her hands under his sweater, anxious to feel his bare flesh against hers. Pushing the soft material up to his armpits, she leaned into him and felt her pulse leap when he intensified his kiss.

His skin felt so smooth beneath her hands. She ran eager fingers down his spine, then waited while he let her go to tug his sweater over his head.

He forced her down onto the pillow with gentle hands and buried his mouth in her neck, his mustache feathering her sensitive skin.

She tried to pry her fingers under the tight waistband of his jeans, and when that didn't work, she searched for the button and released it. She heard him suck in his breath as her fingers brushed against his straining flesh.

"Hilary!"

His voice, hoarse with emotion, fired her own torment. She cried out as he dragged the straps of her nightgown down to expose her breasts, then took an aching peak into his mouth.

He shifted his weight and stretched his body out to cover hers. Lifting his head he looked at her, his eyes burning with a blue flame.

"You learn awfully fast, lady," he muttered hoarsely.

"You're a good teacher," she whispered back.

His smile was rueful. "I think I created a monster." He brushed her lips, teasing them with the light pressure of his mouth. "An exciting, thoroughly irresistible monster."

He captured her mouth again, and she eased her fingers under the waistband of his jeans, pushing them down over his hips. She felt him shudder, then, unbelievably, he lifted his head and rolled off her.

She stared at him, trying to understand, afraid that she already knew.

Simon met her bewildered gaze, knowing he couldn't avoid the truth any longer. He wasn't being fair to her. He should never have allowed his emotions to get the better of him. He should have been strong enough to resist the temptation in her eyes and in the body language he hadn't been able to ignore.

She would never know, he thought wearily, what it had cost him to regain his control. He pulled his sweater back over his head without speaking. He knew what he wanted to say. His heart and his soul longed to say the words that would keep her in his arms until they had to leave.

But to do that would be to imply something he couldn't give. He was a wanderer. He lived his life according to his rules, not the rules society laid down for him.

She wanted a partner, someone to share her life, to become part of her in thought, word and deed. He couldn't do that. It would mean trusting his life to her, his happiness and his future.

Somehow he had to get that through to her. "We don't have time for this," he said, keeping his voice casual. "You have a plane to catch." He stood and buttoned his jeans, striving to hide his despair behind an expressionless mask.

"You don't have to feel obligated about the scorpion," he went on deliberately. "I did it because I figured it was the only way I could be sure you would go back to Bangkok and let me get on with my job."

There were all kinds of pain, he discovered. He'd had no warning that this kind would hurt him so much. He saw the devastation in her eyes a second before she looked away, and he knew he would never forget it as long as he lived.

He couldn't leave her like this. He felt his control crumble like a demolished building, and, helpless to stop himself, he caught her chin with his fingers.

"Hilary." She met his gaze steadily, but he could see the pain dulling her eyes. "You know I care for you," he said, his voice dropping to a whisper. "Those hours we spent together in the village were the most wonderful—the most beautiful moments of my life."

Her expression didn't change, and he struggled on, his voice husky with the force of his emotion. "You are a warm, giving, passionate woman. You need a man who can give you his love without reservations, without holding anything back. A man who is capable of giving more than he takes, a man willing to share his life with you, physically and mentally, in every sense of the word. I can't do that, Hilary. I wish I could."

"I know." She looked at him with a sadness that echoed agonizingly in his heart. "I never expected you to."

He had to get out of there, he told himself urgently, before he was tempted to make promises he couldn't keep.

He jammed his thumbs into his pockets to stop his hands from reaching for her. "I'll be back in an hour," he said quietly. "I bought your ticket last night. You have a little over two hours to wait in Bangkok before your flight leaves for L.A."

She nodded. "What about the scorpion? Shouldn't the arts department be informed?"

"I'll take care of that later." He hesitated, knowing there was nothing more to say, then spun on his heel and went through the door.

Hilary sat for long minutes on the edge of the bed. Sunbeams beginning their long climb in the sky crept over her shoulder to play across the box that contained the scorpion.

She lifted it onto her lap and opened it. She should be happy. She'd recovered the scorpion. Her father's last wishes would be granted, and the carving would remain in the Somerset museum in honor of his memory. She touched the silk cushion with gentle fingers.

Memories. She would never again be able to look at the scorpion without the pain of remembering. She'd lost so much. The loss of her father had hurt deeply, but losing Simon was even more painful than she'd feared.

A tear splashed onto the scorpion's back, followed by another and yet another. She'd been a fool to hope. She'd been a fool to love him, knowing he would never return it.

She dashed at her eyes with the back of her hand, impatient with herself. She'd known what she was getting into. He'd told her he never made any promises.

And no matter how bad she was feeling now, she couldn't regret any of it. It had been a wonderful experience with a beautiful man, and she hadn't done anything she hadn't wanted to.

Now it was over, and she still had a job to do. And since she had to be ready in an hour, she told herself as she got wearily to her feet, she had better get dressed.

She barely had time for a cup of coffee before Simon returned. The sight of him dressed now in his lightweight pants and a yellow sport shirt brought fresh pain to her aching heart. Following him down to his car, she decided that the sooner she got the goodbyes over with the better.

She answered his perfunctory remarks with a vagueness that finally made him lapse into silence on the way to the airport, for which she was thankful.

If she could carry this off for a little while longer, she told herself, he would never have to know how very much she would miss him.

She watched him check in her luggage and pick up her tickets without having to speak to him, but then, all too soon, it was time.

He stood looking down at her, his face expressionless, his eyes cool blue and empty. People jostled all around them, but in that moment Hilary felt as lonely as if she'd been left on the moon.

"Thank you for everything, Simon." She'd managed to say that without her voice breaking, but her hand shook when she held it out.

She braced herself for the moment he would clasp it, then felt her composure desert her when he grasped her shoulders without warning and pulled her against him.

Oblivious to the travelers swarming past them, he gave her a quick, hard kiss and let her go. "Be happy, Hilary," he said huskily, and then was gone, swallowed up in the crowd.

She stumbled onto the plane, fighting back the embarrassment of tears. Alone in her seat, she stared blindly out the window until the plane swept into the blue sky, and she watched the gleaming spires and domes of the temples dwindle into tiny specks of gold.

Bangkok felt unbearably hot and humid when she walked down the steps from the plane. She thought of the cool forest breezes of the hills and then wished she hadn't when an almost unbearable pain hit her beneath her ribs.

Simon. Would she ever forget him? The pain would lessen in time, she knew, but the memories would always remain crystal clear, no matter how many years she spent without him.

Walking into the crowded terminal, she thought of May Song and Chen. She envied them the years they'd spent together, and she hoped they had many more to come.

She wondered if she'd ever know how it all turned out. She'd wanted to ask Simon to let her know, but her pride had prevented her from saying anything that might be construed as an excuse to see him again.

This was how he wanted it. There was one thing he could never take away from her, she thought sadly as she scanned the information boards behind the counter. The memories. Those would always be hers.

She looked at her watch. Two hours to go. Two hours left of an unforgettable trip to an unforgettable place. There would be many memories, and in spite of the danger, in spite of the snide attitude of that fool at the arts department, she would always remember Thailand as a beautiful, exotic country with warm, friendly people.

Thinking of Phong brought back her resentment of the man. There was nothing she hated more than not being believed, especially when she knew she was right. And now she would have to leave without having the satisfaction of telling him how wrong he was.

Or would she? Her frown disappeared as she hunted through her shoulder bag. The address of the arts department was still tucked inside, with the phone number written underneath it.

She would call him from here, she decided. It was nine-thirty; he had to be there by now. She would feel a whole lot better after she'd told Mr. Phong exactly what she thought of his treatment of visitors to his country.

It took her only a few minutes to find a vacant phone, and then she was dialing the number.

By the time she heard the answering click on the end of the line she was already having second thoughts. But she remembered Phong's attitude and the way he'd threatened her, and the memory strengthened her resolve.

The feminine voice answered in Thai, and then in English when Hilary stated she wished to talk to Mr. Phong. After a short silence the clipped voice of the official came on the line.

"Miss Barlow? I am surprised to hear from you. I thought you would be in the United States. Unless you're calling from America."

Hilary rolled her eyes to the ceiling in silent disgust. "Not quite. I'm still in Thailand. I am leaving today, but there's something I wanted you to know before I leave."

"Oh?"

His tone jarred her nerves for some reason, and she began to wish she hadn't been so impulsive. It would have been better, she thought belatedly, to have written to him from the States when all this was settled.

"Yes," she said firmly. "I want you to know that I was right about the scorpion. I have the real one. The one I showed you was a fake, as I told you. My friend will be filling you in on the details in a few days, but I wanted to be the one to inform you of your mistake, since you had such a hard time believing me."

If she was waiting for an apology, she would have a long wait, she realized. The silence went on for so long she was about to hang up when Phong's voice came smoothly over the line.

"I'd really like to see the scorpion, Miss Barlow. Do you have it with you?"

"Yes." She hesitated. Two hours wasn't going to give her much time. Besides, without the copy, he probably wouldn't be convinced there actually were two scorpions. He'd think she was just trying to pull a fast one again.

"Unfortunately," she said, her voice deceptively pleasant, "I won't have time. My flight leaves Bangkok in less than two hours. Goodbye, Mr. Phong. I really wish I could say it's been a pleasure."

She replaced the receiver with a thump that shook the bracket and, feeling somewhat appeased, went to find a comfortable seat to wait for her flight.

Less than an hour later a hand grasped her arm, and her heart surged with a treacherous hope, but when she turned, it was to look into the dark eyes of a complete stranger.

"Miss Barlow?" He touched his cap. It was a very official-looking cap and matched his uniform, Hilary realized with an uncomfortable lurch of her stomach.

"Yes?" She tried to pull her arm free and was alarmed when the man held fast.

"Mr. Phong sent me. He wishes to see you."

Hilary relaxed slightly. "I'm sorry, but I told Mr. Phong I don't have time to see him. Tell him I will write and explain everything when I get back to the States and that he will be officially informed about everything very shortly."

"I'm sorry, Miss Barlow. I have orders to bring you to him. It is only a ten-minute ride. He will see that you do not miss your plane." The man gave her arm a slight tug.

Hilary gave a desperate look around. She couldn't see anyone likely to help her. Even if there was, they would probably tell her to go with the guard. The arts department did have a certain authority where antiques were concerned; she would probably have to go and sort this mess out now before she got clearance to leave. She could just see Phong calling customs to tell them her papers weren't in order.

Wishing fervently that she hadn't given in to her little spurt of revenge, Hilary allowed the man to escort her out of the terminal.

"My plane leaves at eleven-thirty," she said coldly, once she was seated in the long black car that waited at the curb. "I expect to be on it, or your Mr. Phong will have a lot to answer for."

The guard averted his face and remained silent during the entire ride to the arts department.

The coolness of the shadowy hall did nothing to ease Hilary's discomfort as she walked slowly with the guard to Phong's office.

She was ushered inside, and her stomach churned again when she saw the empty chair behind the desk. She took the chair opposite and glanced at her watch. It was almost ten-thirty. She still had an hour. As long as Phong didn't drag this thing out, she could make it.

To her relief the guard left, and she spent the next fifteen minutes squirming on the chair while her nerves wound themselves into tightly sprung coils.

Where was he? How dare he keep her waiting like this! She would give him a piece of her mind when he finally condescended to turn up, she fumed.

Her irritation was fueled by the intense pain she felt every time she thought about Simon. Somehow she would have to find out what happened when he went in after Chambers. She couldn't spend the rest of her life wondering whether Simon had been successful—or, worse, whether he'd come through unhurt.

Maybe she could call the DEA when she got back to the States, and ask them. She looked at her watch again. Ten fifty-five.

She jumped up, her nerves stretched to the screaming point. She'd give him five more minutes, she told herself, and then she was getting out of there. The only way they could stop her from getting on that plane would be by brute force.

She wanted to go home. She wanted to be in familiar surroundings again, with people she knew. Somewhere she could nurse her wounds and get on with her life.

Her head snapped up as the door opened suddenly, filling her with a mixture of relief and apprehension. Phong nodded at her politely before crossing to his desk.

He gestured for her to sit down, and she did so, impatiently.

"Mr. Phong," she said as soon as he was seated, "I have a plane to catch in just under thirty minutes. I hope we can dispense with any unnecessary details.

Phong looked coldly at her. "Do you have the scorpion?"

"Yes." She patted her bag. "It's in here."

He stretched out a hand that had unnaturally long nails, she noticed for the first time with a little shiver of distaste. "I'd like to see it," he said quietly.

Letting out a meaningful sigh, Hilary opened her bag and withdrew the box. "Since you couldn't see the disparity between the copy and the picture of the genuine carving," she said, handing it over, "I doubt that you will see much difference in the carvings now. But if you insist—"

"Do you have the copy?" Phong said sharply.

Hilary snapped her mouth shut. For the first time she was beginning to understand the ramifications of what she had done. Any word about Chambers to this man could start an investigation that could wreck Simon's chances of picking up the criminal.

"No, I don't," she said stiffly. "And frankly I can't see what you're so worried about. I made a perfectly legitimate exchange with the museum. They have the Buddha, and now I have the scorpion. I'm sorry I can't fill you in on all the details, but as I've told you, you will be fully informed in a few days. Now, if you'll excuse me, I have a plane to catch." She stood and held out her hand for the carving.

"You have to understand, Miss Barlow," Phong said, lifting the lid of the box, "that if there has been some kind of criminal activity concerning this valuable antique, naturally I would like to know more."

He looked down at the scorpion for a long moment, then snapped the lid shut. "For instance, who is this friend who is going to bring me this information?"

Hilary met the cold gaze without flinching. "I am not in a position to tell you." She could feel it closing in around her: a cold, frightening sense of danger.

Again she held out her hand. "I have to leave now," she said, putting into her voice as much forcefulness as she could manage. To her intense relief, Phong handed her the box, just as the phone at his elbow pealed sharply.

She thrust the box back into her bag, ignoring Phong's quiet voice speaking in to the phone. He replaced the receiver and looked at her.

"I must ask you to wait just one moment more," he said, making it sound like an order. "There's someone who wants to ask you some questions."

The hairs on the back of her neck stood at attention. "I've told you everything I can," she said, backing toward the door. "If I don't leave right now, I'm going to miss my plane and—"

She broke off when the door opened behind her, shattering the last of her frazzled nerves. She froze, some sixth sense warning her that danger had arrived.

In the fleeting moment before Phong spoke, she reminded herself that this time Simon couldn't help her. He thought she was safely on her way back to the States.

It was with a strange feeling of detachment that she heard Phong say, "Miss Barlow, I'd like you to meet a friend of mine. Mr. Frank Chambers."

Chapter 10

Simon glanced impatiently at his watch once again. The plane was late, and he'd had enough of hanging around the airport. The hours had dragged painfully by since he'd said goodbye to Hilary, and he couldn't wait for the guys to arive and help take his mind off her for a while at least.

Two-thirty. She'd be on her way to the States by now. She would arrive in Seattle around noon Pacific time for her connecting flight to L.A. That would make it the early hours of the morning in Chiang Mai.

He scowled and jammed his hands in his pockets, hunching his shoulders. He had to forget Hilary Barlow. He had bigger problems to deal with right now.

He slumped down on a vacant bench and sighed. There was a time when the adrenaline would have been pumping through his veins at the prospect of the next couple of days. He was close enough to victory to smell it. He had Chambers cornered, and provided there were no last-minute itches—and he couldn't think of one possibility—everyhing was set to go.

All he had to do was go over the plan with the guys when they got there, tighten everything down, and at long last he'd have his hands on that piece of garbage.

It wasn't that he wasn't looking forward to putting Chambers away, he told himself. He was; he'd waited a damn long time to do it. But it was different now. It was that same lack of enthusiasm that had prompted him to give up this life two years ago. The excitement of the chase, the thrill of pulling off the seemingly impossible, the tremendous high in achieving his goal, all that had blunted, like a knife that has been used too many times.

He stirred, giving himself a mental shake. He was just depressed; it would pass. It would have to pass, he told himself grimly, if he was going to—

"Well, get a load of this happy face. What did you do, have one beer too many last night?"

At the sound of the cheerful voice, Simon looked up, his frown changing to a wide grin as he met the laughing gray eyes of the man standing in front of him.

"Ty, you old rebel, you get uglier every day." He jumped to his feet, grasping the other man's hand in genuine delight. "How long has it been, four years?"

"All of that, pretty boy. I see you still haven't put any permanent marks on that magnificent profile. I don't know how you guys do it. If I didn't know you better I'd say you were bucking for a modeling career."

Simon laughed. Tyson Goodwin was shorter than he by two inches, but his husky build and solid muscles, combined with the lightning reflexes of a martial arts expert, made him a valuable ally in a dangerous situation. And a lethal enemy.

"Where's Blake? You did bring him with you?" Simon looked past Ty's shoulder, searching for the dark head he knew would be towering above the crowd.

Blake Townsend's head easily cleared everyone else's.

The big man's smile flashed as he caught sight of Simon and Ty, though his green eyes looked stormy when he fi nally reached them. He sent Simon a narrow-eyed glance, then grabbed his hand and pumped it. "You're looking a bit down," he said, frowning. "Trouble?"

Simon shrugged. He'd forgotten Blake's uncanny knack of sensing a person's mood. "Not so far. Welcome to Chiang Mai. You got luggage?" There were some things he intended to keep to himself, he reflected as he led the way to the baggage claims area.

An hour later, with the three of them crammed into his tiny room in the rooming house Simon studied his friends with satisfaction.

He'd filled them in on all of it—all of it except for Hilary's involvement. As far as he was concerned, that part of it didn't have any bearing on what they had to do.

Blake stared at Simon thoughtfully, his thumb stroking the frosted surface of his beer can. "All right," he said, "we have Chambers and his men, who are the bad guys, against us three and the Chinese carver, right?"

"Right." Simon took a swig of his beer and pushed himself away from the wall. "Except that Chen is an old man. We can't expect help from him."

"Great," Ty muttered. "We have to watch out for an old man and a bunch of kids, as well as take on a gang of thugs."

Blake's green eyes narrowed as he looked at Simon. "What about the law here? Will they help?"

"As soon as I get the extradition papers back, I'll contact them. Once they see the set of pictures I've got, they'll lend us all the rangers we want."

Blake frowned. "You've got to wait for the papers?"

"Yeah." Simon stepped over Blake's legs and sat down on the end of the bed. "The Thais will take one look at those pictures, and they'll want to move. They're not going to let us mastermind this gig, or even go with them, unless we have the papers to take Chambers and his boys back. And I don't trust anyone else to bring that snake in. He's too slippery."

He scowled at the can in his hand. "The first thing we've got to do is take out that helicopter he's got stashed behind the refineries, or he'll be out of there before we know it."

"So when do we get the papers?"

Simon shrugged. "I sent the negatives to the States. There's enough evidence on them to convince the boys to serve papers on Chambers and bring him in. They'll send the papers back by special courier. We should get them in a couple of days."

"A couple of days?" Ty sat up, his face brightening. "Well, that gives us time to do a little socializing."

"Forget it." Simon shook his head in warning. "Tonight we're going to take a look around Chambers's little sin city and find out what we're up against. It'll take us a couple of days to set up this exercise and round up the gear we'll need. By that time the papers should be here."

They both gave him their complete attention, and he switched off the thoughts of Hilary before they could begin. He had a job to do, and he would do it. Only then would he let himself think about her. . . .

Simon was reminded of that thought as he lowered his body wearily onto his bed shortly before dawn the next morning. Apart from an odd hour or two, he'd been without sleep for two nights in a row.

Exhausted as he was, sleep still eluded him. He was satisfied with the night's mission. While Ty and Blake had scouted the jungle around Chambers's headquarters, he'd risked sneaking back to Chen's house. He'd been hoping to have another chat with him and get some inside information.

It bothered Simon to find the house empty. Maybe Chen worked at night, he thought, or maybe he slept in the big house when he was working.

Simon turned onto his back, envious of the snores from the two men sleeping on his floor. They weren't home free yet, not by any means, he reminded himself.

He knew from experience how many things could go wrong. Still, it looked good. Hilary should be arriving in L.A. by now.

He swore silently. Those thoughts of her kept creeping in when he least expected it, disturbing his concentration. It was a good thing this was his last assignment. There was no doubt about it; he was getting soft. And he wouldn't stay alive in this business by being soft.

He sighed and closed his eyes. He would not think of Hilary, he told himself. He would not.

The phone blasted sleep from his body less than twenty minutes later. Ty swore loudly and profusely as Simon fumbled for the receiver in an effort to quiet the jangling noise.

Shaking his head to clear the fog, he mumbled, "Yeah?"

The voice on the other end of the line was brisk. "Adams. She wasn't on the plane."

"What?" he felt for the lamp and switched it on, squinting in the dim light at his watch. Six-fifteen. She had to have been on the plane.

"Are you sure?" His head was clearing now. Fast.

"Yeah. I've been calling you every hour since noon my time."

"I just got in a little while ago. Did you check the passenger list?"

"Yeah. She's listed. Her luggage is here, but she never boarded."

Simon swore. Across the room, Blake raised himself on his elbow. Simon met his piercing gaze and shook his head. "I'll look into it," he said into the phone. "I'll get back to you."

"Right." The line clicked, and he was left listening to the dial tone.

"What is it?" Blake's green gaze cut across the room, and Simon swallowed the nausea that the unaccustomed fear had produced.

He'd been scared for her before. But never like this. Dear
God, never like this. His brain seemed numb, and he pulled
himself into a sitting position, burying his head in his hands.

When he most needed to think, the thoughts wouldn't
come. What could have happened to her? He was afraid—
horribly afraid—that he knew. But how?

He swung his legs from the bed and strode to the tiny re-
frigerator. He pulled out a beer and lifted the tab, then
poured the cool liquid down his throat until he coughed and
choked.

"What the hell?" Blake was on his feet, struggling into
his jeans, while Ty sat rubbing at his eyes, still swearing.

Simon regained his breath and walked back to the bed.
"We've got trouble," he said shortly, and reached for his
pants. "I'd better fill you in on the rest of it."

He sat on the bed while Ty sat cross-legged on the floor
and Blake paced back and forth in the narrow space left to
him. He told them everything—except how he and Hilary
had spent one particular afternoon in a remote tribal village. "She should have arrived in Seattle at noon. That was
four hours ago," he said, combing his hair with unsteady
fingers.

"Who was that on the phone, then?" Blake said, stopping his pacing to look down at Simon "A relative? Maybe
they just missed her. Maybe she's safely home in L.A."

Simon shook his head. "That was Adams. He was supposed to meet Hilary off the plane in Seattle." He closed his
eyes and tilted his face to the ceiling. "She had the negatives," he said, his voice sounding like a groan. "I put them
in the box with the scorpion. Underneath the cushion."

Ty whistled softly as Simon's words hung in the air. "You
think she gave Adams the slip? Is she in with this Chambers guy?"

Simon moved without thinking, coming off the bed with
his fists curled. "She didn't even know she was carrying
them," he said, his voice biting off the words. "I didn't tell
her because I know how transparent she is. Customs would

take one look at her and know she was hiding something. I didn't want to take the chance of putting her through a search and a bunch of explanations. As for that idea about Chambers, you'd better put it where it belongs before I do it for you. I would trust that woman with my life.''

"Take it easy," Blake muttered as Ty lifted a hand to protest.

"Whoa. Sorry, pal." Ty scrambled to his feet. "Why didn't you tell us it was like that?" he added in a soft voice.

Simon stared at him, still thinking of the words he'd just spoken. *I would trust that woman with my life.* "I didn't know," he said slowly.

Ty raised his eyebrows and looked at Blake, who cleared his throat. "Let's sit down and think this out," he suggested quietly. "So you think Chambers has something to do with this. But how would he know the negatives were in the box?"

Simon shook his head. "I don't know. I had the film developed the evening before Hilary left, by a DEA contact. He was cleared by the agency. I checked on him first. I put the negatives in the box as soon as I got them back, and I had the box with me the whole time after that. Chen saw me exchange the carvings, but he didn't know about the negatives." He looked at Blake in despair. "No one did."

"Then maybe you're wrong. Maybe Chambers has nothing to do with this." Blake scratched his head. "She could have missed the flight and had to wait for the next one."

"She had two hours. I can't see how." Simon looked at his watch. "If she did, she's still here." He pulled his wallet from his back pocket and found the scrap of paper, then reached for the phone and dialed the Bangkok hotel.

The familiar voice of the clerk answered. "Yes, Mr. King. I remember you," he said to Simon's question.

"Do you remember Hilary Barlow?" Simon said urgently.

"The American lady. I remember."

"Did she come back to the hotel?" His stomach muscles ached with tension, and he made an effort to relax.

"No, Mr. King. I not see her. But there is message for you."

"Message?" His heart leaped. "She left me a message? What does it say?"

There was a slight pause, then the clerk spoke again. "Message not from Miss Barlow," he said carefully. "You want I read?"

Simon could feel the sweat forming on his brow. He sank onto the bed, his fingers closing around the hard plastic of the receiver until they cramped. "Read it."

"It says—" again the voice hesitated "—you want it, you know where to find it. Come alone or it dies." The clerk's voice shook. "It has *F* and *C* on the bottom."

Simon's eyes closed briefly. "Thank you."

"Mr. King? You okay?"

"Everything's fine." He drew in his breath slowly. "Just a friend of mine with a strange sense of humor. Thanks for your help." He replaced the receiver and looked up to meet two pairs of eyes.

"Chambers has her," he said hollowly.

The eyes, one pair cold gray, the other hard green, gleamed with the light of battle.

Ty said, "Then he had to know about the negatives somehow. Somebody must have tipped him off. Why else would he grab her?"

Blake lowered his body into the armchair. "So, it looks as if we'll have to change our arrangements."

"I can't figure it," Simon muttered. "How the hell did Chambers know Hilary was with me? He didn't know I was even in the country."

"He must have." Ty moved to the end of the bed and sat down. "He had to be pretty sure you'd call the hotel, for him to leave a message there."

"He probably figured I'd call there once I found out Hilary was missing. His boys have left messages there before.'' Simon pounded the table with his fist. ''Damn him. If it hadn't been for Adams meeting the plane, I would never have known she wasn't back in L.A.''

He caught the glances Blake and Ty exchanged, and shrugged defensively. ''We didn't have any future plans,'' he muttered, knowing what they were thinking.

''So that's what the story is with you and her,'' Blake said softly. ''Was that her idea or yours?''

Simon shot him a warning look, and Blake raised his hands. ''All right. It's none of my business. The important thing is what do we do about it?''

''We go get her.'' Simon got up from the bed and pulled open the top drawer of his shabby dresser. ''And Chambers.'' He lifted up a khaki shirt and shook it out. ''And,'' he added, his voice harsh with angry fear, ''if he's so much as touched her, don't worry about taking him alive.''

Hilary stared at the sunlight forcing its way through the slits in the bamboo walls and tried not to think about the dogs pacing around outside.

There were three of them—black Dobermans—and they looked every bit as vicious as their reputation. Not that she was in any position to challenge the dogs anyway. She grimaced as she tugged at the rope that bound her wrists behind her back.

It was a useless gesture, as she'd found out hours ago, and it only chafed her skin, which already had to be raw. She shifted her hips, trying to find a more comfortable position on the narrow cot.

Lying down had been uncomfortable all night, though she'd managed some fitful sleep in spite of the fear that hovered at the edges of her consciousness.

Sitting up brought some relief. At least her mind felt clearer this morning, she thought thankfully.

Ever since she'd turned and looked at the man standing in the doorway in Phong's office the day before, her mind had seemed a fuzzy blank.

She vaguely remembered Chambers questioning her on the flight back to Chiang Mai, telling her over and over again what she already knew, that she was on her own and Simon couldn't help her now. He thought she was back in the States.

In spite of Chambers's promise that he would release her if she told him where to find Simon, she'd stubbornly refused to say anything. She'd closed her mind against his softly spoken threats and prayed that she could hold out long enough for Simon to launch the raid and find her.

She stared at her ankles, which were also bound by the thick rope. She couldn't help remembering that Simon had told her Chambers had held him for five days bound hand and foot.

Five days. It had been only one night, and already she was a mass of pain. She lifted her ankles from the bed and winced as pain knifed up her legs.

How long would it take Simon to organize the raid? she wondered. She had shut out the fears that had plagued her through the long night, burying them under memories of the past few days.

But now, in the pale shadows of the morning, she forced herself to face them. Chambers had promised to make her cooperate and had gone into horrifying details of the methods he planned to use.

Even if she survived until the raid, Simon would be bringing armed men with him. He would have no way of knowing she was in the middle of it all, so she could very likely die in a gun battle.

She had to get out of here, she told herself desperately. She couldn't expect any help from Chen. She wondered what they'd done to him. He was an old man; he wouldn't be able to stand up to them.

Guilt swamped her when she thought about Chen. None of this would have happened if she hadn't called Phong.

She stiffened. Her head jerked toward the door as it opened, letting in a pool of light. Her stomach lurched as the tall figure of Chambers stepped into the hut and walked toward her.

His physique was remarkably trim. His silver hair, which was still thick and luxuriant, fell back from his forehead in neatly combed waves, but the deep wrinkles and the folds of loose skin on his jowls betrayed his age.

It was his eyes that bothered Hilary the most. Something about them filled her with a sick panic. They made her feel as if she were looking into the eyes of the devil.

"I hope you slept well," Chambers said in his well-modulated voice. "Perhaps you feel more like answering my questions this morning."

Hilary pressed her lips together. She'd been through this once the afternoon before, a long, grueling session in the sticky heat. He hadn't touched her physically, but his soft voice reciting the atrocities he planned had sickened her, and she'd finally passed out with shock and exhaustion.

She dimly remembered having been carried into this hut and having her hands and feet tied, but not until she'd been brought a drink and some kind of rice dish had she felt her strength returning.

She cringed backward as Chambers leaned over her.

"You could save yourself a lot of discomfort, Miss Barlow, if you would just answer my questions. How long has Simon King been in Thailand? Where is he staying? Who does he have working with him besides you? How did you find out about the jade thefts? How long has Chen been working for you?"

The same questions, Hilary thought wearily. She'd heard them over and over again. She clamped her mouth shut and stared into the black eyes with defiance.

Chambers sighed. "I have nothing against you personally, Hilary," he said quietly. "I like women. I'd hate to see you hurt." He reached out a well-manicured hand and ran a finger down her cheek before she could jerk her face away from him.

"Such a pretty face," he murmured. "It would be a shame to spoil it with ugly scars."

Hilary swallowed and kept on swallowing as his eyes gleamed at her with a dark evil.

"I detest violence," Chambers said as if talking to himself. "It's so...messy. It would be so much more pleasant if you were nice to me."

Hilary's eyes widened with a new fear. This was the first time he'd suggested anything of that nature.

Chambers smiled, a thin movement of his lips that had nothing to do with amusement. "I could make you forget Simon King. You have to understand that I can't let him live. He has become too much of a nuisance to me. Now that he knows where I am, I have to relocate again, and that's always a nuisance."

He sighed and moved away from her, giving her stomach a chance to settle again.

"I was just getting used to this place," he muttered. "I'm tired of all this upheaval." He turned back to her, his face a cold mask of anger.

"Simon King is going to die," he said, making it sound like a fact, "so you might as well make it easy on yourself. You have until tomorrow morning to tell me what you know. If you are sensible, then you can leave with me, looking just as pretty as you do now. If not, I will use some of my other methods, which I'm sure you remember me telling you about."

Hilary fought the sudden lurch of her stomach and forced herself to look at him. She had to try something. Anything. If Simon didn't get here before the morning, Chambers would once more slip out of his grasp, and she would probably be dead—or wishing it.

"I'll give it some serious consideration," she said, making no effort to control the tremble in her voice. "But I'm too uncomfortable to think about anything right now. I really need to go to the bathroom."

Chambers's expression changed. Whether he believed she might talk or not, he apparently believed her urgency. He nodded, turned on his heel and left the hut.

She waited, her heartbeat shaking her body, as the minutes ticked slowly by. When she heard the footsteps approach the hut, she held her breath, then let it out with relief when she heard a feminine voice give a sharp order to the dogs.

The door opened and a young, attractive woman walked into the hut. She avoided Hilary's eyes as she leaned over to untie the ropes that bound Hilary's ankles.

Hilary looked at her face, which was half-hidden by the long dark hair swinging across her shoulders. "Who are you?" she said, feigning an indifference she was far from feeling. "Chambers's girlfriend?"

She winced as pain coursed up her legs from her freed ankles. She winced again when the woman drew a gun from the belt of her pants and motioned with it for Hilary to move.

"I guess that answers my question." Hilary slid her feet to the floor and gasped as slivers of pain cut through them. "Do you have a name?" she said painfully as she tried to balance on her uncooperative legs.

The woman jerked the gun at the door, her eyes hard and unfriendly.

Hilary shrugged and shuffled toward the door. "I could do this a lot better if you'd untie my hands," she grumbled.

The woman didn't answer, but when Hilary stumbled, the woman grabbed one of her arms to steady her. Hilary immediately shook her off. "I can manage," she said, preferring her unsteady gait to the feel of the woman's hand on her arm.

By the height of the sun, Hilary judged it to be around nine o'clock when she stepped outside. Apart from the dogs, who rolled their eyes at her until her guard snapped an order, the village appeared to be empty.

They were all probably at the refineries, Hilary thought uneasily. She glanced at the big house in the center but could see no sign of movement. Chen's house, as far as she remembered, was on the opposite side of Chambers's village.

She wondered if he was a prisoner inside, then forgot about him when the woman nudged her toward the trees. Hilary had been worried she'd be taken to the big house, and was relieved that she was expected to use the primitive facilities of the forest.

She managed to edge the woman several yards away from the houses by pretending to look for a suitable place. By the time her guard had lost patience and indicated with a sweep of her gun that Hilary was to go no farther, the houses were hidden from sight by the trees.

"You'll have to untie my wrists," Hilary insisted, turning her back and wiggling her hands to emphasize her meaning. "I can't manage with them tied like this.

When the woman didn't move, she looked imploringly over her shoulder. "What are you worrying about? You have a gun. I'm not going to argue with that."

Again she wriggled her hands. The woman probably didn't understand a word she was saying, she thought hopelessly. She was about to try again when the woman tucked the gun back into her belt and began tugging at the rope around her wrists.

The pain in her arms made her cry out when she pulled them forward. She rubbed at them fiercely with her hands to get the circulation moving again while the woman watched her with a stoic expression on her face.

"All right," Hilary muttered when the gun was jerked at her again. "But the least you can do is turn your back."

The woman looked blankly at her.

"Turn your back." Hilary twirled her fingers to illustrate her meaning.

The woman hesitated, then compromised by turning her head.

Hilary had seen the branch and knew what she had to do. There was a brief moment when she wondered how she would bring herself to use it, then she thought about Chambers. She snatched the branch up, and brought it down hard on the woman's head.

She'd never hit anyone in her life and was shocked at how easily the woman went down. At first she was deathly afraid that she'd killed her, but she found a strong pulse in the slim neck and felt sick with relief. Her gaze fell on the gun lying in the grass, and after a moment's hesitation, she picked it up by the barrel and pushed it into her pants pocket.

How Simon did this sort of thing all the time she couldn't imagine, she thought as she leaped through the undergrowth in what she hoped was the direction of the river.

She had to make it fast, she told herself. She probably had a few minutes' head start before her guard was missed. She would have to follow the river upstream, go through the gorge and make it to the road. Someone would surely give her a ride into Chiang Mai. If not, she thought with a surge of determination, she would darn well run all the way into town.

The heavy brush and thick ferns seemed denser than when she'd followed Simon through there, and when she didn't arrive at the riverbank in the next few minutes, she began to panic.

To be lost in that jungle would be exchanging one crisis for another that was equally as dangerous. She made herself stop and take a look around.

In which direction had the sun been when she'd come through here before? She frowned, trying to concentrate. It had been later in the day then; that would make a difference.

The soft sound behind her warned her, and she spun around, her heart plummeting as she saw the tall man standing a few feet away. He stood with his legs braced apart, his rifle sitting in the crook of his arm and pointed straight at her.

"Well, well," he said in a low drawl, "what have we here?"

She thought of the gun in her pocket and knew she wouldn't have a chance to use it. She twisted away from him, determined not be taken again by Chambers's men. Her second step faltered as another man, also carrying a rifle, stepped from the undergrowth.

"Hold it, darlin'," he said softly. "You're not going anywhere."

Hilary's gaze darted desperately from one man to the other as she backed slowly away. She moved one step, then two, and then her breath came out in a tiny scream as she backed into a solid wall of flesh.

A hand descended on her shoulder, and she froze, her defeat so bitter she could taste it.

"Damn it, Hilary, you have a way of turning up in the most unexpected places."

Stunned, she twisted her head until she could see over her shoulder. His face looked relentless, but the expression in his ice-blue eyes betrayed his relief at seeing her.

"Simon." She barely breathed the word, still unable to believe he was actually standing there. Then, with a cry, she flung herself at him, regardless of the two men who watched the whole procedure with interest.

His arm closing around her felt like a band of steel as he pulled her against him. She would have been happy to stay there forever.

For a moment he held her, crushed against his chest, his mouth inches from hers, then he let her go. "Let's get out of here," he said, shouldering his own rifle, which Hilary had just noticed. "You've got a lot of questions to answer."

The gun reminded her of the one in her pocket. She pulled it out and handed it to Simon with a shudder. "Here—you take this. Guns make me nervous."

He looked surprised but took it without comment and shoved it in his belt. She stayed as close to him as she could get, while the four of them scrambled through the tangled undergrowth in the opposite direction Hilary would have taken, finally emerging at the riverbank.

"I'm glad you came along," Hilary said as Simon helped her into an inflatable rubber raft that had been cleverly hidden beneath some bushy ferns. "I never would have found the river."

The raft rocked as the three men climbed in, filling it to capacity. "We've set up camp on the opposite bank a half mile upstream," Simon said, handing paddles to Ty and Blake. "You'd better tell me how you got away, and talk fast—I need to know how much time we've got."

She told him quickly, leaving out most of what Chambers had said. Simon's expression was already ferocious enough to make her nervous.

The two men paddled with an easy strength that moved the raft at a fast pace through the water. They had reached the curve in the river when they first heard the spine-chilling howl of the dogs.

"They can't follow our trail once they hit the water," Simon said as Hilary looked at him anxiously. "Chambers won't know we were with you. Hopefully he'll think you've gone upstream. None of his rafts are missing, so he may not figure you've crossed the river to the other bank."

"Unless I swam."

He shook his head. "You wouldn't have had time. The dogs know where you went into the water, and the opposite bank is too steep for you to climb out."

"How did you find me?" She wanted to touch him, to feel his arms around her again. Only the presence of the other two men stopped her from reaching for him.

"You weren't hard to spot. You were charging through the forest making more noise than a herd of elephants."

She gave him a withering look. "No, I mean how did you know where I was?"

"I called the hotel in Bangkok when I found out you weren't on the plane. We were taking a preliminary scout around when we heard you crashing around in there."

He waved a hand at the other two men. "I guess you'd better meet these two ruffians. Blake Townsend is the tall Texan, and that's Tyson Goodwin, known to all his friends as Ty. I won't tell you what his enemies call him."

"The ones that can still talk, you mean." Ty grinned and lowered an eyelid in a wink. "We've been hearing some nice things about you."

"Oh?" Hilary felt the blush creeping over her face and glanced quickly at Simon before turning to Blake.

The Texan returned her friendly smile with a quick nod. "Pleased to meet you, ma'am."

She had to wait until they'd beached the raft and dragged it into the bushes before she could ask the questions burning in her mind.

"How did you know I wasn't on the plane?" she demanded as soon as they were settled on the ground in the shade of lofty teak trees.

"What happened to the scorpion?" Simon countered.

"Chambers has it." Hilary couldn't suppress the shiver that attacked her spine. "Not a nice man, your friend Chambers."

"Did he hurt you?" Simon said quickly.

Hilary shook her head. "It was more what he implied. Something about his eyes—I don't know—he just gives me the creeps."

"I know what you mean." Simon reached for her hand and swore when he saw the rope marks on her wrist. In a quick gesture that took Hilary by surprise, he pressed his lips to the chafed skin and let her go.

Ignoring the grin that spread across Ty's face, he added, "How did Chambers find out about the negatives?"

"Negatives?" She stared at him. "What negatives?"

"Oh, my," Ty murmured, "she still doesn't know." He shrugged off Simon's fierce look.

Hilary listened in growing dismay as Simon explained about the negatives. "I don't know anything about them," she said when he'd finished. "I thought Phong wanted the scorpion to give it back to Chambers."

Simon frowned. "Where does Phong come into this?"

"Who's Phong?" Blake said, looking at Ty.

Ty shrugged. "Beats me."

Hilary sighed. "I'd better start at the beginning." She told them everything that had happened from the moment she'd arrived back in Bangkok.

"So that's how Chambers got on to you," Simon murmured. "Phong is in on the deal."

She nodded. "I don't think he's all that involved. He's just taking bribes to turn a blind eye. He must have had a shock that first time I walked into his office. According to a remark Chambers made, Phong didn't know until that moment that I existed."

"So," Simon said thoughtfully, "when you told Phong you had the real scorpion back, he realized you must have switched it. He called Chambers—"

"—And delayed me long enough for him to get there from Chiang Mai," Hilary finished. "Chambers has a helicopter. It took him ten minutes to get to the airport, and an hour by his private jet from there."

"Yeah, I saw the helicopter. So that's how he knew you were with me. You told him."

Hilary looked at him miserably. "You know better than that. I admit I did a pretty stupid thing, and I feel terrible about it now, but I didn't tell anyone about you. Chambers already knew. Hal and Jerry saw your gallant rescue outside the arts department. They recognized you and reported to Chambers, who ordered them back to Chiang Mai. He didn't want you following them."

"He thought we were working together and was hoping that Jerry's threats would cause you to send me back to the States, out of harm's way. Then he'd have only you to deal with."

Simon swore. "So he knew I was here all along."

"Yes." Hilary absently brushed a fern from her pant leg. "But he didn't know we were on Hal and Jerry's trail. He thought they'd lost you in Bangkok. Until Phong called him and told him that I had the scorpion. Then he knew we'd been to his village."

She twisted a long blade of grass around her finger and pulled it out of the ground with an angry tug. "I'm afraid he knows that Chen helped you. It was the only way you could have slipped into his house. I don't know what happened to Chen. I haven't seen him since they brought me back here."

"Wonderful." Simon ran a hand through his hair. "So Chambers has the scorpion and the negatives and Chen."

"And," said Blake, "we can't get any help on this without the papers. Which we can't get without the negatives."

"Plus," Ty added in a mournful voice, "we have to rescue an old man as well as a bunch of kids."

"You don't have to rescue me now," Hilary said in a small voice. She looked at Simon. "It looks as if I'm going to be in the finale, after all."

Chapter 11

"Forget it, Hilary," Simon said harshly. "I'll do my best to bring the scorpion out with me, but you are staying out of it."

"Wait a minute!" Blake ignored Simon's scowl and leaned forward. "If she doesn't come with us, what are you going to do with her? Leave her out here on her own?"

"I can take her back to town," Simon said stubbornly. "We can reschedule the raid for tomorrow."

"You can't do that." Hilary saw three pairs of eyes swivel to her face. "Chambers is leaving in the morning. In fact, now that he knows I've gone, he may even leave sooner."

Simon let out a sigh. "That thought had occurred to me." He rubbed at his eyes with the backs of his hands. "What I don't understand is why he didn't leave yesterday, when he knew we were on to him."

"Because," Hilary said soberly, "he has a huge shipment of heroin he wants to get out before he closes the refineries down. I heard him talking to Phong about it when they were discussing what to do with me."

Simon punched at his knee. "Of course. It takes time to get a shipment like that ready to roll, and he probably flies it out on the helicopter. He wouldn't leave without it, unless he was forced to."

"And that's why he left the note for you," Blake said slowly. "He probably figured you'd be on him with a trigger-happy bunch of lawmen. He grabbed Hilary to stall you long enough to get his shipment out."

"Or long enough to make me tell him where to find you first," Hilary said with a shiver. "His threats were pretty convincing."

Simon muttered something unintelligible.

"He may not even know he's holding the negatives." Ty shook his head in disbelief. "Can you beat that?"

"All right," Simon said irritably. "We'll have to go in now. I guess you go, too, Hilary. But I'm going on record as saying I don't like it. And—" he glared at each one of them in turn "—I'm relying on you to see this lady doesn't get hurt."

"We'll guard her with our lives," Ty promised cheerfully.

"You may have to. At least the dogs seem to have given up for the moment." He fixed his intense gaze on Hilary. "As for you, I'm going to give you specific directions. Follow them to the letter if you want to come out of this in one piece."

"I will." She couldn't help the grin, even if her insides were churning with fear and her hands felt cold.

She was surprised to find she could eat when Simon shared the rations they'd brought with them. As the men worked out their plans, she listened eagerly and answered their questions when she could.

Simon repeated her part in it again and again, making her recite it until she knew it by heart.

"You have to know it well enough that you will act automatically," he told her. "When you're under pressure, it will be hard to think."

She nodded soberly, praying she wouldn't let them down. She wondered if the men had the same quivery sensations in their stomachs. Watching them quietly discussing the details of the raid, she decided they couldn't possibly look so calm if they felt half as nervous as she did.

An hour slipped by while Simon taught her the simple words of Thai she would need to carry out her role. Working with him in that way made her profoundly aware of her feelings for him. He was so patient, gently prompting her again and again until she had it right, quick to praise her when she succeeded.

Finally, everything was set. Ty had been sent on a reconnaissance and had come back to report that all appeared quiet. "I couldn't see Chambers," he told them, "but the helicopter is still there. And the dogs are back at the refineries. They must have given up on searching for Hilary. They're probably too busy getting ready to move out."

Simon nodded briefly. "All right. You know what to do." He placed his hands on Hilary's shoulders and looked down at her, his eyes intensely serious.

"Just follow orders," he told her, "and for God's sake be careful."

She nodded, too nervous to speak. She climbed into the raft with the three of them, repeating over and over in her mind what she had to do.

Her orders were to try to round up the children once the raid got under way. When she'd herded them safely back to Simon's camp, she was to stay with them until one of the men came for her. If things didn't go as planned, it was up to her to get out and inform the authorities. It all sounded so simple and at the same time so utterly impossible.

So many things could go wrong, she'd told Simon earlier. He'd merely shrugged, saying that was the way it usually was. She wondered again what made them do it. What made men like Simon and his two friends risk their lives for the sake of law and order?

This was the Simon she didn't know, she thought as she watched Simon jump ashore and beach the raft. This tough, professionally trained gunman biting off terse orders was a far cry from the man who'd held a silver bell in his hand and told her he would always remember her.

She forgot her memories when Simon reached out his hand. His grasp was firm around her fingers as he helped her ashore, and for a moment he held on to her, his eyes probing hers. "You okay?"

"I'm fine," she assured him, and walked past him to join the others, afraid she would blurt out something inappropriate.

They moved in single file, stealthily creeping through the trees, using the bushy undergrowth as cover. Hilary had to admit she was being a lot quieter than when she'd blundered through there earlier—though she was sure Chambers could hear her heart pounding from wherever he was.

She was relieved to see that the woman she'd left lying on the ground had disappeared. Probably trying to sleep off a giant headache, she thought guiltily.

Just short of the nearest house, Simon held up his hand. Without speaking, Ty nodded and slipped off to the right.

Simon worked his way around the edge of the village until they were on the other side, where Blake also left them. Hilary could hear the hum of the generators as Simon led her closer to the refineries.

When he halted, she saw the thatched roofs through the trees. The expression in his eyes when he looked at her made her stomach churn with apprehension.

"Do what you can," he said quietly, "but don't waste time feeling guilty if you have to make a run for it. Use your judgment. I'm relying on you if things go wrong."

She laid trembling fingers on his mouth. "It won't go wrong," she whispered. "But you know I won't let you down."

"Yes, I know that now."

She frowned, wondering if there was a deeper meaning to his words, but he slipped away from her before she could question him. She crouched in the ferns, every nerve in her body quivering as she watched him creep toward the dogs.

The first one started to its feet with a low growl, which immediately died when a large piece of meat landed near its nose. Within minutes all three dogs were lying on their sides. Asleep, Hilary hoped.

Simon disappeared, leaving her alone with the throbbing serenade of the jungle resounding all around her. She watched a butterfly flit across the bush in front of her, a kaleidoscope of color with its bright red-and-yellow wings.

The fragrance of the ferns wafted gently around her as she waited in the moist warmth. When the shot came, it shocked her so badly she rose unthinkingly to her feet.

The first shot was followed by another, then a whole barrage of shots echoed cruelly through the forest, destroying the quiet tranquility as birds shrieked and monkeys hooted their warnings.

Hilary spun around in the direction of the shots, her heart pummeling her ribs, then she dropped to her knees as she heard shouts and the pounding of feet.

Peering through the leafy ferns, she could see men running from the refineries—eight, ten, twelve of them, then three more and still another four behind them.

She felt sick, wondering if Simon had been hurt in the battle that was now raging from the village. How could three men stand up to this many? Should she get out now, while she could, and try to get help?

Even as she considered it she knew how futile such a move would be. It would all be over before she'd reached the road.

She looked back at the refineries, her blood freezing as her decision was made for her.

Children, more than a dozen of them, were filing out from the long huts. Hilary cautiously rose to her feet, looking in all directions.

All the men had raced toward the village. If she was going to move, it had to be now. Staying as low as she could, Hilary stumbled toward the refineries, willing the children to stay where they were.

When she broke out of the trees and raced toward the forlorn group, they stared at her, openmouthed. She pictured what she must look like. In her rumpled shirt and slacks, hair sticking out at all angles, probably dirt-streaked from her trips through the jungle, she probably didn't appear too reassuring, she thought wryly.

She reached the first child, a boy of about twelve, and grabbed his arm. Trying to remember the Thai words Simon had taught her, she gabbled them at the boy, who stared at her in terrified bewilderment.

Inflection, Simon had impressed on her, made all the difference to the meaning of the words. She tried again, pitching her voice at different levels as Simon had taught her.

To her relief the expression in the boy's dark eyes changed, became wary but comprehending. Another barrage of shots galvanized her into action.

She repeated her words and tugged at his arm. She could have wept with relief when the boy nodded and spoke rapidly to the rest of the children.

Taking the hand of the smallest child, a frightened-looking girl who couldn't have been more than eight, Hilary led them back into the trees to the point where Simon had left her.

Giving the boy instructions, which she fervently hoped he understood, she indicated she was going back to make sure all the children were out.

Leaving him in charge, she ran back to the three huts that stood side by side at the river's edge. After a heart-stopping few moments while she looked inside, she saw, to her intense relief, that all three appeared to be empty.

Hardly daring to believe that it had all gone so smoothly, and praying that Simon and his men were having the same good fortune, she sped back to the children.

Somehow she had to get them past the village and down to the rafts. Pre-occupied with her strategy, she didn't see the stocky figure until he stepped out in front of her.

The children cowered back, their eyes on the rifle that was pointed at her heart.

"We meet again, Miss Barlow," Jerry said, baring his teeth in a repulsive grin. "You should have done what I told you and gone back home."

Hilary made a quick signal to the boy she'd elected as leader, hoping he would understand and make a run for it with the children. Her heart sank when Jerry jerked the rifle in their direction and rasped out an order.

The children froze.

"Don't get any more ideas like that," he snarled at Hilary, "or I'll drop you right where you stand."

"Wrong, my friend," said a cheerful voice behind him. "I'm the one doing the dropping."

Hilary stared in stunned surprise as Jerry swung around and met the full force of Ty's booted foot in his throat. The rifle clattered to the ground as Jerry choked, made a horrible gurgling noise, then collapsed in a heap.

"Gotta go," Ty said quickly. "Can you handle the kids?"

Hilary nodded, still too shocked to speak.

Ty gave her a quick grin and disappeared back into the trees.

Hilary looked after him, desperately wishing she'd had time to ask him if Simon was all right. The boy tugged at her hand, reminding her she had more urgent problems to take care of.

She said the Thai word for "come" and felt pleased when the boy apparently understood. Taking hold of the little girl's hand, she led them in a wide arc around the village, flinching every now and again when shots zinged into the trees.

She would not let herself think about Simon. She would go to pieces if she started imagining one of those bullets tearing into his wonderful body, taking him from her even more irrevocably than his own volition.

Her charges seemed docile, as if they accepted as routine all that was happening. With a sense of outrage Hilary wondered what sort of treatment these children had received that had made them so unmoved by the violence all around them.

Hilary found her way to the river without hesitation this time, and they loaded the smallest children onto the rubber raft in a matter of minutes.

The boy, who told Hilary his name was Hahn, knew a smattering of English, which helped a great deal in getting the rest of the children onto one of the bamboo rafts.

With Hilary paddling the rubber raft and Hahn guiding the bigger raft with a pole, the small procession slowly made its way upstream to where Simon had set up camp.

Hilary spent the next hour or so teaching the children a modified version of several camp songs, with the small girl perched on her lap and the rest of the children clustered as close as they could get.

She encouraged them to sing at the top of their voices in an effort to drown out the sound of gunfire, which she suspected bothered her a lot more than it bothered the children.

Then it was her turn, and, amid much laughter, she mastered the difficult words of a Thai song. The sound of a helicopter overhead almost drowned her out, frightening the children into silence until she persuaded them to resume their lesson. They were all singing lustily, then one by one the children's voices died away.

Hilary, realizing that she and the child on her lap were singing on their own, looked up. Following the children's gazes, she glanced over her shoulder. Simon stood behind her with his arms folded and with a warm expression on his face that quickened her pulse.

"You seem to have made yourself at home," he said, his voice sounding husky.

She heard the silence and knew the fighting was over. Relief, and an overwhelming rush of love, made her light-headed.

"Are you all right?" she said quickly. "What about Blake and Ty? Did you get Chambers? He didn't get away, did he?"

He gave her a tired smile. "Whoa! One at a time." He slid the rifle off his shoulder and propped it on the ground against his leg. "Ty is holding a gun on Chambers. He took a bullet in the shoulder, but he'll be all right."

"Chambers?"

Her expression changed when he shook his head. "No, Ty. Chambers came out of it unscathed, as usual." He pushed his hair off his forehead with the back of his hand. "Blake is flying them both to Chiang Mai in the helicopter. The rest of the gang—what's left of them—is locked in one of the refineries. Thanks to Chambers's practice of forced labor, the locks are on the outside."

"Chen," Hilary cried, "is he—"

"He's fine. He's sitting outside the refinery with a rifle trained on the door. Just in case anyone gets any ideas."

"Chen? It's hard to believe that frail man could lift a rifle, let alone fire one."

"He's quite an expert. He learned how to use one in Cambodia, as a matter of survival."

Simon walked around in front of her and lifted the little girl into his arms. He was rewarded with a shy smile as the child put an arm confidently around his neck.

Hilary hoped her feelings weren't showing on her face. "The father image suits you," she managed to murmur, then had to look away when his eyes met hers.

"I radioed the Thai rangers," he said. "They arrived a short while ago and are waiting for us at Chambers's house. They're taking everyone in by helicopter."

"They are?" Hilary looked at the curious faces of the children. "What will happen to them?"

"The authorities will take care of them." He spoke to the children in Thai, and they scrambled to their feet.

Hilary stood and brushed off her clothes. "Is Ty all right?"

"He's fine." Simon gave her an intent look. "You're really worried about him, aren't you?"

She smiled, delighted to see the suspicion on his face. "Not in that way. I'm simply concerned over the health of a nice man, that's all."

"Nice, as in *pretty*?"

She took hold of two of the children's hands. "Not as pretty as you, if that's what you're worried about."

"Worried?" He strode ahead of her, carrying the small girl. "Who says I'm worried?"

Hilary followed, torn between a desire to laugh at his show of male egotism and cry because that was all his jealousy was. She didn't have time to speak to him again until much later.

He left on a different helicopter, and on arrival at the Chiang Mai airport, she was put on a bus with the children and taken to a building in town.

There the children were questioned by a friendly faced young woman who managed to get smiles from most of them before she was finished.

With her limited English, the woman explained to Hilary that the children would be taken to a hostel and an attempt would be made to locate their parents. Further than that she would not speculate, and Hilary left, wishing she felt more secure about their future.

A soft-spoken ranger drove her to a nearby hotel, saying only that she had a room booked there. He either knew no more or was not telling her, and she had to be content with accepting a key from the clerk behind the surprisingly modern counter. She was tired, she realized as she followed a uniformed boy up to the second floor.

Once inside the room, she lay down wearily on the bed. She assumed that Simon had arranged for the room and that he would be in touch with her. She curled up, tucked her head in her arm and fell into an exhausted sleep.

She woke a couple of hours later to a polite tapping on the door. Disoriented at first, she had to take several moments to find her feet and make her way to the door.

Her disappointment when she saw a woman standing there instead of Simon must have shown in her face, as the woman looked at her worriedly.

"Miss Barlow?" she said, pronouncing the name with care.

"Yes." Hilary looked at the boxes the woman was carrying. "But I don't think—"

"Mr. King sent me. I come in?"

"Oh." She stepped back, allowing the woman to enter.

The woman laid the boxes on the bed and pulled off the lids. "Mr. King say you have anything you like. He take care of money."

Hilary put her hand on her throat and stared as the pretty dresses spilled onto the bed in a riot of color. "Wait a minute—" She broke off as the phone across the room interrupted her.

She crossed the floor to answer it, her eyes still on the rich fabrics. Her pulse leaped as she heard the deep voice on the end of the line.

"Did Maila get there yet?"

"If you mean the lady from Goodwill, I guess she did."

Simon's chuckle started her pulse jumping again. "Let me tell you," he said, "that was the most expensive shop I could find. Just pick out what you want. I figure the United States government owes you that, at least."

"Oh, I couldn't—"

"Yes, you can." His tone warned her not to refuse. "They're paying for your room, too. I know your luggage is sitting in Seattle, and I didn't think you'd want to come dancing with me tonight in what you're wearing."

"Dancing?"

"If you feel up to it."

Hilary closed her eyes. She'd walk barefoot to Bangkok for a chance to be in his arms again. "Oh, I think I can manage it," she said lightly.

"Good. I'll pick you up for dinner at seven. Find something pretty. I don't want to outshine you."

"Simon, what about—"

"I'll fill you in on everything later. Don't keep me waiting. I'm hungry."

So am I, she thought, replacing the receiver with a smile. Her rush of excitement pushed everything else from her mind, and, with an enthusiasm that was rare for her, she threw herself into the task of selecting a suitable dress.

After much discussion, she and Maila decided on a sleeveless white dress in Thai silk, which was delicately embroidered in pastel shades around the hem of the full skirt and at the scoop neckline.

Hilary chose a filmy peach wrap to go with it and had to be content with a pair of white ballerina flats, the only suitable shoes Maila had in her size.

Cool cotton underwear completed the purchase, and although Maila offered a strand of peach-and-white beads, Hilary decided her jade scorpion necklace complimented the dress perfectly.

She couldn't wait for Maila to leave so that she could begin her preparations for the evening. Feeling refreshed and invigorated by her cool shower, she was ready long before the appointed hour.

When the tap finally came on her door, she was surprised to find herself apprehensive about opening it. She'd given herself a stern lecture stating all the reasons why she should not pin any hopes on this coming evening.

Simon was merely taking her out to dinner, like the night that now seemed so long ago. He'd given her an indisputable argument for ending their relationship, and while she'd detected a certain amount of regret behind his statements, she could not deny their validity.

He simply was incapable of making a commitment, at least to her. Or probably to anyone. That gave her a small measure of comfort but did nothing to ease the ache of losing him.

At least he'd been honest with her, she acknowledged as she crossed the floor. As for this evening, she would take everything from it she could, and add it to the memories that would keep his spirit alive forever.

She opened the door, her heart turning over at the sight of him. She hardly recognized him. The stubble that had covered his chin earlier was gone, and his hair, for once, was neatly combed in place.

Dressed in light gray slacks, white shirt and black linen jacket, he looked like one of the prosperous clients she chauffeured around Los Angeles.

His gaze moved over her in warm approval, making her blood tingle as she stood back to let him in. He eyed the furnishings of the spacious room without commenting, then looked down at her.

"That was the dress I would have picked for you," he said softly. "You look wonderful. I guess we do have similar tastes in some things."

"In a lot of things." Feeling self-conscious, she moved over to the bed to pick up her bag. It was the first time they'd been alone together since he'd told her he couldn't love her. She didn't want to think about that, yet it was there, between them, a vague shadow of regret.

"Thank you for the dress," she murmured. "That was very generous of you, and I love it."

"Don't thank me. Thank the United States government." His voice was casual again, as if he regretted his weakness of a moment ago.

She pushed the thought out of her mind and made a vow to enjoy this evening. She would put off the hurt until tomorrow. Tonight the lion was hers, with or without his heart.

She looked up at him, her smile wide and genuine. "I don't know about you, but I'm starving."

He crooked his elbow at her and grinned. "How does someone with your waistline have such a ravenous appetite?"

She placed her hand in his elbow. "It's easy when you only eat one meal a day."

He laughed and led her through the door into the hallway. "I guess we have been skimping on meals lately."

"Yes." She hid her sudden pang of nostalgia with a feigned scowl. "And, Mr. Simon King, I intend to see that you make up for that."

"And I intend to satisfy your every whim," he assured her solemnly as he closed the door.

Hilary had strong doubts about that but kept her thoughts to herself as he escorted her to the elevator.

She'd been afraid to hope that he would take her to the same restaurant as before. When he turned off onto the road that led to it, she was filled with a mixture of excitement and sadness.

Last time there had been hope, and the thrill of what could be. Now she knew, and it would be very difficult to be close to him, knowing that it would be for the last time.

He had even ordered the same table, on the veranda overlooking the river, and in spite of her efforts to overcome her dejection, her eyes misted as she seated herself.

Although there were several questions she wanted to ask him, Simon insisted on finishing the excellent meal before he agreed to tell her the details.

He waited until they had been served coffee and brandy, then lifted his glass in a toast. "To a successful mission," he said, "and to the beautiful lady who helped me accomplish it."

She smiled and touched her glass to his. "And to the handsome man who helped me accomplish mine. The Walter Somerset museum and I will forever be in your debt."

"Oh, I think we evened things out pretty well." His eyes met hers over the rim of his glass, and she looked away quickly, before he could read the longing she knew must be burning in her gaze.

"So tell me," she said when she was sure she had control of her voice. "What happened to Chambers? And Ty? Is he all right?"

He put his glass down with a sigh. "You're not going to forget Ty, are you?"

She wished that sigh had been for real. "I just want to know if he's going to be all right."

"He's going to be fine. He's in the McCormick hospital here in Chiang Mai and expects to be flown home tomorrow. Blake is in Bangkok with Chambers, who is being held in custody until the papers arrive for me to arrest him and take him back to the States."

"And Phong?"

"He's been arrested, along with the curator of the museum. Chen, you'll be glad to hear, is back with May Song, and although I couldn't get any promises, the government has agreed to take into consideration the fact that he was forced to work for Chambers. It looks as though he'll be acquitted of any charges."

Hilary let out a small cry of delight. "I am glad."

"I knew you would be." He stared into his glass, his expression unreadable. "What about you? Are you going back to your chauffeur job?"

"For a little while." She stirred her coffee, trying to ward off the depression that threatened her. "I've learned a lot about myself these past few days," she went on determinedly.

"I've decided that I'm capable of bigger things. I'm going to open my own business when I've saved enough money. A little shop, I think, specializing in handcrafts from Thailand. I think they'd do well in the States, and it will give me an excuse to come back to Chiang Mai."

Her voice almost broke on the last word, and she cleared her throat.

He looked at her then, with the same warm expression in his eyes that could make her blood tingle and her heart fill with treacherous hope. "I think that's a wonderful idea. That's why I wanted you to have one last night in Chiang Mai, because I know how much you love it."

Do you know how much I love you? her heart cried. "That was a nice thing to do," she said, managing a smile.

"Oh, it wasn't an entirely unselfish gesture." He drained his brandy glass and set it down. "I'm flying back to Bangkok in the morning with you," he said quietly. "I want to put you on the plane myself this time."

Irrationally, she wanted to leave. She wanted to get it over with, to say goodbye to him and try to forget how much she loved him.

And yet she was relieved when he raised his hand at the waiter and ordered more coffee. She sipped at her brandy, her eyes on his face, trying to commit every inch of it to memory.

The faint lines on his forehead and at the corners of his mouth. The way his mustache tilted when he smiled. The dark blond brows winging above his wonderful, sky-blue eyes. The way his hair insisted on falling across his forehead.

Then she remembered the question she wanted to ask him. "How long have you worked with Blake and Ty?" she said abruptly.

His expression seemed wary when he looked at her. "A few years. Why?"

"You seem very close. It's more than just a working relationship, isn't it?"

"You could say that." He hesitated, then appeared to come to a decision.

She listened while he told her about his two friends and some of the experiences they'd shared.

"We go back a long way," Simon said, his gaze on his empty glass, "and there's no one I'd rather trust with my life than those two men."

"What made you join the DEA?" Hilary said, shivering at the thought of how many close calls he must have had in his lifetime.

"I was taking pictures of a drug raid for a local newspaper several years ago. I saw a young boy, thirteen years old, blown out of his mind by the overdose of heroin he'd shot into his arm. I felt helpless. I wanted to do something, but there was nothing anyone could do. Then I met Blake, and he told me about the DEA. I signed up for training soon after that. I figured that helping to put a stop to this vicious industry was something I could do."

The waiter brought the coffee at that moment, and she was glad of the diversion. The more she learned about him, the deeper her love grew, and she was finding it increasingly difficult to look at him without blurting out her feelings.

The music drifted to her from the dance floor, intensifying her longing as it had once before. He must have been tuned in to her thoughts. She watched him rise and hold out his hand. Part of her wanted to refuse, for she was afraid to be close to him.

"Dance with me," he said softly, and she put her hand in his and walked with him to the dance floor.

The music, melancholy and nostalgic, fitted her mood, but had a slow, sensuous beat that made her wish she'd had the strength to refuse his offer.

And then his arms closed around her, and despite the pain, she knew that not for anything would she trade these last few minutes in his arms.

He drew her close until her entire being was filled with the essence of him: the musky fragrance of his after-shave, the firm warmth of his body, the touch of his hand at her shoulder blades and the strength of his fingers holding hers.

She tried to keep some space between them at first, but as the music seeped into her soul, she surrendered to the pressure of his hand.

Her breasts tingled where they rested against his chest, and her breath caught as he lowered his face until his jaw touched her cheek.

She tightened her fingers on his shoulder when his thigh gently collided with hers. When she felt the solid strength of his shoulder beneath the smooth fabric of his jacket, she remembered vividly his naked body leaning over her.

Unable to control the urge, she moved her fingers to the back of his neck and burrowed them into the soft hair that covered it.

He lifted his head and looked down at her, his gaze seeming to penetrate every nerve in her body. His mouth was so close to hers she could feel his breath on her lips.

"Hilary?" His lips had barely moved, her name a soft whisper on them, yet the question exploded in her brain, sending slivers of excitement to every nerve end.

The question was repeated in his eyes, in the pressure of his arms holding her tight against his body. Then it became undeniable when he shifted his hips and she felt the full impact of his arousal.

She knew what he was asking. And she knew what she should say. Yet in spite of her conviction that she was being an utter fool, she knew she could not refuse him.

Where he was concerned, things like pride and common sense didn't matter. What mattered was right now, this moment. He wanted her, and she wanted him, more than she'd ever wanted anything in her life. What else was there to think about?

She didn't have to tell him; he read it in her eyes, and the answering flame in his fired her blood.

He guided her back to the table, settled the bill and seated her in the car without speaking. He drove fast, as if afraid she'd change her mind.

As if she could. Her whole being was a tingling, shivering mass of expectation. Never in her life had she felt every second so intensely. She was aware of every movement he made, every breath he took.

Even that walk from the waterfall in the jungle had not been charged with such intense vibrations. By the time he pulled up at the hotel she felt light-headed with the turbulence of her emotions.

He strode around the hood of the car and pulled her door open. She almost fell into his arms, and he steadied her, holding her against him for a brief moment.

"This is what you want?" he whispered, his eyes searching her face.

"This is what I want."

His smile swept from her mind any lingering doubts, and in a haze of need and anticipation she let him lead her to the privacy of her room and close the door on the outside world.

Chapter 12

This wasn't something he'd planned, Simon thought as he closed the door. But now that it was started, he could not stop it. Even if he'd wanted to.

His body shook with the power of his need as he gently drew the wrap from Hilary's shoulders and laid it on the bed. He pulled his jacket off and dropped it, his eyes locked with hers.

She stood waiting, though her face was flushed and the quick rise and fall of her breasts revealed her emotions.

He lifted his hand and traced the curve of her cheek, and his stomach tightened when she drew a sharp breath through her parted lips.

He watched the path of his fingers as they moved down the soft skin of her neck to the hollow of her throat. A pulse fluttered against his fingers like a frightened bird, and his heart melted.

He slid his hand to the back of her neck and pulled her forward, unresisting, until he could feel the taut peaks of her breasts pushing against his chest.

Her hands rested on his biceps, and he could feel his muscles flexing against her fingers as he wrapped his arms around her yielding body and covered her mouth with his.

Her lips were warm and responsive and as eager as his. He relaxed the pressure of his mouth before her urgency could sweep him away, out of control.

He wanted this to last. The memory of it might have to last him a very long time. He traced the outline of her mouth with his tongue, then brushed her parted lips with his open mouth, using a light, teasing pressure that fired his own excitement as well as hers.

She pulled away from him, breathing rapidly, but he followed the movement of her head, holding her close, his mouth brushing hers one more time before traveling to her neck.

He nuzzled the back of her ear and felt her quiver against him. She lifted her chin, giving him access to the line of her throat, and he took advantage of it, pulling his mouth down the length of her neck.

His tongue found the hollow of her throat, and he felt the convulsive grip of her fingers on his arms. Then she surprised him by slipping her arms around his hips and pulling him against her soft belly.

Her murmur set off an answering surge of need, and he felt his control slipping. He straightened, pulling away from her in an effort to hold on a little longer.

Her fingers moved immediately to the buttons of his shirt and undid them quickly. He watched her face as she concentrated on her task, then held his breath as she spread her fingers out across his bared chest.

"I love touching your body," Hilary said, watching her fingers make paths through the crisp dark blond hairs.

"I love you touching me."

She heard the tremor in his voice and looked up quickly. She still found it hard to believe that she could produce this effect on a man who was normally so controlled, so powerfully confident.

His fingers traced the neckline of her dress before reaching behind her for the zipper. "I also love touching you."

She let him pull the white silk dress from her arms and slide it over her hips to the floor. Stepping out of it, she took hold of his hands, preventing him from undressing her further.

"It's my turn," she said unsteadily, and saw his nostrils flare as he dragged in his breath. She took her time, her excitement mounting as she pulled off his shirt, then his slacks.

His briefs couldn't hide the intensity of his need, and her hands shook as she eased them down over his hips. She would never forget the magnificence of his body, she told herself. Or the feel of him.

He removed the rest of her clothes in a fever of impatience and bore her down on the bed with the weight of his body. "Hold still," he growled throatily, "or this'll be over before I've begun."

In answer she ran her hands down his back to the crease of his buttocks and smiled when he groaned. "I just want to touch you," she whispered.

"And I want to touch you." He did so, bringing a sharp moan from her as his fingers found one of her most sensitive spots. He took advantage of her vulnerability and shifted his weight, lowering his mouth to her breast.

She forgot everything except the intense, compelling pleasure his lips and tongue provoked in her aching body. The pressure deep inside her began building steadily, and she dug her fingers into the smooth flesh of his back.

She moaned again when she felt the soft brush of his mustache travel down her belly to her thighs.

She gasped out his name and a shudder shook her body. She had never imagined anything remotely resembling the sensations he was producing, and the burning pressure became unbearable.

He must have sensed her agony, for he raised his head, and she cried out again as his fingers found her, increasing her urgency until her senses exploded in a torrent of release.

She felt the slight roughness of his fingers stroking her belly as she let her body drift slowly down from the dizzying heights.

When she could look at him, she found him watching her face, his features tense.

"Do you have any idea how erotic it is to watch you like that?" he said, his voice raw with emotion.

"No." She shifted onto her side and pushed him onto his back. "But I intend to find out."

She saw the passion flare in his eyes as she ran her fingertips through the springy hairs of his chest. He bore her touch without a murmur, though his mouth tightened when she brushed her thumbs across his hardened nipples.

She felt his muscles contract as she moved her fingers over his stomach to his navel, then traced the narrow ridge of hair down.

A gasp forced its way between his lips as she lowered her head, her hair brushing his belly.

"Hilary," he breathed, then groaned and grasped her arms, dragging her up his body.

Eager for him again, she straddled his hips and lowered herself onto him. Supporting herself with her hands on his shoulders, she watched his face as she moved slowly on him until his thrusting hips picked up the momentum.

His hands gripped her thighs while his eyes burned into hers, his expression melting her soul. She'd thought her love for him was all it could be—until he drove into her with a desperate cry to join them in one last violent shudder of agonizing pleasure.

She knew then, as she lay spent and satiated on his heaving chest, that she could never belong to another man. If she lived to be a hundred years old, she would go to her grave loving this man and no other.

She woke from a restless sleep to find the lamp still blazing. She was pressed against Simon's back, her knees tucked behind his.

He held her hand to his chest, his fingers entwined with hers, and she could feel as well as hear the steady rhythm of his breathing. She was sure she'd never heard a more beautiful sound.

She lay a long time, absorbing the feel of his body against hers. There would be many nights, she thought with a rush of pain, when she would wake up and ache to have him close to her like this.

How long would it be, she wondered, before that ache became bearable? Her face was wet with tears when she drifted off to sleep again.

The next time she opened her eyes, the room was dark. Simon must have turned off the lamp, she thought in the first few fuzzy seconds of waking.

When she reached for him and found him gone, her pain was so acute she pulled her knees up to her chin in an effort to deal with it.

She would not cry, she told herself. It was time to begin the process of learning to live without him. Dry-eyed and hurting, she watched the dawn dissolve the shadows of the night.

He'd left a note for her, she discovered when she'd made herself sit up. Scribbled on the back of the restaurant bill, it was short and to the point.

"Plane leaves at eight-thirty. Will pick you up at seven-thirty," she read aloud. "All right, Mr. King. I'll be ready."

She picked her dress up from the floor and shook it out. She didn't want to wear it, but her pants and shirt were in no condition to travel in.

She would wear it this last time, she decided, and then she would pack it away, out of sight. Maybe one day she'd be strong enough to give it away.

She showered quickly, refusing to let her mind walk the path of memories. The thought of spending an hour on the plane with Simon was almost too much to bear, but, she told herself, she would do it—and with a smile—if it killed her.

She managed the smile through the long morning that followed. Simon kept up a constant stream of small talk as though afraid of touching on anything personal.

That hurt her more than anything—so much so that she found enough pride to look him in the eye and say goodbye without falling apart.

He made no suggestions to keep in touch, nor did she expect any. In all the time they had been together the night before, he had said nothing to indicate he had changed his mind about anything.

She always seemed to be saying goodbye to him, she thought with a stab of pain as she boarded her plane in Bangkok. At least it was the last time. The thought gave her little comfort.

The shock of arriving in the cold damp November weather in Seattle did nothing to alleviate her misery. She was surprised to be met by a kind-faced man who told her he was a friend of Simon's. He had her luggage waiting for her and saw her onto her connecting flight to Los Angeles without saying very much at all.

Not that she wanted to talk. She appreciated Simon's thoughtfulness, but any thoughts of him brought more pain than she could deal with, and it was with a tremendous sense of relief that she finally arrived back at her apartment.

The first few days that followed were difficult. She found it hard to concentrate on her driving, and twice came close to rear-ending a car, because her mind was somewhere else entirely.

Her worst moments came when she unpacked and found the yellow parasol. She stored it away, out of sight, along with the little elephant Simon had given her and the embroidered dress.

A ceremony was held at the Walter Somerset museum to celebrate the delivery of the scorpion, and it was all she could do to stay there until it was polite to leave.

She wondered constantly whether Simon was back in the States and whether Chambers had been safely delivered. She couldn't stop herself from scanning the newspapers every day in the hopes of finding a news item about it, even though she knew how unlikely that was.

Before long, the Christmas season was in full swing. The sight of all those cheerful faces, arms loaded with presents, children jumping with excitement everywhere she looked and the constant sound of ringing bells outside the lavishly decorated stores all deepened her depression.

Her job helped keep her mind occupied. With all the parties, concerts and special events being held in the city, she worked long hours into the night, arriving home bleary-eyed and exhausted. Eventually, there came nights when her exhaustion allowed her to fall asleep.

The week before Christmas, her mother called. Hilary had always hated the noisy crush of people her mother insisted on entertaining throughout the holiday.

Normally she would have endured it, feeling obligated to join the family. She surprised herself by refusing her mother's invitation, and was pleased to feel no guilt in doing so.

She was making progress, she told herself the day before Christmas Eve. She was actually getting through entire days without feeling the dreadful ache that could cut off her breath without warning.

The memories still haunted her, but she was getting better at shutting them out before they engulfed her in a suffocating misery.

She had slept late that morning and was finishing a leisurely breakfast when her doorbell rang. Frowning, she went to answer it. Apart from the dispatchers at work, she had few friends—none of whom would be calling on her in the middle of the morning.

She pulled the door open—and felt as if the entire world had rocked beneath her feet. She tried to speak but choked on the words and could only look up at him helplessly.

He looked just the same as he had the day she'd said goodbye to him in Bangkok, with his dark blond hair tumbling onto his forehead and that same smile, which tilted his mustache in that familiar way.

He looked virile and rugged in his jeans and yellow sport shirt. Only his eyes looked different. There was a guarded look in them, a certain caution, that was in stark contrast to the confidence she was used to.

"Hello, Hilary," he said quietly. "You were tough to find."

She had imagined this scene so many times in those first awful days. She'd played it so many different ways in her mind but had never expected to feel like this.

A burning resentment had taken the place of her initial blinding joy at seeing him. Why now? Why, just when she was beginning to heal, did he have to come looking for her?

"This is a surprise." She forced a smile but made no move to invite him in. *Maybe he'll go away,* she thought desperately, and in the next second hoped just as desperately that he would stay.

"Can I come in?" he said, and looked pointedly past her.

She considered the state of her apartment. There hadn't seemed much point in worrying about it lately. She must look pretty drastic herself, she realized in despair. Her jeans had seen better days, and her sweatshirt had been a favorite staple of her high school days.

As for her hair, she had washed it that morning, but had simply let it air dry. It had to be a mess. She ran a hand through it self-consciously and reluctantly stepped back. "Of course. I'm afraid it's not too tidy."

"Don't worry. I should have called."

Why didn't you? she asked silently. *Maybe I would have had the strength to hang up on you.*

She watched him walk past her into her small living room and knew just how futile that thought was. Whatever progress she had made, she hadn't stopped loving him. Not one tiny fraction less.

Even now she found it hard to believe he was actually standing in her living room, looking around him with the polite interest of a stranger.

"Nice," he observed. "Quiet and understated."

Like me, she thought, and was immediately angry with herself and with him for destroying her newfound security.

"Thank you," she said, noticing with relief that it wasn't untidy at all. Some habits must be automatic.

He laid his jacket on the back of her comfortable armchair, then sat down. He looked so out of place that she almost forgot her resentment.

"You have an unlisted number," he commented, as if that should have come as a surprise to her.

"Yes." She crossed to the couch and perched on the arm. "I got tired of men calling me, asking to meet my sister."

He raised his eyebrows. "Is she that beautiful?"

In answer she leaned forward and picked up a magazine from the coffee table. Flipping it open, she handed it to him.

He studied the picture of the tall, lithe blonde for several seconds, then put it down. "I guess she is, if you like the sophisticated type."

His tone implied that he didn't, a fact she would have argued with if he hadn't looked at her just then with a smile that reminded her of just how much she still loved him.

"I have coffee on, if you'd like some." She stood up abruptly, barely waiting for his nod before she hurried into the kitchen.

A quick glance in the small oval mirror on the wall didn'
do much to soothe her agitation. She looked a mess, she
thought miserably. No makeup, hair flying everywhere and
faint shadows still underlying her eyes.

What was he doing here? Surely he hadn't just breezed
into town expecting her to fall straight into his arms.

He probably did, she acknowledged with a twist of her
mouth. Wasn't that exactly what she'd done ever since she'd
met him? He'd only had to look at her, and she'd melted.

She lifted two mugs from the cupboard and set them on
the counter. Well, not this time. No more goodbyes. She'd
had enough. More than enough.

This time she would be strong. She would not put herself
through that misery again. Not for one more moment in his
arms. Not even for one more night.

She poured the steaming coffee into the mugs and prayed
for the strength she would need. She pulled in a deep breath
and heard it come out shakily as she picked up the mugs.

She'd come a long way in the past few weeks, she reminded herself. She was her own person now, in control of
her destiny. Now was the time to prove it.

He sat where she'd left him, absently leafing through the
magazine. He looked up at her when she handed him the
mug, and she had to make herself turn away. She felt secure enough to sit on the couch, and did so, placing her mug
carefully on the coffee table between them.

"So, what are you doing in Los Angeles?" she asked,
hating the brittle note in her voice, yet unable to control it.

"I came to see you."

She ignored that, incapable of dealing with it yet. "How
did you find me?"

"I called every limousine service in the book. Yours was
the last one. I had the devil of a job talking your boss into
giving me your address. I finally had to go there in person."

Hilary made a note to have a talk with her boss that eve-
ling. Although, since her boss was female and particularly
usceptible to good-looking men, it was difficult to blame
ier too much. Especially if Simon had turned on his dev-
·stating charm. She knew only too well what that charm
ould do when he was really trying.

She crossed her legs in a defensive gesture and picked up
er mug. "I take it you got Chambers safely back to the
'tates."

"Yes." His eyes demanded that she look at him, but she
licked her gaze away.

"He's in jail," he added, "along with the rest of his cro-
.ies—the ones who survived.

"What about Hal and Jerry?" Hilary sipped at her cof-
-ee, studiously avoiding his gaze.

"I didn't come here to talk about Hal and Jerry."

The sharp tone in his voice made her raise her head. His
yes glinted at her, and for the first time she saw a desper-
tion in them that threatened her resolve.

She put her mug down quickly, before she could suc-
umb to the temptation nagging at her. She had to get this
ver with, and now.

"So what did you come to talk about?" she said, putting
very ounce of her resentment into her voice.

Simon stared at her, wondering how he could possibly
andle this. He hadn't expected her to throw herself at him,
ut neither had he expected this wall of resistance.

She was a stranger. Had he been mistaken about the way
ie felt about him? If so, he was about to make a colossal
ool of himself.

He set his mug down on the table, knowing he would have
) risk it. He was willing to risk a lot more, if he could only
et through to her.

"I came," he said slowly, "to give you a Christmas pres-
it. And to offer you an invitation."

He had unsettled her. He saw the flicker of warmth in her eyes before she had time to subdue it, and he saw some thing else. Something she had hidden until now. Something he recognized. He'd been through that kind of pain him self.

Hope swamped him, and he knew then what he had to do He pushed himself off the chair and sat down next to her on the settee.

Seeing her flinch, he made himself stay where he was. He dared not touch her. Not yet. "I have some things to tell you first," he said, willing her to meet his eyes.

When she did look at him, her gaze was as cool and empty as the mountain peaks. He tasted fear and reflected rue fully that the few times he had felt real fear, it had been over her.

"Is this going to take long?" She looked at her watch. " have to be at work in an hour."

He winced inwardly. "I'll make it as quick as I can. But want you to hear me out. Deal?"

She shrugged, portraying an indifference he was almos sure she didn't feel. Almost.

"I'm not very good at this, Hilary, so you'll have to bea with me." She didn't answer, and he struggled on. "I fin it very hard to talk about some things, but in order for yo to understand, I'm going to try."

She looked up quickly. "Haven't we been all through thi before?"

It was there then, vibrant in her voice. The pain that h knew well. Encouraged, he told her. Everything. How he' felt when his mother had died when he was twelve years old How angry he'd been and how desperately afraid. He'd shu everyone out, especially his father and his sister.

He'd buried his emotions under a series of daring esca pades, each one more dangerous than the rest. He'd close off his deepest feelings, leaving only surface ones. Those h could deal with.

"From then on," he told her, "I lived only for the moment. I'd learned what it was to lose someone you love, and intended never to be that vulnerable again. I decided that was futile to invest in a future, if you never knew when it ould be taken from you."

Hilary's heart ached for that lonely, brokenhearted boy. His explanation didn't heal her own pain, but it helped to nderstand why he was the way he was.

"Thank you for telling me," she said quietly. "I know ow difficult it must have been."

She steeled herself to look at him and saw a raw, aching eed in his face that almost destroyed her.

"I thought it was enough," he said, his voice dropping to husky whisper. "I thought that as long as I was free, I was afe. And then I found out that freedom isn't freedom at all, your heart belongs somewhere else."

Her breath caught, and she struggled to release it. *No,* she ld herself frantically, *don't start hoping again. Not now.*

"Hilary." He reached for her hand, and she was power- ss to pull it away. "I'm trying to tell you that I love you."

She gulped, tried to speak, and couldn't. She searched his ace, trying to read his expression. His eyes told her before is hesitant words could confirm it.

"I think I knew it from the moment I first danced with ou," he said huskily, "but I couldn't admit it to myself, let lone to you. I don't want to live my life without you, Hi- ry. I want to go to sleep every night holding you in my rms, and I want to wake up every morning and see you niling at me.

"I want to spend whatever time we may have together ving you, in the best way I know how."

She felt the tears on her face and reached blindly for him. I love you, too," she whispered brokenly. "Oh, Simon, I ve you, too."

His mouth smothered the last words as his kiss swept h
away to that indescribable world that contained only the tw
of them.

When he lifted his head at last, she was breathless an
light-headed with happiness.

His eyes burned down at her, warming all the places i
side her that had been so very cold. "I have a Christm
present for you," he said, and let her go so he could le
forward and reach for his jacket.

He pulled a square package from the inside pocket an
handed it to her. She took it with a frown of dismay. "
didn't get anything for you."

"You don't have to." His lips touched hers in a qui
hard kiss. "I have everything I want."

She unwrapped it slowly, then lifted the lid of the bc
Nestled in a bed of white cotton lay a perfect gold bell.

She murmured her delight when she held it up to hear
musical chime.

"Look inside," Simon said softly.

She did so, and her heart leaped as she read the words i
scribed in tiny writing: *Marry me, Hilary. I Love You,*
mon. She looked back at his anxious face and smiled. "Hc
could I refuse such a romantic proposal?"

Grinning with relief, he pulled her back into his arms an
kissed her until she laughingly protested.

"What would you have done if I'd refused?" she sai
shaking the bell again to hear its chime.

"I don't know." He sighed. "It would have taken me
long time to find another Hilary."

He laughed when she lightly punched his chest. "I'll ha
the date put on as soon as we settle it," he said, taking t
bell from her. "How does Valentine's Day sound? Chia
Mai is beautiful then."

Her gasp of delight drowned out his next words. "For
honeymoon?"

"A working honeymoon. I thought you might like to order stock for your store."

"My store?" She stared at him in confusion.

"Isn't that what you want? Or would you rather stay with the limousines?"

"I'd rather have the store, of course, but—"

"I'd like to finance it. I think a wife should work until she has children, don't you?"

When she'd recovered from the thought of having his children, she flung her arms around his neck. "You're going to make a wonderful husband and an even more wonderful father," she whispered in his ear.

She sat back as a thought struck her. "What about the DEA? Do they allow fathers in their organization?"

"I'm no longer with the DEA." He looked guilty as he faced her. "I haven't been for two years. I came out of retirement to go after Chambers. I didn't tell you before because it was easier to pretend it was my job that prevented me from making a commitment."

He pulled her back into his arms. "I kept telling myself that I was too fond of my freedom to settle down, instead of admitting that I was afraid to love you because I was scared of losing you."

"You'll never lose me—and that's a promise." She confirmed it with the firm pressure of her mouth on his. "So what are you going to do now?" she asked him when he finally lifted his head.

"I'm a free-lance photographer—" he brushed her lips with his "—who plans to go into a nice, steady photography business."

She gave him a worried look. "Is it going to be enough? Won't you miss all that excitement? The travel and the danger?"

"Are you kidding? I won't have time, with a wife and kids to look after."

She wriggled out of his embrace. "No, seriously, Simon. Maybe this is something we should talk about."

"I won't miss it," he assured her. "I made up my mind a long time ago that I was tired of it. I've been happy the past two years without it, and now that I have you, I don't have a single doubt. Now, that's enough talking."

His kiss prevented her from answering.

A long time later she called her office on Simon's insistence and told them she wouldn't be back. She would be too busy making preparations for the wedding, he told her.

She sighed happily as she put the phone down. "I guess this is going to be a good Christmas, after all."

"It would be a better one in Oregon." He came up behind her and wrapped his arms around her waist. "Come back with me tomorrow. My sister and her husband have room for us at their resort. You'll love it. There's snow on the mountains and Christmas trees growing along the lake. We'll have our own private cabin, and you can get to know my sister and meet my nephew."

He went on talking enthusiastically, but Hilary was only half listening. She'd already made up her mind. She'd go anywhere he asked as long as she could be with him.

He was right; she loved everything about Oregon. His sister, Lee, and her tall, handsome husband, Nick, welcomed her with open arms. His nephew, Michael, nicknamed Midge, was an eighteen-month-old bundle of energy who adored Simon and spent most of the time trying to follow him everywhere.

The lodge where the family lived was rustic and beautiful, and they all spent Christmas Eve in front of the enormous log fire, where they were joined by the resort's other guests.

Hilary stared at the stately Christmas tree with its glittering lights and simple snowflake ornaments and thought about her mother's lavish parties.

This was what Christmas was, she thought blissfully, cuddled in the comforting circle of Simon's arms. Singing carols in front of a crackling fire, with warm, friendly people and the person you loved most in the world beside you.

Later, as they walked on the crackling snow toward their cabin, Simon drew her to a halt and turned her toward the mountains. The moon shone on the snow-covered peaks, giving them a ghostly glow against the black sky.

The crisp, cold air stung her cheeks, but she felt warm with the glow inside her.

"It's beautiful, isn't it," he said softly.

"Yes." She leaned against him, feeling his solid warmth at her back. "You love it, don't you?"

"Yes." She felt his breath on her cheek as he laid his face against hers. "I've been all over the world, but this will always be home."

She turned to look at him, hugging him close. "I'd like it to be my home, too."

The look on his face was her reward. "You mean it?" he said carefully. "I thought you liked California."

"I do. But I like Oregon, too. And anyplace in the world is home if you're there. Besides, I'll have less competition for my shop here."

He gave an exaggerated sigh. "The businesswoman already." He lifted his head. "Listen."

She'd heard it, too. The faint sound of church bells ringing out their message from the valley. "Merry Christmas, my love," she whispered, and lifted her face for his kiss.

His mouth claimed hers in a silent promise that she knew he would keep. The lion had given his heart at last, and she would hold it safe forever.

* * * * *

Keepsake

Harlequin Books

You're never too young to enjoy romance. Harlequin for you . . . and Keepsake, young-adult romances destined to win hearts, for your daughter.

Pick one up today and start your daughter on her journey into the wonderful world of romance.

Two new titles to choose from each month.

COMING NEXT MONTH

#269 ONCE FORGOTTEN—Jan Milella

Claire's marriage to Jack had fallen apart several years ago. Now she was losing her daughter, too. Little Meghan needed a kidney transplant, and time was quickly running out. Jack was a doctor, perhaps the only one who could help Meghan. Soon Claire found herself hoping that together they could heal old wounds and remember a love once forgotten in this desperate race against time.

#270 STRANGER ON THE SHORE—Carol Duncan

Sarah Wilson possessed a "sixth sense," but she couldn't forsee any profitable outcome from a relationship with free-lance writer Jordan Matthias. The man had a reputation for exposing psychic frauds, and she wasn't about to reveal her own special abilities to him. But he did have an uncanny effect on her other five senses, and she wondered if he'd be interested in the secrets locked in her heart.

#271 REBEL'S RETURN—Sibylle Garrett

Afghani Prince Ahmed Khan was a rebel with a cause. In his fight for his country's freedom, he had sacrificed everything—family, title, wealth—and found imprisonment in his self-imposed isolation. But when he met Toni Prescott, he knew that only her love could set him free.

#272 KNIGHT SPARKS—Mary Lynn Baxter

As Carly's superior officer, Captain Rance Knight was off-limits, so she tried to ignore the sparks that flew whenever he was near. But then they were thrown together on a case, and even though their forbidden love could end their careers, Carly was willing to be seared by his fire.

AVAILABLE THIS MONTH

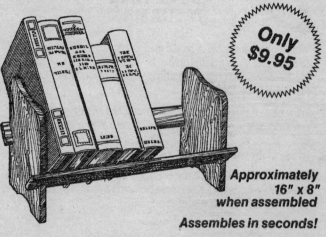

1989
IS THE YEAR
OF THE MAN!

What makes a romance? A special man, of course, and Silhouette Desire celebrates that fact with *twelve* of them! From Mr. January to Mr. December, every month spotlights the Silhouette Desire hero—our **MAN OF THE MONTH.**

Sexy, macho, charming, irritating…irresistible! Nothing can stop these men from sweeping you away. Created by some of your favorite authors, each man is custom-made for pleasure—*reading* pleasure—so don't miss a single one.

Diana Palmer kicks off the new year, and you can look forward to magnificent men from **Joan Hohl**, **Jennifer Greene** and many, many more. So get out there and find your man!

Silhouette Desire's

MAN OF THE MONTH…

MAND-1